THE LUSTFUL LORD

The strikingly handsome, infinitely elegant gentleman was clearly drunk—but not so drunk that his strong arms could not hold Florence in an iron embrace. Then Florence felt his lips nuzzling her neck with practiced skill.

"Sir, I am a married lady," she cried. "My husband . . ."

He silenced her with his lips, her final words trailing off in a muffled mumble.

It was then that the wedding guests poured into the room. They promptly burst into cheers and applause for what should have been the shocking scene before them.

And Florence had her first dreadful inkling that this lustful lord—most surely not for better but for worse—was now her legal master . . .

MELINDA McRAE holds a master's degree in European history and takes great delight in researching obscure details of the Regency period. She lives in Seattle, Washington, with her husband and daughter.

D1459965

MARRIED BY MISTAKE

Melinda McRae

A SIGNET BOOK

SIGNET
Published by the Penguin Group
Penguin Books USA Inc., 375 Hudson Street,
New York, New York, 10014, U.S.A.
Penguin Books Ltd, 27 Wrights Lane, London W8 5TZ, England
Penguin Books Australia Ltd, Ringwood, Victoria, Australia
Penguin Books Canada Ltd, 10 Alcorn Avenue, Toronto, Ontario, Canada M4V 3B2
Penguin Books (N.Z.) Ltd, 182-190 Wairau Road,
Auckland 10, New Zealand

Penguin Books Ltd, Registered Offices:
Harmondsworth, Middlesex, England

First published by Signet, an imprint of New American Library,
a division of Penguin Books USA Inc.

First Printing, May, 1992

10 9 8 7 6 5 4 3 2 1

Copyright© Melinda McRae, 1992
All rights reserved

 REGISTERED TRADEMARK—MARCA REGISTRADA

PRINTED IN THE UNITED STATES OF AMERICA

For Kendall Elisabeth,
who wanted to have her
name in a book.

Chapter 1

"You have the devil's luck, Alford!" Jeremy Trent tossed his cards upon the green baize table in disgust.

A slow smile crept over the face of Thomas Beresford Swinton, Viscount Alford. He cocked one dark brow. "Blasphemy from you, Trent?"

"Picking all the winners at Newmarket, then taking all the hands this night," Trent grumbled. "It's uncanny."

Alford raised his glass in a toast. "To luck," he said with a grin, then drained his glass in one gulp.

"Yours will run out one day," the man on his left, Seb Cole, warned. To punctuate his words, he upended an empty bottle over Alford's glass. "Brandy's gone."

"Then uncork another, you ass," Lewiston Hervey muttered while he gathered up the cards for another hand.

"Gentlemen, allow me." Alford was on his feet with fluid grace. "As your host, it is my duty."

Only a slight hestitation in his gait as he crossed the room hinted at the amount of brandy Alford had already consumed. He grabbed another bottle from the sideboard, grimacing at his reflection in the mirror above. He passed the low settee pushed up against the wall and none too gently lifted the head of the baby-faced man lying there, then let it fall back against the padded cushion.

"Almhurst's still gone," he announced to no one in particular before he stumbled back toward the table with his prize. He presented the bottle to Cole with a flourish before retaking his seat.

"Hardly unexpected," Cole said. "Lad's never had a head for liquor."

"Leastways he quit snoring," Hervey said, dealing the cards around the table.

As if on cue, Almhurst began a nasal rumbling.

"Damnation." Alford took his long discarded cravat from the arm of his chair, wadded it into a ball and lobbed it at the settee, where it bounced off the young lord's nose. The men laughed but the snoring continued.

"Maybe we should toss him out on the walk?" Cole asked hopefully.

"With our luck he'd develop an inflammation of the lungs, die, and we'd all hang for it," Trent said, his expression glum as he examined his cards.

Alford slouched further down in his comfortably worn armchair, studying the cards in his hand. His expression remained impassive.

"Has anyone heard more about the new dancer at the opera?" Cole asked while he sloppily refilled everyone's glass.

"She's been deucedly coy, from what I hear," Trent replied. "Either she's already got a protector lined up or she's a foolish chit."

"Perhaps," said Alford, shifting slightly in his chair, "she is looking for a gentleman of refinement and taste."

Trent guffawed. "I suppose you think you would be more successful?"

"I know I would be," Alford replied, an enigmatic smile lighting his face.

"Monkey says you won't."

Alford's smile widened. "So certain are you of my failure?"

"My money's on Alford," Cole said. "Ain't never yet seen a female who's refused him."

"Well, Alford, what do you say?" Trent prompted him. "Think you can storm her castle?"

Alford picked up his glass and gestured in salute to his cronies. "No bets on this one, gentlemen. The lady and I have already enjoyed a very satisfactory interchange."

"As I said, the devil's own luck," Trent mumbled.

With a laugh, Alford slapped Trent on the back. "Perhaps it will rub off one day."

"My lord?" Alford's valet appeared at the door.

"What is it, Rawlings?"

"Some papers from your father, my lord."

"At this hour?" Alford frowned. "They can wait till later."

"They are regarding your brother's wedding," the valet said. "He has been trying to locate you for three days."

"Any fool would know I'd been at Newmarket." Alford shook his head. "Bring them here."

"So Kit's really going to seal his doom, eh?" Hervey joked as play halted.

"More the fool he," said Alford, squinting at the papers in his hand. "Rawlings! Bring the damn candles over here. Can't see a thing in this light. And a pen. And ink."

"Yes, my lord."

"What does he need a wife for?" Cole asked.

Alford turned back his cuffs and meticulously rolled up his sleeves. "Don't ask me what maggot got into his head— although it was most likely my father. Probably convinced the idiot he would not get a decent post unless he had a wife."

"Who's he marrying?" Trent asked.

Alford shuddered at the memory. "Washburn's chit."

"Washburn? Don't remember a Washburn. What's the matter with her? Does she have a squint? Or freckles?"

"Probably," said Alford as he scrawled his signature across one page. "I haven't seen her since she was a pestilential brat of nine or ten. Washburn's kept her hidden on the Continent for years, so something must be amiss."

"Shouldn't someone warn Kit?"

Alford gave a careless wave of his hand. "It's his life to ruin as he will."

"Kit's marrying a girl he hasn't seen in what—ten years?" Seb Cole was aghast.

"Kit's managed to see her here and there, from what I gather," Alford replied blandly as he flipped through the papers.

"How come Kit's seen her and you haven't? Not like you to ignore the ladies."

"Now, Trent, think on it." Alford absently rubbed the bridge of his nose. "How many days have I spent under my father's roof in the last ten years? Five? Ten? Whereas Kit, dutiful son that he is, was constantly underfoot at that house. He would have been around whenever Washburn and the girl made an appearance.''

Cole and Hervey exchanged dubious glances.

"Couldn't you talk to Kit," Cole asked. "Make him see reason? There are all kinds of ways to get out of the noose."

"Ah, but there will be no opportunity to speak with Kit." Alford leafed through the remaining papers, halting once to scrawl his name again. "That is the beauty of the arrangement. He is unable to get leave to come home for the wedding. The marriage is to be done by proxy. By the time he realizes what he's in for, it will be far too late." He collected the papers and handed them to the waiting Rawlings, who bowed his way out of the room.

"Who's going to stand proxy for him?" Hervey said.

Trent gave him a withering look. "Alford, you clunch," he said.

"A rum hand to deal your own brother," Hervey muttered.

"You wound me," Alford said, placing a hand over his breast. "It was my dearest brother's express wish that I stand in for him. I am honor-bound to accede to his request."

"Seems to me a real brother would help him get out of it," Hervey continued.

"Kit's a strapping big laddie now," Alford said, mimicking the ancient Scots groom who had taught them both to ride. "He can do what he wishes with his life."

"Maybe we should investigate the chit," Hervey offered. "We ought to be able to catch a glimpse of this Miss Whatever-her-name-is. Make sure Kit's doing the right thing."

"And how do you propose to locate 'Miss What's-her-name' when you don't even know it?" Alford demanded.

"You'll tell us where she is." Hervey's face brightened.

"I am sorry to disappoint you, my friend, but I have no idea where the future Mrs. Swinton is residing." Alford grinned wickedly. "Although there is a good chance it is in London. It shouldn't take you more than five or six weeks to locate her.''

"Your father would know," Cole pointed out.

Alford shrugged carelessly. "More than likely. But what are you going to do when you find her? Inspect her like some piece of horseflesh at Tattersalls? She might allow you to examine her teeth, but I highly doubt she will appreciate a thorough examination of her hindquarters.''

Trent's loud snicker rent the air.

Hervey adopted the air of injured innocence. "We was just trying to help your brother. He won't want to get shackled to an antidote.''

Cole and Trent nodded in agreement.

"Gentlemen, it is a matter of supreme indifference to me what my brother plans to do with himself. If he wishes to marry at his tender age, who am I to say him no?'' There was an edge to Alford's voice.

Cole and the others wisely kept silent.

Alford looked around the table, the sharp look in his icy blue eyes belying his languid pose. "Now, gentlemen, where were we, before this untimely interruption?''

Almhurt's loud snore punctuated the question.

"Drat this pen!" Florence Washburn tossed down her quill with disgust. "That is the fifth point to splinter.''

"Perhaps if you wrote with a lighter hand . . .'' her Aunt Agatha suggested.

Florrie scowled. "It is only that there is so much to take care of, and so little time to accomplish it. I cannot believe Kit is behaving so abominably.''

"Now, Florrie," her aunt cautioned. " 'Tis not his fault he could not get home for the wedding.''

"But what a miserable way to get married," Florrie wailed. "First my groom is unable to attend, and now I find I must have his odious brother standing in as proxy. It is enough to make me scream.''

"I am certain Lord Alford will play his role admirably.''

"You wait," Florrie warned, her hazel eyes flashing. "He

will find some way to ruin the whole day for me. I loathe the man. I *detest* him. It is the one bad thing about marrying Kit—I will be connected to that oaf.''

"You have not seen the boy in ages," Agatha reminded her. "I am certain he has grown into an admirable young man."

Florrie stared at her aunt as if she had sprouted wings. "Do you not ever listen to gossip, Auntie? Alford's name is on everyone's tongue. He is a dissipated gamester who chases anything in skirts. His ladies are legion. But then, I hear he has a fondness for older women, so perhaps you and he will deal well together."

"Florrie!"

She grinned impishly. "Well, perhaps he will behave himself at such a solemn occasion." Florrie sighed, absently twining a lock of her dark blond hair around her finger. "It will be a rather sad affair to be a married lady without a husband. Even when I arrive in Portugal there is no guarantee Kit will be able to join me. I wish he would sell out and take up a Foreign Office position sooner rather than later."

"You are both still young with plenty of time ahead," Agatha said. "A year or two in the military will seem as nothing one day. And you yourself said it was only gaining Kit more connections."

"I know," Florrie said, turning with resignation back to the pile of invitations to be addressed. "And I am certain Portugal will prove interesting. I will be able to learn Portuguese and Spanish at the same time."

"As if you did not have enough languages," her aunt groaned.

"A diplomat's wife must be accomplished," Florrie reminded her. "Just think how dreadfully boring it would be if I only knew English. I would miss out on all manner of exciting conversations."

"Which would probably be all the better for you," her aunt warned. "Your father told me about that incident in St. Petersburg."

"Oh, pooh," said Florrie. " 'Incident' is far too strong a word. It was merely a minor misunderstanding. And had my Polish been up to the mark, it would not have happened at all. I simply thought we were going for a drive in the country, not eloping.''

"All the more reason to see you safely wed, my dear." Sir Roger Washburn strode into the room and planted a kiss on his daughter's brow. Despite the fact he had just passed his fiftieth year, his form was as trim as it had been at twenty. Only the hair that was now more gray than brown gave a hint of his years. "As a married lady, you will be less of a candidate for these foreign intriguers. You will have a husband to protect you."

"Which will do me an endless amount of good when he is hundreds of miles away," she complained with the slightest hint of a pout.

"I am certain that *Mrs. Swinton* will be able to handle herself with aplomb," Sir Roger added. "Have the invitations been addressed yet?"

"Almost," Florrie replied. She ticked the list off on her fingers. "The food order has been placed with the caterers, the flowers are ordered, I go for my final dress fitting tomorrow, and the musicians have been engaged."

"Good job, my dear. As always. I am having dinner with the earl tonight, to discuss the final settlements. Barstow informs me that Alford has finally signed the proxy papers, so it appears everything is in order."

Florrie wrinkled her nose at the mention of her future brother-in-law, a gesture not missed by her father.

"Now, Florrie," he warned. "How can you expect to be an effective diplomatic hostess when you make your aversions so well known? Personal opinion has no place in diplomatic circles."

"Neither does Alford, thank goodness. If Kit and I are very lucky, we will find ourselves posted to all manner of exotic capitals and I will not even have to think about Alford for another ten years."

"I doubt Barstow will let you get that far from him. Remember, little one, Kit is next in line until Alford marries and produces a son. And if rumor is correct, he shows no intentions of settling down anytime soon. Barstow will want to keep a close eye on Kit until the succession is secured.''

"Perhaps you can arrange a proxy marriage for Alford.''
Florrie brightened at the thought. "Find some ignorant thing
who has not heard his name. All he needs is one son and
Kit is free."

"What, you do not relish the idea of being a countess one
day?" Sir Roger's eyes twinkled with teasing.

"Oh, I hope to be at least that,'' she retorted with a smug
expression. "But Kit will have his own title, thank you, as
reward for services extended to the Crown. Alford is
welcome to become Earl of Barstow."

"We shall see,'' her father said, rising. "Since you ladies
have everything so well in hand, I'm off to the club. I'll tell
you about the meeting with Barstow tomorrow.''

Florrie airily waved her papa out of the room and turned
her hand back to addressing the remaining invitations.

She really did look forward to this marriage. Oh, not
because she was top-over-tails in love with Kit. She regarded
him much more as a slightly elder brother, for that was the
role he had played during most of their time together. But
Kit would make an amiable companion, and that counted for
much in the diplomatic circles they would find themselves
in. And even if he was just starting out in his career, she
would rather align herself with him than an older, more
experienced hand. For after acting as hostess to her father
since she was fifteen, Florrie rather liked the idea that she
would be much more familiar with diplomatic life than her
husband. Kit would turn to her for advice and information.
The two of them would make an excellent team.

Still, there was this business with Alford to get through.
She shuddered slightly at the thought. Alford had never made
an effort to hide his contempt for her when they were
children. He had always refused to allow "a girl" to play
pirates or soldiers with him and Kit. And when words had
not been enough to discourage her, he had subjected her to
the full force of his creative torments. If she never set eyes
on him again during her lifetime, it would not be long
enough. And now she was not only going to be forced into
the same room with him, but must repeat her marriage vows

to him instead of Kit. For the hundredth time, she wished she could sail to Portugal and marry Kit there. But with her father off to Sweden, there was no one willing to take the responsibility of chaperoning an unmarried young lady for any length of time. Marriage to Kit would give her the respectability and freedom she needed to travel on her own.

And if it took seeing Alford again to achieve that, it was worth it, Florrie thought. She would be as polite as could be to her future brother-in-law—in public, at least. But she could continue to think what she would about him in private.

The rest of the household was fast asleep by the time Sir Roger sat in the library of his hastily rented London townhouse, staring for an inordinate amount of time at the papers he held in his hand. Did he dare act on them?

He shifted in his chair and took a welcome swallow of port from his glass. He considered his options. His main goal was to do what was right for Florrie. As her father, it was his duty to see that she was properly settled. With no wife to guide him, he had to make the decision he thought best. That was why he had brought his daughter back to England now. The Continent was no place for a young, single woman with the Corsican poised to wreak havoc again.

Plus, it was time his daughter had a life of her own. He would miss her skills as a hostess, but it was time she set up her own establishment. He had thought this marriage to Christopher Swinton was an ideal solution to the problem of Florrie. "Problem" was too harsh a word—dilemma, perhaps. The chit had an innate knack for the diplomatic life. She was still young, and a bit impulsive, but with a few more years behind her, she would soon be a force to be reckoned with. It was imperative that she wed a man equal to her talents.

Kit Swinton was a logical choice. He had the advantage of having known Florrie since she was a babe in leading strings. They were amiable companions. And Kit would go far, Sir Roger had no doubt. Although young, he was ambitious and talented enough to aim high. After some much needed seasoning as a staff officer, he would be able to step into an assistant ambassadorship without difficulty. And with Florrie at his side . . . they would be an imposing team.

But how much more power could Florrie wield in a similar position here in England? As wife of a sitting Lord, or cabinet minister . . . The possibilities were endless. And Sir Roger held in his hand the route to that end.

Alford's carelessness did give him pause. Sir Roger had investigated the man most carefully, and much of what he learned did not give him pleasure. The truth of Alford's existence more than corroborated his reputation. The lad was well on his way to a life of dissipation and waste. But that chat earlier with Barstow revealed another side to the story. Washburn could not approve of the way Barstow held his heir on such short rein, and it was only logical that Alford chafed at the strain. True, he had not shown any of the ambitions of his younger brother. But with a skilled hand to guide him . . . There was more than one politician whose wife held the true power.

Sir Roger again leafed through the proxy papers in his hands. An honorable man would return them immediately to the earl. An honorable man would not attempt to trick both his daughter and her future in-laws. An honorable man would abhor the action he contemplated.

But honor went only so far. When it came up against opportunity, the lines blurred. And was not diplomacy the art of taking advantage of opportunity?

Still, it was highly possible his plan would not work. All might be uncovered beforetimes, and corrected. And what would happen later, when the deception was revealed? He must plan very carefully. There had to be a way to make certain that the results could not be challenged. It would take careful doing, but he might be able to manage the arrangements. It was a delicate matter, with innumerable potential for error. But Sir Roger had not risen as high as he had in diplomatic circles without acquiring a number of devious methods. He had a few tricks up his sleeve.

Chapter 2

"Of all the rude, intolerable, rag-mannered starts!" Florrie swept past her aunt with a furious swish of her skirts. "I told you he would find some method of ruining this day."

"Now Florrie," Agatha began. "Alford is only a trifle late. He will be arriving at any moment, I am certain."

" 'Twill be an awkward wedding reception if there is no wedding," Florrie said, stomping across her bedroom. "Perhaps this is merely his idea of a novel approach—first the celebration, then the wedding. I am supposed to be greeting guests in half an hour!"

"The ceremony will not take long." Aunt Agatha attempted to soothe her.

Florrie plopped onto the gilt chair by the window. "I should have gone straight to Portugal. I could have wed Kit there without any fuss."

Her aunt gently pulled Florrie to her feet and straightened her lace overskirt. "You will wrinkle your dress, dear."

"As if anyone will notice," Florrie grumbled. "It will be my continued status as *Miss* Washburn that will draw all the attention. How could he do this to me!"

"Florrie?" Sir Roger's voice came from the corridor.

"Come in," Florrie replied wearily, frowning into the pier glass on her dresser. She looked a fright. A dark, angry flush stained her cheeks and all her agitated wanderings had caused half her curls to tumble down about her shoulders. This was all Alford's fault!

"I have been speaking with the vicar," Sir Roger said upon entering. "He states there is no difficulty in substituting another proxy for Alford."

"You mean we do not have to wait for that miserable creature?" Hope dawned on Florrie's face.

"You may wish to adopt a more politic method of describing your future brother-in-law," Sir Roger chided her gently.

Florrie shot him a look of disgust. "After he ruined what there is of my wedding? I can only hope he does not arrive at all, now. Who have you recruited to take his place?"

"Simmons," Sir Roger replied. "He is here already, picking up the last of the papers for the Foreign Office."

Florrie sighed. "He will do as well as anyone, I suppose." At that point, Mad King George could stand in for Kit and she would not care. She only wanted to get this ordeal over with.

"Then let us proceed with haste to the drawing room," Sir Roger said, offering his arm to his daughter. "We shall have this wedding yet before the guests arrive."

"May I offer a toast to the new Lady Alford?" The vicar beamed from behind his glasses upon the completion of the ceremony as the footmen poured glasses of champagne.

Florrie laughed. "I am sorry to have to deflate myself so, vicar, but I am only plain Mrs. Swinton. Alford's my brother-in-law."

The vicar looked confused. "I had thought . . ."

"A toast to the newlyweds," Sir Roger interjected hastily, and the small gathering lifted their glasses.

"My best to you, *Mrs.* Swinton," Simmons teased. "I am certain your father is relieved to have you safely wed at last."

"Along with Wellesley," joked Sir Roger. "He will no longer have to fear an international incident involving Florrie and some enamored European princeling."

Florrie endured their good-hearted teasing. She knew it was a relief for her father to hand her safely into another's hands. With the Continent in such turmoil, a young daughter was not the best companion. Sir Roger had left more than one post earlier than other diplomats, fearing for her safety. Florrie hoped he would not take any unnecessary chances now that he would be alone. With Napoleon's army dominating Europe, anything could happen.

"Another toast to my new daughter-in-law," Lord Barstow said. He kissed Florrie gently on the cheek. "You will be a welcome addition to the family, my dear. Kit is a lucky lad."

"Thank you," Florrie beamed with pleasure.

"No, I was right."

They all turned toward the vicar, who crossed the room with the marriage papers in hand, a perplexed frown on his face.

"It says quite plainly that Florence Amelia Washburn, spinster, has wed Thomas Beresford Swinton, Viscount Alford, with George Simmons standing as proxy."

"What?" Three voices exclaimed at once.

"Let me look at those." Sir Roger grabbed the papers from the vicar. "My God, it is true. Look here." He stepped next to Barstow and pointed out the incriminating signatures. "Looks like your boy missigned the paperwork. I did not even think to examine it beforehand!"

"I don't believe it," Florrie snapped, snatching the papers from her father's hands. A quick perusal only confirmed his words. "This is insane."

"It will only take a few moments to straighten things out," Sir Roger assured her. He took the papers and returned them to the vicar. "Cross out Alford's name and write in Christopher Swinton. Can't have my girl married to the wrong man."

The vicar smiled weakly. "I am afraid I cannot do that, sir."

"What?" Barstow demanded.

The vicar cleared his throat. "I have just conducted a legal wedding, my lord. With Viscount Alford's signature here," he pointed to the line on the page, "and the proxy's signature there, this is a perfectly legal document."

"Then tear it up and start over," Barstow growled.

"I cannot do that," the vicar said, defensively holding the papers close to his chest. "That would make Miss Washburn —I mean Lady Alford—subject to bigamy charges."

A loud crash resounded in the room. The men turned to stare at Florrie, who stood over the shattered remains of a crystal vase.

"Florrie," her father began warningly.

"Under no circumstances will I consent to this farce of a marriage," she announced with a defiant tilt to her chin. She whirled on the vicar. "You will change those papers and you will do it now."

The vicar protectively moved the papers behind his back as Florrie approached him.

"I cannot do that," he said again, blinking rapidly.

"Agatha, perhaps you would take Florrie upstairs so she can compose herself before the guests arrive," Sir Roger said. "Gentlemen, let us repair to the library where we can discuss this matter more thoroughly. I am certain there is a reasonable solution."

"I will not marry Alford," Florrie reiterated as her aunt dragged her out the door.

After Florrie's departure, Sir Roger dismissed Simmons and guided the vicar and Barstow into the library. When they were settled comfortably, he turned to the vicar. "Well," Sir Roger began, "what must we do to straighten this tangle out?"

"I am certain there are ample grounds for an annulment," the vicar replied nervously. "Under the circumstances . . . I would be quite willing to go over to Doctor's Commons right away and look into it."

"A good idea," said Sir Roger, dispatching the vicar with a wave of his hand. When he was gone, Sir Roger turned to the earl. "Is that heir of yours always so careless?"

Barstow shook his head in disgust. "It is a constant trial to me," he said. "I had thought he would outgrow his youthful escapades, but he seems to be hell-bent on proving he is as wild as ever. I knew I should not have relied on him to do this properly."

"You do not think he did this on purpose, as a prank?" Sir Roger's eyes were wide in questioning. "Is that perhaps the reason he is not here?"

"I do not know," Barstow moaned. He drained his glass in one large gulp. "I tell you, Roger, be glad you have only the girl. Sons are a deuced nuisance. Kit's as steady as they come, yet Alford's my heir and I cannot be easy about his manner of living. Every time I try to talk a little sense into him, he ignores my suggestions and goes his own way." He scowled darkly.

Sir Roger studied his glass. "Sounds like the lad could use a strong, steadying influence," he said carefully.

"I've tried to convince him to marry, hoping a wife might settle him down. Now I'd be content to see him wed just to ensure the succession, but he only laughs in my face at the suggestion," Barstow said. "It was one of the reasons I was so pleased to see Kit married. Assuming he and Florence have children, that matter would be taken care of no matter what Alford does."

"Do you think marriage would be enough to settle Alford down?" Sir Roger asked with a deliberately innocent expression.

"Certainly, if he tied the knot with the right chit. One who would not let him have his own way all the time, who would rein him in from his excesses, and encourage him to take up some other pursuit beside gaming and sporting."

Sir Roger looked pensive. "Florrie has a strong personality," he began hesitantly. "It takes a determined fight to thwart her wishes."

Barstow frowned. "Are you saying we should let this marriage stand?"

Sir Roger shrugged. "I must admit, it does not look like the most auspicious match right now. But if Alford and Florrie could be persuaded . . . She certainly has the strength of will to keep him in line."

The earl pondered his friend's words. "But what about Kit?"

Sir Roger waved a dismissive hand. "We both know this was no love match. It was a political union—the future diplomat with the perfect diplomatic hostess. I am certain Florrie thinks of Kit more as a brother than a husband."

The earl slowly nodded his agreement. "But how in the world do you intend to persuade your daughter to comply? She sounded rather adamant in the drawing room."

"You leave Florrie to me," Sir Roger assured him. "Once she sees the benefit of such a match, she will be of a more receptive mind. I am more concerned about Alford."

"No problem there," said Barstow smugly. "I'll just threaten to cut his allowance. His stable alone eats up half of it. He'll think twice about the matter if he's forced to give up his sporting pursuits."

Sir Roger retained his doubtful expression. "At the same time, I cannot be easy about this. I do not want Florrie tied to a man who will not treat her with the respect she deserves. Or who will only be one step ahead of the duns."

"Alford knows how to go on," Barstow growled. "Present him with this as a *fait accompli* and he will knuckle under. Mayhaps I can throw in a few horses or a new carriage to sweeten the deal. He can be made to see reason."

"Still . . ." Sir Roger feigned reluctance. "Florrie has her heart set on becoming a diplomatic hostess. Alford's interests run more to sport and games. . . ."

"Oh, Alford could hold his own in the political arena if he put his mind to it," Barstow assured him. "He's been after me for years to give him one of the parliamentary seats. Didn't think it necessary, before. Who wants to sit in the Commons?"

This revelation surprised Sir Roger. Was it possible that Alford *did* have a political bent? The news could not be better. Florrie could certainly give Alford an extra push in that direction.

"Perhaps, once the initial shock wears off, they both might listen to a reasoned explanation," Sir Roger said. "I will leave you to explain the situation to Alford, and I will deal with Florrie. It will take them a deucedly long time to go through all the legal rigmarole for an annulment in any event. We shall have plenty of time for artful persuasion."

. Barstow grinned in a conspiratorial manner. "To the newly wedded couple," he said, raising his glass. "Lord and Lady Alford."

Sir Roger found the brandy particularly satisfying.

Alford sat impatiently in the worn leather chair, his fingers beating a restless tattoo on the arm. How much longer was this going to take? He frowned at the glass of claret he held. This was not the finest vintage he had ever tasted. In fact, it came close to being one of the worst. But there was little else to help pass the time in this tumble-down inn. It boded ill for the remainder of the day.

"You certain we will still make London in time for the wedding?" Lewiston Hervey asked with apprehension.

"They can't hold the wedding without me, can they?" Alford asked, taking a long swallow of the ruby liquid. He stared glumly at the parlor door for the hundredth time. "How long can it take to reshoe a horse?"

"Told you we should have gone up yesterday," Hervey protested. "Would have been in London with plenty of time to spare."

"And missed the mill this morning?" Alford snorted his contempt. "Don't be a fool, Hervey, or I shall be tempted to leave you here when that bloody horse is finally ready to go. You made a tidy sum on the match."

The young man opened his mouth to protest, but then shut it quickly at the grim look Alford directed at him. He refilled his glass instead.

Alford's frown deepened. He had not wanted to have anything to do with this deuced wedding. If Kit was foolish enough to become a tenant-for-life, let him. But why drag his brother into it? Now Alford was forced to race back to town after a perfectly ripping mill in order to stand proxy at this ridiculous ceremony. *Anyone* could have stood proxy.

Alford did not hold with any sentimental twaddle about standing in for his brother. In fact, he suspected the idea was his father's doing. He scowled deeper at the thought. He and Kit were four years and poles apart. Kit was the son who could do no wrong, the one who was free to do what he pleased with his life, while his elder brother was bound to the useless role of heir. Unencumbered by a title and an estate, Kit had the freedom to choose his own path. While

Alford could do nothing. His own life could not start until his father was dead, until the inheritance passed to him— that is, his life could start if the boredom of waiting did not kill him in the intervening years.

"Do you ever wish, Hervey, that you were not an only child?"

Hervey blinked at him uncomprehendingly. "Why should I?"

"Just imagine," Alford suggested. "If you had an older brother, he'd become the new viscount when your father died and you could be anything you wanted."

"What else would I want to be?" Hervey asked.

"A rag peddler in Covent Gardens, you clunch," Alford said with irritation. "You could be with Wellington on the Peninsula, or trapping beaver in North America, or . . ."

"Sounds cold and wet and nasty to me," Hervey shivered. "I like it here."

"Then how about being a sitting Lord or a member of the Commons? Anything. Something."

Hervey shook his head. "They'd probably be in the middle of some crisis or another just when the next season at Newmarket comes. Can't walk out on the Prime Minister to watch a mill. Besides, you'd have to make speeches. Write them. Read them." He grimaced.

Alford shook his head in disgust. He should have known better than to ask Hervey, whose greatest ambition in life was to own a top-of-the-trees wardrobe and the horses to match. He had no concept of the frustration Alford experienced. No one of his acquaintance did. They were all content to waste their lives on frivolous pursuits while waiting to come into their inheritances. They had no lofty ambitions.

But he did. Or at least thought he did. It seemed his interest grew less and less each year as the reality of his situation sank in. It was only now, with Kit's marriage a reminder of how he was in the thick of things on the Peninsula, that the old resentments arose. Even that stupid Washburn chit had done more than he, spending time at nearly every court in Europe. Alford took another long look at the claret, then drained his glass. Damn life.

Alford's groom stepped through the door. "The horse is shod, my lord."

"It is about time," Alford grumbled. He nudged Hervey. "Time to go." He reached across the table and took hold of the half-empty claret bottle. "We'll take this with us. The roads are terribly dusty this spring."

Hervey grinned.

Chapter 3

By the time he stopped at his rooms at Albany and changed into formal clothing, Alford was willing to concede he *was* late for the blasted wedding. But after splitting not one, but three bottles of claret with Hervey during the last miles to London, Alford did not give a damn how late he was. No one had asked him if he wanted to be at this damned ceremony. They could damn well wait until he was ready.

A ruby fob attached to its chain put the finishing touches on his garb. Waving his valet aside, Alford entered the front room. Finding Hervey with a freshly cracked bottle, Alford insisted on a round of toasts before they departed for Washburn's rented residence.

"To the groom," Alford saluted. "Damn fool idiot that he is."

"To the lovely bride," Hervey mumbled.

"How do you know she's lovely?" Alford demanded querulously. "No one's seen the chit yet."

Hervey shrugged. "Just being polite."

Alford shook his head and laid a companionable arm on Hervey's shoulder. "Politeness will only get you into trouble, *laddie*. No one respects politeness. Rudeness is the key." He raised his glass. "To the bride—may she have spots, freckles, and a squint." He downed his drink in one swallow. "Now, let us seal Kit's doom!"

The lurching motion of the carriage as it jounced over the bumpy London streets caused Alford to realize just how much claret he had consumed. Considering the amount of spirits they had downed the previous night, it was doubtful he had ever been quite sober today. But he rapidly realized he was a bit more muzzle-headed than he would have preferred.

Alford could only guess at the look on his father's face when his elder son arrived at the ceremony totally mopped. T'would serve the old man right for dragging him into this.

Hervey nearly tumbled out the carriage door when it was flung open by the overzealous footman in front of Washburn's rented house. Alford descended more sedately, then climbed the steps to the townhouse with the carefully exaggerated tread of a man who was in his cups. Letting the brass door knocker fall with a resounding thud, he waited impatiently for the door to open, his body swaying slightly as he strove to maintain his balance. The transition from lurching carriage to rock-hard steps was disconcerting.

"Where is this deuced wedding supposed to be?" he demanded loudly of the butler who opened the door.

"To the left at the top of the stairs," the butler replied.

Alford turned back to Hervey, who lagged behind. "Come on, lad. Pick up the pace."

"I was not invited," he demurred.

"Of course you were," Alford insisted. "By me. Come along."

The sight that lay beyond the doors was not exactly what Alford had expected. He noted with dismay the numbers of people who stood about the drawing room. He had thought this was to be a small, private affair. It was ridiculous enough that he was being forced to go through with this inane proxy marriage. He did not want to do it in front of a crush of witnesses.

"Alford!" Lord Haverstoke bore down on him. "How like you to be late for your own wedding."

"Not my wedding," Alford grumbled, nervously grabbing a glass of champagne off a passing footman's tray. "Kit's."

Haverstoke smiled smugly and slipped way.

"What the devil?" Alford looked quizzically at Hervey. "Is Haverstoke bosky?"

Hervey shrugged.

A resounding thump across his shoulder blades nearly caused Alford to choke on his champagne.

"Alford, you sly dog," chortled Seb Cole. "Putting out that this was to be Kit's wedding when all along—"

"Kit's not going to have a wedding if I can't find the damn bride," Alford said curtly. "Who are all these people?" he asked with a wild sweep of his arm that threatened to overset several guests.

Seb took him carefully by the arm and drew him to the side of the room. "Have you seen your father since you arrived?"

Alford shook his head, downing the remainder of the champagne in one gulp. He looked about for another.

"Perhaps you should find him," Seb suggested.

"Can't hold the ceremony without me." Alford shrugged.

"Alford, you certainly took everyone by surprise." Another tulip of the *ton* presented himself before Alford's blurred vision. "Suppose this means you'll give up your rooms at Albany. Put my name on the list."

"Mine too," chimed in another.

"I asked first," the tulip insisted.

"I'll throw in a monkey."

"Two."

"Four."

Alford sauntered away. He'd never let either of those idiots have his rooms. But why should he be giving his rooms away? Where else would he stay? Those two were surely in their altitudes to even suggest such a thing. Wearily he scanned the room, looking for his father. One would think more consideration would be shown to a key member of the wedding party. He sipped his champagne slowly, listening to the conversation swirling around him.

"I heard the bride was livid," one matron said in a voice loud enough to be overheard.

"Wouldn't you be?" her companion replied. "A title would be small recompense for life with one such as *him.*"

"Do you think they will be able to annul the marriage?"

Alford shook his head. Some poor girl had obviously found herself married to an unsuitable *parti.* Parental pressure, no doubt.

"Found your father yet?" Seb reappeared at Alford's side.

He shook his head. "Maybe Kit came to his senses and called the thing off."

Alford felt an elbow dig into his ribs.

"Can't blame you for looking so downcast," Lord Exham said with a sly smile. "Cheer up. My uncle's a solicitor and I am certain he would love to take the case."

"What in God's name is everyone talking about?" Alford turned to Seb.

Seb's smile widened. "You really do need to find your father. I am sure he will enlighten you. Try the morning room. Second room on the left across the corridor." He strolled away.

Alford stared at his departing friend with growing bemusement. He knew he had imbibed more than his wont, but it was not nearly enough to account for his confusion. He did not mistake the odd looks and stifled snickers directed his way. No one he had yet spoken with made any sense. That was what came of being so generous with the champagne for the guests. They were all three sheets to the wind. Alford grew convinced he was the soberest man among them.

Where was his father? It was odd no one had come searching for him, late as he had been. A wicked smile crept over his face. Maybe the bride herself had been in the champagne.

Several futile moments of searching led Alford to believe that his father, as well as the bride, had disappeared. If they were in no hurry to find him, Alford was in no hurry to get on with this ridiculous farce. Half of London must be here at what he had been told would be a "private" wedding. He was damned if he was going to stand amid this crush and be gawked at. Alford appropriated another glass of champagne from a passing footman and went in search of some privacy.

The Washburn chit must be more of an antidote than even he thought, that she would hide herself away on her wedding day. His brow wrinkled in concentration as he tried to conjure up some remembrance of her face, but all he could recall was her plaintive, whiny voice as she begged to trail behind him and Kit. Kit had succumbed to her pleas, but Alford had not. In fact, he recalled with a grin, he had rather effectively taken care of her annoying presence. *That* had been worth the punishment that followed. She still had the sense to stay out of his way.

A few false explorations and the back stairs finally led him to the solitude of the library. Alford flopped his tall frame into one of the comfortably worn chairs before the cold fire grate and sipped at his champagne. Time and enough to worry about Kit's intended later.

Florrie peered cautiously around the corner, making certain no one was in the entry hall. Finding it empty, she hurried across the corridor and into the dining room. If she encountered one more person's false congratulations, she would go mad.

She pushed open the door to the library with a hesitant hand. Relief flooded her face when she found the room empty. Slipping quickly inside, she shut the door behind her.

"The devil and damnation," she muttered, plopping down on the sofa. This had to be the most miserable day of her life. And it was all Alford's fault.

"My sentiments exactly," drawled Alford from his chair in the far corner.

Florrie swore again, silently, at having been caught out in such an unlady-like display of temper in front of this stranger. "I beg your pardon," she said. "I had no idea you were there."

Alford saluted her with his glass. "You are more than welcome to stay. The room is large enough for two." His eyes swept over her in an admiring glance. Damn if this chit wasn't a beauty. His gaze took in her flawless cream complexion, the honey-blond hair, and the very enticing display of bosom above her fashionably low-cut gown. Damned nice.

Florrie eyed the stranger warily. He was handsome enough, his dark hair artfully tousled in the current style, his clothes well-tailored in a fashionable mode. But his good looks were not enough to overcome her irritation at finding her haven occupied.

"Who are you?" Florrie demanded.

"Only a man in search of quiet and solitude," Alford

replied with careful enunciation. He rose and walked with studied care across the room to stand before her, wishing he had thought to bring his quizzing glass. This lady bore further inspection.

Flushing at his avid perusal, Florrie sought to rein in her temper. "I would ask, then, sir, that you respect my need for the same."

"I see you, too, have found today's revelries wearying," he said. He sat beside her without invitation, eyeing her with increased interest.

Florrie groanèd inwardly. She had been looking for some quiet retreat, away from all the curious eyes and snickering congratulations of their guests. Good God, how could anyone think that marriage to Alford was an enviable state? And now this odious man—who looked to be well on his way to drunkenness—was leering at her like a French sailor.

"I beg you to leave, sir," she ordered in annoyance.

"Leave?" Alford took her hands in his and drew them to his chest. "The most beautiful woman in the house suddenly appears before my eyes and begs me to depart? Alas, fair lady, I cannot bear to be cast so gracelessly from your presence." He brought one hand to his lips.

Florrie tried to pull her hand away, but he only clenched it harder. There was no question, the man was foxed. Trust her to have wandered into his lair. "I must protest, sir. We have not even been introduced."

"There will be time and enough for that later," he said, slipping his other arm about her waist and pulling her nearer.

The first faint twinges of unease spread through Florrie. Surely this drunken lout was not going to attack her in her own house? Why, someone could walk in at any moment. Was he mad as well as drunk?

She planted a false smile upon her face. "I am dreadfully thirsty," she said. "Could you perhaps bring me a glass of something refreshing?"

"And can I ask a favor from you in return, fair lady?"

"Oh, certainly," she replied. She would make her bolt for the door the instant he released her.

"I have some perfectly wonderful champagne just over

there.'' He nodded toward the corner. "But I should like to claim my reward first.''

He leaned toward her in a most alarming manner. Florrie edged away. "First the champagne, then the reward," she countered.

"All right."

Florrie misjudged her timing by the merest fraction. When the stranger removed his arm and dropped her hand, she leaped to her feet. But before she could take her first step, she found herself grabbed about the waist and unceremoniously plunked down upon the man's lap.

"Thought to trick me, did you?" He chuckled as he wrapped his arms tighter about her.

Florrie felt his warm breath against her neck and fought against her rising panic. She doubted that a scream would be heard amidst all the noise from the celebrants upstairs. How frightfully ironic to be in such an awkward situation in her own home!

She jumped when she felt the man's lips nuzzling her neck. "Let me go," she cried, and began to struggle in earnest. This man had rapidly changed from a rather overbearing drunk into an obnoxious lecher.

"I like a lady with a little spirit," he said, holding her flailing arms tightly in his.

"Sir, I am a married lady," she cried. "My husband . . .''

He silenced her with his lips, her final words trailing off in a muffled mumble.

Florrie struggled against his arms, unable to free herself from his hold. She could not even yell for help now, with his mouth pressed against hers.

Even in his drunken state, Alford was not too far gone to recognize the lady's real reluctance. He had no intention of hurting her and quickly loosened his hold. But before the lady took advantage of her freedom, the library door creaked open.

"Good Lord!"

"Thomas!"

The shocked tones of Sir Roger and the Earl of Barstow

reached Florrie's ears. Taking advantage of the disgusting lecher's surprise, Florrie twisted away and stared at her father.

"Looks as though they are eager to get things off to a good start," joked the Earl of Barstow, standing next to Sir Roger in the doorway.

Sir Roger laughed. "I own I was worried that he would entertain some concern about the mix-up. But he seems to have the situation well in hand."

Alford suddenly sobered, feeling an overwhelming sense of dread. "Will someone please explain what is going on?" Alford pleaded. He turned to the woman still clasped in his arms. "Who are you?" he demanded.

"Miss Florence Washburn!" she retorted.

A grimace of dismay crossed his face and he hastily pushed her off his lap back onto the couch. Florrie immediately balled up her fingers into a fist and punched him in the nose.

"You disgusting pig!" she shrieked as she clambered off the sofa.

"My nose!" Alford felt, rather than saw, the blood dripping from his nose, and he scrambled frantically in his pocket for a handkerchief to stem the bleeding.

"A bleeding nose is the least of your worries," Florrie sneered. "My father will be more than anxious to deal with you."

Sir Roger cleared his throat. "Florrie, dear, I fear perhaps you have not recognized your old friend. Kit's brother. Viscount Alford."

Florrie stared in amazement at the man on the sofa. His face was obscured by the large, red-stained handkerchief he held to his nose. His pale blue eyes glared at her from over the edge of the linen. Alford? Wrinkling her nose, she tried to picture the obnoxious youth he had been when she last saw him. Florrie turned a puzzled look to her father and the earl.

Barstow grinned from ear to ear. He elbowed Sir Roger in the ribs. "Looks like he was just a bit too eager to claim his husbandly rights."

It was that which made Florrie realize they were telling the truth; this was Alford. "You oaf!" she yelled, striding over and giving him a firm box to the ears.

"Ow!" Alford recoiled in pain. "Call off this hell-cat, Washburn, before she kills me."

"Now, Florrie, this is no way to treat your husband," Sir Roger cautioned, trying to hold back his mirth.

"Husband!" In his surprise, Alford dropped the handkerchief.

"For God's sake, get that linen back on your nose. You're bleeding like a stuck pig," Barstow said. "Didn't anyone tell you?"

"Tell me what?" Alford demanded.

Barstow heaved a sigh of exasperation. "Thanks to your carelessness with the proxy papers, you've managed to get yourself married to your brother's intended."

"What?"

"You signed where Kit's signature was to go," Sir Roger explained. "You became the groom."

"He will be my husband over my dead body!" yelled Florrie.

"It would be a pleasure," Alford mumbled sourly from behind his handkerchief.

Sir Roger and the earl exchanged conspiratorial glances.

"Perhaps we should allow them some time to become re-acquainted," Barstow suggested. "I am certain Alford can be trusted to behave in a more gentlemanly manner with his *wife.*"

"Not bloody likely," the viscount muttered.

Ignoring his son, Barstow took Sir Roger by the arm and they left the library, shutting the door behind them.

Alford cast one withering glance Florrie's way, then tilted his head back against the cushions, keeping his nose elevated.

"Is it broken?" Florrie asked at last.

"How the hell should I know?" he said, his voice muffled.

Florrie looked away. "I really did not mean to break it, you know," she said with a hint of apology. "But you certainly deserved it." She looked sideways at him again. "If you pinch the nostrils, the bleeding might stop."

"This is not the first bloodied nose I've had," he snapped. "I know what to do."

"It certainly does not look like it," she returned with a scathing glance. "Dabbing at it like that will only keep it bleeding longer."

"Oh, I suppose you are a trained physician in addition to being a lady of science?" he sneered.

She began laughing and he glared at her again.

"I can't help it," she gasped, her mirth spilling out. "You look so amusing!"

He shifted on the sofa and turned away from her.

"Oh, don't be so peevish, Alford. You have to admit you well deserved it. What were you thinking of, to grab a lady so? You are lucky it was I, or you would be facing an irate father or husband over the end of a pistol in the morning."

"I can think of worse fates," he grumbled.

"Like being married to you?" She snorted. "You have only yourself to blame for that, *my lord*. 'Twas your misplaced signature that did the deed."

"I do not believe it. This is some scheme cooked up by you or your crafty father."

"Hardly," she replied coldly. "No one in their right mind would wish to be married to you."

"You were eager enough to have Kit."

"Kit is my friend," she said. "I would not have you if you were the last man on earth. Leading apes would prove a better fate."

"They probably would not want you either," he said.

"Hah!" she retorted. "I could have wed any number of men these past years. I am marrying Kit by choice, not necessity."

"Damned convenient he is out of the country," Alford said snidely. "If he spent half a fortnight in your company, he'd change his mind quick enough."

"It takes only five minutes in *your* company to be certain I would not even want to be in the same house with you."

"That can be most easily arranged," he said.

They lapsed into angry silence, marred only by Alford's labored breathing.

He truly could not believe this was all happening. Through some fantastic chain of circumstances, he was wed to this odious witch—it had been corroborated by not only his father, but hers as well. But he clung to a glimmer of hope—certainly a person could not be married against their will in this day and age. All he would have to do is explain the situation to someone in authority and the union would be dissolved. He would not stay married to this shrew no matter how lovely she was.

He twisted slightly and watched her through half-closed eyes. If he had seen her across a room at a rout, and been told she was Florence Washburn, he would have called the man a liar. When he had last seen her she was a raggle-taggle hoyden, with hair done up in braids, her dress torn, and her face dirty. She had been, in fact, a pestilential brat who would not give him or Kit a moment's peace. To think that ragamuffin child had grown into *this*.

For one quick moment he envied Kit. Kit, who had seen her during the years she grew up, and probably knew what a beauty he was capturing. Kit never took a wrong step; Alford should have remembered that. He would never have wed anything less than perfection.

Perfection indeed! Hah! She may have the face and form of an angel, but she had the temper and tongue of a Billingsgate fishwife. Kit was welcome to her. Alford would escort her to the damned dock himself if it meant she was off to Portugal the quicker.

He carefully lifted away his stained handkerchief, dabbing at his nose with one unsullied corner to see if the bleeding had at last stopped. Satisfied it had, he turned toward her again.

"Would you be so kind as to bring me my glass of champagne, Miss Washburn?"

"Miss Washburn? Do you always treat every woman you attack with such formality after?"

"What would you prefer?" he asked sarcastically. "Lady Alford?" He winced at the sound and he felt a new trickle of blood start down his lip. "Damn."

Florrie stood in front of him, grabbin the handkerchief

from his hands. "Trust a man not to know how to do this properly." She twisted one corner into a narrow wad and stuffed it up his bleeding nostril. "Now leave it there!"

"I can't breathe," he complained.

"Breathe through your mouth," she ordered. She crossed the room and procured Alford's glass. Walking back to where he sat, she could not help but laugh at the sight.

"Glad I can amuse you," he said, taking the glass.

"You have to admit you look a fright, with your handkerchief hanging out of your nose." She grinned.

Ignoring her, he carefully pushed the cloth away from his mouth and took a long swallow from his glass.

Florrie sat in a chair, watching him with an assessing eye. He had grown from the gawky adolescent she remembered into a tolerably good looking man. Well, perhaps better than tolerable. The lashes that were closed over those icy blue eyes were indecently long. His face was lean without being thin, and for all the rumors she had heard about his dissipated lifestyle, not a trace of it showed in his face. But no manner of good looks could overcome his odious personality. Florrie almost hoped she had broken his nose—it was unfair that such male perfection hid an unconscionable rake.

Alford's eyes flew open, scowling at the sight of her. "Are you still here?" he groaned. "I had hoped you would be gone by now."

"I thought we should discuss our next step."

"What next step?" he asked suspiciously.

"Getting out of this ridiculous marriage, you idiot."

He sighed. "I assume father's solicitor can take care of it."

"Are you so certain that your father will do so? He sounded suspiciously happy when he was here."

Alford sat upright. "There is no way on earth I will remain in this marriage," he said. "And since we seem to think alike on that point, I think we should proceed immediately to getting the matter disentangled. I will hire my own lawyer if I have to."

Florrie breathed a hidden sigh of relief. Despite all of Alford's protestations, it was *he* who had missigned the papers. It must truly have been an accident.

"Fine," she announced, standing up. "I shall leave matters in your capable hands. Inform me when the matter has been taken care of."

"With pleasure," he grumbled before collapsing back against the cushions again.

Chapter 4

Florrie stood with hands on hips amidst the chaos of her bed chamber, glaring at her maid. Clothes lay in disordered piles on every surface, while two yawning trunks took up much of the floor space. Marie stared back at her with defiant black eyes.

"I have no weesh to go to theese sea coast," the maid protested. "The country—bah!"

"The English countryside is a sight more civilized than Portugal and you had no objections to going there," Florrie retorted.

Marie gave a disdainful sniff. "Portugal is at least close to France. I never heard of theese Hartland."

Florrie tossed up her hands in disgust. "Well, you will not get to Portugal with me if you do not accompany me on this journey first," she stormed.

"Fine weeth me," the maid replied. "I weel find myself a new position in London."

"That you will," Florrie said, shaking with rage at the girl's impertinence. "Out of my sight. Now."

She sank down on the bed as the maid shut the door none-too-gently behind her. The situation went from bad to worse. First the botched marriage to Alford, then her father's insistence that she leave town to still the gossip, now this. She was being shipped off to some horridly isolated corner of the island without even her own maid to accompany her. She'd probably end up having to use some bovine farm girl who did not know which end of a needle to thread, let alone how to care for Florrie's clothes. Not that that haughty French creature had been much better. She had far too great an opinion of herself for a maid. Typical French arrogance.

Florrie set her mouth in a stubborn line. She would not

do it, she decided. Either her father sent her to some location that was at least on the fringes of civilization, or she would insist on staying in London until she was free to join Kit on the Peninsula. She would not be stuffed away in some desolate back corner of the country as if she had done something wrong. With renewed determination, she marched out of her room in pursuit of her father.

She cornered Sir Roger in the library.

"It is impossible," she announced, "for me to go to Hartland."

"Oh?" Setting his pen aside, he looked inquisitively at his daughter.

"My maid just quit. I shall have to remain in town. I certainly cannot depart on such a lengthy journey on my own."

Unless, of course, you wanted to, Sir Roger thought. "That problem can be easily resolved. We shall find you another maid. I am certain London has an ample supply."

"But how can I train a new one properly in the *country*?" Florrie pronounced the word with about as much enthusiasm as an exiled member of the Bourbons would say "Napoleon."

"I am certain you will find some way to manage, my dear." Sir Roger suppressed a chuckle. He had expected his daughter's protests to start earlier than this. It was an indication of how unsettling this whole marriage confusion had been to Florrie that it had taken her so long to come up with her excuses.

"And, of course, there is the additional difficulty of finding a maid who will also be willing to travel with me to Portugal."

"Not an easy task," her father agreed.

"So I think it would be best for me to stay in London," Florrie continued. "I can interview for a new maid and prepare her for the trip to Portugal when this blessed annulment comes through."

"I do not think that is the wisest course," Sir Roger said, putting on his sternest face. "My first concern has to be for you, Florrie, and for your reputation. We have been abroad for too long. The London matrons are not familiar with you, and have no other way to judge you but by hearsay. It behooves you to behave as circumspectly as possible until this little matter is dealt with.''

"But . . ."

"Your removal from the city, as well as Alford's, will dampen even the busiest of tongues. Later, after the annulment is finalized, you will be able to come back and once again take your place as a young, betrothed lady. There will be no question about your situation.''

"It is not fair!" Florrie fumed. "It was not *my* fault this happened.''

"Of course not,'' Sir Roger said soothingly. "I would like to take a horsewhip to Alford for being so careless. But the deed is done and we will have to wait until it can be undone. Besides, it will be a treat for you to spend some time in the English countryside.''

"Why cannot I go someplace closer to London? Someplace that is not the next thing to the end of the earth?''

"Now, Florrie, it was not easy trying to find a suitable place for you to stay. It would accomplish nothing if you were to stay in a neighborhood with close connections to London. In Hartland, you will remain totally free of any gossip.''

"And totally isolated,'' she moaned.

"It will be over soon.'' Sir Roger gave her an encouraging smile. "And you will have plenty of time to study your Spanish grammar. Now decide what requirements you want in a maid and we can go about looking for a new one before you leave.''

Florrie sighed, knowing she had lost the argument. It was exile for her, after all. "All right, Papa,'' she said, bending down to kiss his cheek.

"Won't be the same here without you,'' Hervey mumbled into his brandy glass.

"Quite true,'' drawled Seb Cole, leaning negligently against the mantel in Alford's front room at Albany.

"London is likely to be a deuced bore for the rest of the Season without you here, Alford."

"Don't I know it," the viscount replied. He stared morosely at the flickering fire. "I feel like some naughty boy being sent to bed without supper. Promise me you will come to visit."

Hervey and Cole exchanged dubious glances.

"Devon's a long distance away . . ." Seb began hesitantly.

"And will take you away from the pursuit of your pleasures for far too long," Alford continued sarcastically. "At least now I know who my true friends are."

"It's not like you're going to be there forever," Hervey said. "We'd come down for certain then. But if it's only to be a month . . . We'd spend most of the time traveling to and fro."

"Easy for you to say it's not forever," Alford retorted, sinking even lower into his chair. "Two days in Devon would be enough for anyone. I am looking at weeks."

"You can always hie down to Plymouth if you get bored," Seb pointed out.

"They don't even have roads where I am going." Alfred scowled. " 'Hieing down to Plymouth' would be the equivalent of returning to London."

"Your father'd never know if you left," Hervey said. "You wouldn't see anyone in Plymouth who'd spill the tale. The whole point of this is to get out of London to stop the tattle. Seems to me that Plymouth would do just as well as any."

"You don't know my father," Alford moaned. "I would not put it past him to send an armed guard to accompany me. Face it, men, I will have about as much freedom as some French prisoner in Dartmoor."

"Gossip will die down soon," Hervey said with an optimistic tone. "I ain't going to talk about it anymore. Everyone will forget in a week. You will be back before you know it. Plenty of time left in the Season."

"But there's Newmarket. And Epsom. The Derby." Alford groaned at the thought of all that he might miss.

"I'll run your bets for you," Hervey offered.

Alford pierced him with a withering glance. "I never let anyone place my bets," he said coldly. "And certainly not if I am unable to check on the horses beforehand."

"Don't be so Friday-faced," said Seb, clapping Alford on the shoulder. "Think of all the feminine sympathy you can evoke upon your return from exile. The ladies will be enticed with your mournful tale."

"They'll probably have forgotten my name by then," Alford said glumly. "They'll pass me in the street and not even recognize my face."

"Well, they'd hardly know you now anyway with that nose," Hervey pointed out.

Alford scowled, then winced as the movement pained him. He gently touched his fingers to his nose. Although it was not broken, the appendage was swollen and still hurt like hell a full two days after Miss Washburn had landed that stupendous right. He could only be thankful his eyes had not blackened in the bargain.

"I was thinking," Hervey began, looking around the chamber with an eager glance. "With you being out of town and all, this place is going to sit empty. I could stay here, keep an eye on things if you like."

"Oh, wonderful," said Alford. "Now I know why you are so willing to shove me out of town. You want my rooms. Can I get anything else for you, Hervey? Would you like my valet as well? The curricle? The dancer at the opera?"

"Well, since you won't be able to do much for her while you're in Devon, I—" Seb's sharp jab in the ribs silenced him.

"Perhaps you will find adventure in Devon," Seb suggested. "Smugglers. Or a ring of French spies. You can capture them with brave feats of derring-do and come back a hero."

Alford brightened. "Perhaps I can find a source of some decent brandy," he mused.

"That's the spirit," Seb said with an encouraging smile. "The whole thing will be over before you know it. You'll be unleg-shackled in no time and can once again walk the streets of London a free man."

"I won't feel safe until I know that wretched Miss Washburn is safely on her way to Portugal," Alford said. "I will live in fear of another attack until then."

"Still sure you don't want to warn Kit about her?" Hervey looked concerned. "Can't see how your brother would wish to marry a girl who made a habit of unprovoked attacks on men."

Alford had not confessed the true tale of the events leading up to Florrie's well-placed punch. "Kit's a military man. He can keep her in line with his sword, if need be."

"Must have caught you by surprise. You're pretty handy with your own sword," Hervey snickered.

Alford silenced him with a withering glare. "My one consolation is that if Kit's diplomatic career flourishes, I may never have to see her again."

"Wouldn't mind seeing her again, myself," Seb said, pouring a generous measure of brandy into everyone's glass. "She is certainly no antidote. I'll give Kit credit for his taste."

"You'll probably have ample opportunity to ogle the witch," Alford said acidly. "She'll probably be all over town, flaunting my folly." He sighed. "Why should I be the one forced to leave?"

"It's your nose," Hervey suggested. "Might lead to all sorts of embarrassing questions. You wouldn't want it to be known that she popped you one."

Alford felt tempted to pop one of his own—at Hervey. "Devon," he groaned again. The end of the world.

Chapter 5

Alford stared blankly at the opposite wall of the coach, his discomfort growing with each revolution of the wheels. Blast the English rain that kept him cooped up inside. His fingers drummed restlessly on the seat beside him. Would this interminable journey never end? The two days spent on the road already seemed like weeks.

The coach lurched as it hit another rut and Alford's stomach lurched with it. He should never have eaten breakfast at the inn this morning. He knew better. But he had ignored his mental warnings and wolfed down the thick slices of ham and the freshly baked bread dripping with butter and marmalade, then washed it all down with the good local ale. Now the whole meal was a roiling mass in his stomach.

He turned his gaze to the window, searching for some distant landmark to focus upon, to gain the illusion that the whole world was not moving along with him. But the lane was bounded with close-growing hedges which slipped past his eyes in a dizzying manner, further serving to emphasize the motion of the coach.

Alford took a deep breath and swallowed heavily. Closing his eyes, he leaned his head back against the padded cushion. It did not help. In the enveloping darkness, the spinning in his head magnified itself until he felt as if his whole body whirled within the close confines of the coach. His eyes snapped open and he lunged for the window. Jerking it down, he stuck his head through the opening, taking in the fresh, outside air in large, tortured gulps. He had an instant to realize that he had delayed for too long and then his breakfast decorated the peaceful Somerset countryside.

The coach lumbered to a halt, but by the time Alford was able to fling the door open and jump to the ground, his stomach had been thoroughly emptied. Ignoring the misting rain, he leaned weakly against the side of the coach, grateful to have solid, unmoving ground under his feet again. He fought against the waves of dizziness that still washed through his head.

''You want to ride up top for a bit?'' the old coachman asked with a sympathetic smile.

Alford shook his head. It had been a number of years since he had suffered such a severe bout of motion-sickness, but he knew, now that his stomach was empty, the usual cure would work. He reached back into the coach and pulled out the chased silver flask of brandy from the side compartment. He spit out the first swig to cleanse his mouth, then he took a long, deep swallow. From experience, he knew that if he consumed enough brandy, the movement of the carriage would no longer bother him. The unsteadiness brought on by the spirits seemed to counteract the external motion. As he tipped the flask back a second time, Alford welcomed the scalding burn down his throat. This was what he should have had for breakfast.

With his stomach settled by the brandy and the swirling in his head halted by the stop, he climbed back into the coach and signalled the driver to proceed. Steadily sipping brandy, Alford kept his eyes firmly focused on the interior of the coach, and in a short time, the soothing numbness flowed through his veins and he felt much more the thing.

At least, he did until his thoughts strayed to the person who had brought all this down on his head. It was bad enough to have been forced from town; the indignity of this miserable carriage ride only heightened his irritation. He could easily have ridden out the gossip in London. But his father insisted it was better for . . . Lord, what was he supposed to call her? Miss Washburn? He certainly was not going to call her Lady Alford!

Admittedly, she was an intriguing chit. Most women would have succumbed to a fit of the vapors after what he had done to her in the library. Instead, she punched him in the nose. He gingerly rubbed that abused part of his face. At least it was almost back to its normal size. Thank God she had not broken it. He could not bear the thought of having to recall her handiwork every time he looked at himself in a mirror.

Once the lawyers finished their yammering, she could be quietly packed off to Kit on the Peninsula. And Alford could go back to his normal pursuits. But until then, he would be marooned in the furthest corner of Devon, all for the sake of protecting the reputation of a chit he had loathed from the instant of their first meeting years ago. The unfairness of it all irked him. Why should he be put through such torture on her account? Devon, for God's sake. What on God's green earth had persuaded his eccentric ancestor to build himself a home in such a remote corner of the island?

Alford snickered. Probably as an escape from his wife.

"What do you mean, the girl is ill?" Florrie stared at the landlady of the Hare's Tail in an uncomprehending manner.

"The poor girl is just plum out of sorts," the innkeeper's wife repeated. "My Maisie went to wake her this morning and the poor thing couldn't move. Weak as a kitten and all flushed with fever."

No wonder the new maid had been so quiet on the journey from London, Florrie thought. She'd been so relieved to be rid of her aunt's incessant chatter and that insolent French baggage that she hadn't given the poor girl a thought. Sally had probably been coming down with some dreadful disease the whole time. And Florrie had just spent three days in a closed carriage with her. The very thought made Florrie feel hot and flushed.

"Can you summon a doctor?" Florrie asked. He could tell her if the maid was able to travel. The thought of another night at this poor excuse for an inn did not appeal to Florrie in the slightest.

The lady nodded. "Perhaps you can go up and sit with her before he comes."

"Me?" Florrie said, aghast. Whyever would she want to go sit with a sick servant girl she barely knew? "I do not think that will be necessary. Have someone bring my breakfast and send the doctor to me after he has seen Sally. And perhaps you can spare me a few moments of Maisie's time?''

The landlady bowed out of the room, shaking her head as she went.

Florrie picked up the lumpy and misshapen pillow that had so disturbed her sleep during the night and flung it at the chair in the room's corner. This journey was taking long enough as it was, without another delay. At this rate, it would be summer before she even reached her destination.

''I never should have taken a maid in London,'' she moaned in frustration. ''Continental servants know better than to be sick. Particularly when a body is travelling.'' She sank down onto the edge of the bed and thought.

She would have to wait and see what the doctor said. If Sally was able to travel, they could leave without too much delay and perhaps reach Barnstaple by evening. All depended upon the doctor. And Sally. And herself. Florrie could very well find herself in a similar fix by morning, depending upon what illness had felled the maid. The thought of being sick, alone, in only a modest posting-inn like this increased her frustration. If it came to that, she would summon her father and force him to take her back to London.

That thought cheered her so much that Florrie almost looked forward to becoming unwell. She would give anything to return to the city.

Unfortunately, the doctor's words shattered that hope.

''Chicken pox,'' he pronounced.

''Chicken pox?'' Florrie could not hide her astonishment. ''That is a disease for children.''

The doctor shrugged. ''Some miss it early, and it catches them later. She is not desperately ill, but she cer tainly will not wish to travel for several days.''

''Several days?'' Florrie wailed. ''That is impossible. I *have* to leave today.''

The doctor shook his head. ''I would advise against it. Chicken pox is not normally a serious illness, but it sometimes takes a strange turn in adults. You could risk her becoming seriously ill.''

''I have half a mind to pack her back to London on the

next stage," Florrie muttered. She turned back to the doctor. "How many days until she will be fit to travel again?"

"The fever should abate in a day or two," he said. "It then depends on how severe a case of the pox she has. New ones will be popping out for a week. The itching can be fierce, and the movement of the carriage might only make it worse."

Florrie considered her options—which at this point were reduced to one: she could stay here until Sally was well and ready to travel on. The thought was intolerable. But what else could she do? Travelling alone was impossible.

Or was it? Her father would be aghast if she tried such a thing. But he was not here to stop her. And certainly, she would encounter far fewer difficulties travelling alone than remaining in this stupid inn for days on end. Without a chaperon, Florrie should properly remain in her room during her entire stay. And she knew that was an impossibility, yet it would occasion comment if she tried to inspect the town on her own. But if she traveled onward, she would only have to spend one more night in an inn alone. Perhaps she could even borrow Maisie, or some other local girl, to accompany her as far as Barnstaple. Certainly she would be able to find some sort of girl to help out once she reached Hartland or Hartford or whatever that ridiculous place was named.

"Will you be able to come every day to check on the girl?" Florrie asked the doctor.

"Certainly," he replied.

"My business is pressing, and I cannot afford to be delayed," Florrie explained. "If the innkeeper is willing, I should like to leave Sally here. She can travel on when she is feeling better and you feel it is safe for her to do so." She smiled sweetly. "Of course, I will be willing to pay extra for your close attention . . ."

The doctor nodded.

Florrie rang for the landlady. The landlady frowned at the plan, but Florrie persuaded, cajoled, and then outright bribed her to accept the idea. Florrie settled a generous amount upon the doctor, who promised he would take special care of the patient, and she prepared to embark on the next leg of her journey. Maisie could not be spared, but she had a young cousin who would do equally well. By mid-morning, Florrie's coach was upon the road again. She was determined to bring his journey to a swift end.

Florrie wondered what Kit would say to all this when he heard the tale. He would admire her ingenuity, commend her for taking charge of matters, and laugh at her travails. And, once the whole tale had been told, it would appear amusing. Kit had a way of seeing things that way.

How unlike his brother he was. Kit was steady, ambitious, determined, while Alford was content to drink and game his way through life. Her vexation with him rose again. If it had not been for his drunken carelessness . . . She had no doubt he had been in his cups the day he signed the papers. His behavior in the library was ample proof that he could not handle his liquor. She only regretted she had not broken that oh-so-arrogant nose of his when she had the chance. He might not fare as well the next time he crossed her path.

Alford leaned gratefully against the side of the stone-walled house, struggling to catch his breath. What had ever possessed him to take his lunch in Clovelly? He had seen water before; why had he felt it necessary to walk all the way down to the quay? For after the novelty of seeing a town clinging to the side of a cliff wore off, he was faced with the unpleasant realization that there were definite disadvantages to exploring a town whose main street a mountain goat would disdain to climb. His side ached, his legs trembled, and he was only little more than halfway back to the top. If he did not hurry, the carter who waited for him at his starting point would probably turn back to Bideford and leave him stranded here, still miles from his destination.

This was all Miss Washburn's fault. This whole damnable journey was her fault. She was the one who had spread the tale far and wide of their accidental marriage. If she had kept her mouth shut, no one would have been the wiser and this all could have been dealt with quietly, *in London*. But because she had complained so vociferously in public, he now found himself in some isolated corner of the country, in a town that would have brought a smile to the lips of a medieval torturer.

A few more minutes of rest brought some semblance of normality to his labored breathing, and Alford struck out again for the top of the cliff overlooking Bideford Bay. Next time he travelled to some out-of-the-way corner of the country he'd invest in a good guidebook—the kind that would warn a person not to investigate Clovelly at close range.

"Enjoy your visit?" the waiting carter asked when Alford at last regained the heights.

Alford attributed the cheery tone in the man's voice to malicious glee. "Edifying," Alford replied. He did not add that he had rested for a full ten minutes just below the lip of the cliff, so as not to appear winded when he crested the top. How was it that he was so damnably out of condition?

The man moved aside and Alford took up his seat beside him.

"Couldn't never figure it out, myself," the carter mused as the yoked donkeys lumbered down what passed for a road. "Why'd anyone want to carve a town out the side of a cliff when there's perfectly good flat spots to build?"

"Why, indeed," replied Alford. Unless it was to trap unwary fools like himself.

The only bright spot in the entire day was that it had stopped raining. Alford could only guess at the joys of making a fifteen-mile journey in an open cart in the pouring rain. Some God had taken pity on him at last and spared him *that*, at least.

"What, precisely, do you mean by a 'cart'?" Florrie glared at the innkeeper of the Appledore Inn in Bideford.

"A cart," he repeated. "No fancy carriage is going to make it more than a mile or two out of town afore the road dwindles to a cart track. Why, the mails think even the road from here to Barnstaple is too rough for their precious coaches. Them that's heading further west goes either by horse or cart."

"And where, precisely, am I to find this cart in order to book passage upon it?"

The innkeeper shrugged. "Old Mort is probably out on his rounds. He takes the mail and whatever people have ordered from town and makes his circuit. He should be back shortly after supper."

"And then he can take me to Hartland tomorrow?" Florrie resisted the impatient urge to tap her foot while she talked with this infuriatingly obtuse innkeeper.

"Well, now, that all depends on what Old Mort's schedule is. Normalwise he don't go out toward Hartland every day. Depends on what people's ordered."

"I may have to spend days here?"

The innkeeper nodded. "Could be. I'll leave word to have Mort come by tonight when he gets back. P'raps you can work out some kind of arrangement with him."

"Is 'Old Mort' the only person in this town with a cart? There must be another carter who accepts passengers." Florrie knew how many innkeepers steered their customers only to certain drivers, with the profit split between them.

"This ain't Lunnon. Ain't much demand for carts from them that don't have them. I'll send Mort to you when he returns."

"Fine," snapped Florrie, and retreated up the stairs to her room. She had never before experienced a journey that had been such an unmitigated disaster. One expected difficulties on the Continent and planned for them accordingly. But in England she had expected matters to be more, well, *civilized*. And it was proving to be far less than that.

The thought of spending one more day in an uncomfortable inn was enough to make her contemplate turning tail and racing back to London. Except that the coach that had brought her here had already departed on its return journey. She was stranded at this inn until "Old Mort" was ready to take her to her destination.

Travelling in a cart, indeed. There must be another way to reach the coast. Some form of carriage must exist that could handle the primitive roadways. Through the dirt-begrimed window in her chamber, Florrie could see the ominous black clouds that hovered on the edge of the bay. Rain was in the offing, and there was no way she would travel the last fifteen miles of her journey in an open cart during a torrential rainstorm. No earthly way.

Chapter 6

Water dripped from Florrie's sodden garments and pooled upon the flagged stones of the entry at Hartland Hall. Her new bonnet, bought what seemed years ago in London, was ruined. Her feet felt like solid, frozen lumps at the end of her legs, and she suspected it would be days before her fingers worked properly again. And if appearances were anything to judge, the woman who stood before her had just stepped straight from a child's nursery tale—the kind that kept one awake all night in fear. For she looked most suspiciously like a witch.

Dressed head-to-toe in some unidentifiable black fabric, the woman's iron-gray hair was pulled back from her face in such a tight bun that Florrie was certain the woman suffered constant pain. It certainly explained the pinched look on her face. In the dim light of the hall, her eyes looked large and luminescent. But it was her nose that added the final touch. It was long, sharply pointed, and had a wart perfectly placed upon its tip. She was such a personification of the dreaded Baba Yaga that Florrie would not have been in the least surprised to hear a stream of Russian issue from her lips.

Instead, it was pure Devonian. "No one said aught about a lady," she growled.

Florrie accepted this enthusiastic welcome. It was all a piece of this entirely dreadful experience. Of course, they would not be expecting her. How foolish of her to have thought otherwise.

"I am sorry that the communication did not arrive," Florrie said. "I am certain it is all the fault of the mail. But, as you see, I am here and I would like to be shown to my room. And to have a bath drawn immediately."

She drew in a hasty breath and continued before the witch

could speak. "My maid fell ill and she will not be arriving for some days yet, so I shall need someone to look after my things. Perhaps you can assist me today and tomorrow find some local girl who is willing to come in. And," Florrie added, as she stripped off her gloves and watched the water drip from the ruined leather, "I should very much like a cup of hot tea."

Old Mort dropped Florrie's trunk to the stone floor with a resounding thud that made her jump. Florrie whirled and glared at him. "Kindly treat the other one with a bit more care," she snapped. "There are breakable items inside."

Mort ducked his head and hastened out the door.

"Have someone bring the trunk upstairs immediately," Florrie said as she stepped toward the stairs. She turned again and stared at the housekeeper, who had not moved. "Are we waiting for something?"

"No one told us a lady was coming," the housekeeper repeated.

"So you said." It was the crowning touch to an unmitigated disaster. "I assume there must be at least one chamber that is fit for habitation?" Florrie doubted it. The house looked as if it had not been occupied since the Restoration. The sheets were probably still begrimed with the dirt from some Cavalier or Roundhead.

"There's the old mistress's chamber, but—"

"I am certain it will perfectly suit," Florrie said. "Now, Mrs. . . . ?"

"Burgess."

" . . . Burgess, if you could *please* take me there. If I do not get out of these wet clothes I fear I will contract an inflammation of the lungs, and I am certain you do not wish to have an invalid on your hands."

Still shaking her head, Mrs. Burgess led Florrie up the stairs.

Once Mrs. Burgess decided to do something, she was nothing less than determined, and Florrie was nearly forced to run to keep up with her. She caught only brief glimpses of the house as they raced up the stairs and down the corridor. Her dominant impression was of darkness; the house was heavily paneled with wood in the Elizabethan manner. Florrie prayed her room would be free of that, or at least painted.

And indeed, the chamber she entered was surprisingly light and airy. And bare. Curtains, bed hangings, and furniture were all missing. Only the massive poster bed in the center of the chamber remained.

"I shall have the bed prepared first," Mrs. Burgess said in an apologetic tone. "I always keep my linens fresh. It may take a day to restore the hangings and curtains. Mr. Burgess can move some furniture in."

Florrie nodded indifferently. She was so exhausted she could have sunk down upon the mattress and slept round the clock. Curtains and furniture were the least of her concerns. "If I could only have some tea. And the bath. And my trunks."

"I will hasten," Mrs. Burgess said, slipping out into the corridor.

Florrie walked over to the window and peered through the curtain of rain that enveloped the house. The room was at the back of the building, and the window looked out over the rear lawn. On a sunny day, Florrie surmised, she would be able to see the sea, but today all she could see was an unending wall of gray shadow. Wet, gray shadow.

She shivered, and it was not entirely from her wet clothing. Her paps could never have imagined what he was sending her into. That was the only possible explanation for this inhospitable welcome. One would not deliberately send their worst enemy to this place.

Once she had bathed and changed into dry clothing, she would find her paper and ink and quills, and pen a succinct letter to her father, telling him exactly what kind of situation he had cast his daughter into. He might even be moved to come to the rescue himself. Florrie fervently hoped so.

Alford shuffled the cards with the skill and precision of a seasoned cardsman. After laying them out upon the library table in an intricate pattern, he sat back in his chair and studied them, a slight frown marring his face. He reached for the brandy glass at his elbow, his frown deepening when he discovered it empty.

He knew good French brandy when he tasted it, and this had to be one of the best. Seb and Hervey had been right when they predicted he might be in for an adventure. Alford was very certain that no duty had been paid on this beverage. What a triumph it would be to return from his exile with a supply of prime brandy that would be the envy of every gentleman in London. In a few days, when he got to know the couple that cared for the place better, he would begin making inquiries. He could guarantee the suppliers of this stuff a long list of customers.

Alford leaned back in his chair and stretched, then rose. He sauntered lazily to the table sporting the brandy decanter and poured himself a generous serving.

This whole little visit might not turn out so badly after all, he mused. Which was good, since the very thought of making the return journey caused him to shudder. He would be very content to bide here awhile. The house was certainly old enough and full of interesting, if quaint, relics from the past. Exploring it might provide him with amusement for a day or two. After that, he could investigate the neighborhood—if the deuced rain ever stopped. It had started some time during the night, he had discovered to his great discomfort this morning when he awoke—in a bed that was sodden from the incessant drip coming down from the ceiling.

The housekeeper had been properly apologetic, explaining that each and every storm loosened tiles from the roof and it was not always possible to replace them before the next one hit. Alford did not much care how the leak occurred, but he was grateful when she assured him there were plenty of other chambers.

He had inspected his new room only long enough to ascertain that it looked out toward the sea—at least, the old man had assured him the sea was there. Alford could not see through the torrent more than ten feet from the house. It did not matter; he found he rather preferred the cozy warmth of the library, where the blazing fire and exquisite brandy enabled him to sneer at the elements. He could think of worse ways to spend an afternoon.

"My lord?"

Alford turned toward the ancient housekeeper, who had just entered the room. "Yes?"

"Will you be desiring your dinner downstairs again tonight?"

Alford nodded. Eating in the library was not at all that different than eating in his rooms in London. Eating in his bedchamber would only serve to remind him that he was at the other end of the world—alone.

"The bed's been made up in your new chamber. I hope you will find it to your liking."

"I thought it quite satisfactory when I inspected it this morning." Alford forced a smile. "I imagine the view is quite pleasant when it is not shrouded in clouds. That must occur what—once or twice a year?"

The housekeeper's dour expression told him his little jest was not appreciated—or understood. One was never quite certain with these country folk. He shrugged.

"Dinner in the library will be fine," he said with a curt nod of dismissal.

His earlier enthusiasm waned during the long afternoon, when interminable games of solitaire only made him more aware that he was, indeed, *solitaire*. What he would not give for a good hand of whist. Perhaps the butler or estate manager or steward or whatever fancy title he wanted to call himself played piquet, or ecarte. It was abundantly clear to Alford that one day of solitaire was about as much as he could endure.

He flung down the cards and rose from the table. If he was going to sit and be bored witless, at least he could do it closer to the fire. The wind had whipped up outside and the room had taken on a chill. Alford settled himself into the high, wing-backed armchair that faced the blazing warmth. Moodily, he stared into the flames.

"Your tea, ma'am."

Florrie started back from the window and whirled about. Mrs. Burgess had entered the room so stealthily that Florrie had not heard her. Or had she simply conjured herself and the steaming pot of water out of thin air? Florrie did not dismiss the thought out of hand. Baba Yaga's powers were extensive.

"Thank you," Florrie said.

"The bath water's heating," Mrs. Burgess said as she laid out the tea things on the small folding table she brought along. "I'll bring the tub."

"Very well," said Florrie. "And my trunks?"

"Ol' Mort's bringing them along any time now," she said and whisked out of the room as silently as she had come.

Florrie poured herself a cup of tea, uncaring that it had not had time to steep properly. It was hot, and that was all that counted. She clasped the cup with both hands, reveling in the warmth that spread through her fingers, then took a cautious sip.

Instantly, she spit the bitter liquid back into the cup. This was *not* tea. Florrie sniffed it carefully but did not recognize the odor. A herbal concoction, no doubt. But what herb?

A cold fear seized her and she set the cup down with a trembling hand. What if it was something not quite . . . safe? What if Baba Yaga had mixed up one of her magical potions and waited just outside in the hall for the mixture to do its work? She could wish Florrie dead or . . . worse. Florrie shuddered and stepped backward across the room, as far away from the poisonous brew as she could get. Only her father knew she was journeying here. Mrs. Burgess could do away with her with no one the wiser. No one would come looking for Florrie for a month, at least. By then, any evidence of her ever having been here would be long eliminated. It would be as if she had vanished into thin air.

Florrie jumped a foot when the door crashed open. Mrs. Burgess wrestled a large, tin bathing tub through the doorway.

"Water'll be along in a moment," she said in a matter-of-fact tone. She glanced at the full tea cup sitting on the table. "Too hot for ye?"

Florrie nodded.

"It should be cool enough soon," Mrs. Burgess said. "Be good for you to drink. Chamomile is most soothing for those who've just endured a long journey."

Florrie's knees grew weak with relief. Chamomile. Of course. A perfectly harmless herb.

Mrs. Burgess picked up the cup and brought it to Florrie. "I make up my own teas," she said proudly. "This one has just a touch of rosemary and lavender. Rosemary's good for warding off the chill and lavender is most calming."

"Th-thank you," Florrie stammered, taking the cup. She took another sip, feeling like a perfect fool.

It was this house, this journey, the whole dratted mess that had her so overwrought. After a nice, soaking bath, a warm meal, and a good night's sleep, Florrie knew she would be at peace with the world again. Tomorrow would be a much better day.

And indeed, she did feel much more in charity with the world after she bathed and changed into her warm, dry clothing, with the assistance of Mrs. Burgess. Florrie was grateful that she had spent so much time in Russia. Clothes designed for the Russian winter were marvelous for an English spring. She even hummed a little tune as she sat in front of the blazing hearth, drying her hair in the radiated heat.

She felt so good, in fact, that she determined to venture downstairs before dinner. Mrs. Burgess had given her directions to the library, which was, she promised, more of a drawing room than library, the enormous main hall in this Elizabethan house being more suitable for a banquet than a lone lady. Florrie carefully followed her directions and found herself standing before what she hoped was the library door. She pushed it open carefully and stepped into the room.

"Ah, there you are, Mrs. Burgess. Kindly set the tea tray on the table. I shall pour my own."

Florrie could just see the crown of the speaker's head over

the top of the winged-back chair in front of the fire grate. "Who are you?" she demanded.

The man eased himself from the chair and turned to face her. His mouth immediately fell agape.

"You!" he exclaimed.

Chapter 7

Florrie stared in stunned silence at Viscount Alford, whose face she was certain mirrored her own surprise.

"Is this your idea of a jest?" he demanded. "What are you doing here? I thought you had caused me enough trouble back in London. Have you followed me here to plague me further?"

"*I* plague *you*?" Florrie drew herself up indignantly. "Easy words from the man who caused the whole imbroglio to begin with."

"You have not answered my question," Alford said coldly. "What, precisely, are you doing here?"

"I should ask the same of you," Florrie retorted. "My father sent me here to stifle the gossip in London. The gossip caused by your unconscionable carelessness in signing those proxy papers."

"Impossible," said Alford.

"It was not impossible at all," Florrie said. "You signed them incorrectly."

"Impossible that your father sent you *here,*" he explained. "My father sent *me* here to still the gossip."

Florrie glared at him. "It looks as if you have botched this as well as Kit's marriage papers," she said. "Your father probably told you I was coming here to make certain you went somewhere else."

Alford shook his head. "He specifically said he was sending me here because it was so far from town. He should know what he is doing; after all, it is his house."

"This house belongs to your father?"

Alford nodded. "So, you see, it is quite impossible that I am here by mistake. Obviously, your father made the error."

"But he specifically said that I was to go to Devon because—oh!" Florrie stamped her foot. "They did this on purpose! Those conniving . . ."

"I cannot believe that my father would ever be part of such an underhanded scheme," Alford said.

"Oh, no?" Florrie's voice was scornful. "He probably suggested the whole thing. My father would never place me in such an untenable position."

"It does not matter whose ridiculous idea this was," he said. "If you leave now, you should be able to reach Bideford by dark."

"I leave? Why, pray tell, should I be the one to leave? You are the one who tossed us both into this bumble broth. It is up to you to resolve the situation. You can leave."

He looked at her coldly. "I hardly think you are in a position to order me off my own property, Miss Washburn."

"Lady Alford," she corrected with sweet sarcasm. "As your *wife*, my claim is as strong as yours."

He glared at her in exasperation. "Why on God's earth would you wish to stay here?"

"Because I refuse to undertake another torturous, un- pleasant, and miserable journey until I have fully recovered from the first one," she said heatedly. "And the shock of discovering you here has probably added another week to the time needed for my recuperation."

"Fine, then," said Alford. "I'll leave."

"Have a pleasant journey," she said as he slammed out of the library.

Alford had a strong urge to cause physical harm to someone. Not someone, he corrected himself. Florence Washburn. He began to suspect she was some modern-day incarnation of a Greek fury, set on earth to torment him. He could not get away from her fast enough.

Making his way to the kitchen at the back of the house, Alford hastily calculated the time it would take him to return to London. Four, five days at the most with a decent coach and good changes of horses. He would be damned if he would stay away from town after this. Someone in London had a lot to answer for, and he was eager to discover just who was responsible for this latest situation. There was a devilish deep game being played here.

"Burgess," he thundered as he reached the kitchen.

"M'lord?" The wizened man looked up from his tea.

"There has been a royal botch-up in sending that stupid chit here," Alford said. "I am leaving. You and Mort can load up my tunks."

"Mort ain't here," Burgess replied.

"What, left already?" Alford sighed. "What kind of horseflesh do you have in the stable? I can pack a light bag and head back to Bideford on horseback; Mort can come back tomorow for my trunks."

"Ain't no horse in the stable."

"There should be several horses out there," Alford complained. "My father said there were horses here."

Burgess shrugged indifferently. "Gone for years. No one here to ride them. No use for them."

Alford scowled. "I guess I will have to wait until tomorrow for Mort, then," he said and turned to go. "What time does he usually arrive?"

"Mort ain't coming tomorrow."

"What?"

"Mort only comes once a week," Burgess replied.

"Once a week? He's been here for two days in a row."

"Bringing guests, he was."

"Certainly, there must be some way to get word to him to return early."

"Foot," replied Burgess.

"Foot?" Alford asked.

"Foot."

"Burgess, what do you mean by 'foot'?"

"Ye ken walk t'town."

"Walk? It is fifteen miles. Surely, some neighbor has a horse I can borrow. Where's the nearest farm?"

"Horses ain't much use round here. Might find one in Bude. But Bude's a few steps further than Bideford. Now a good pack pony might be had. Or one of the donkeys."

Alford could only picture himself on either animal, his legs dangling to the ground. "You mean the only way I am going to get out of here before Mort's next 'visit' is by walking to Bideford?''

Burgess nodded.

Alford flung up his hands. "This has to be the most ridiculous state of affairs.''

Burgess stared at him blandly. "We ain't much used to comings and goings around here.''

Alford turned on his heel and left the room. He would wait until tomorrow then, and walk the whole damn way to Bideford if he must. He did not want to spend more than one minute longer than necessary under the same roof as Miss Washburn. He might be tempted to punch *her* in the nose this time.

He turned his steps toward the library, then hesitated outside the door. He had no desire to say another word to that witch. And he did not want to see the satisfaction on her face when he announced his departure. He could easily spend the rest of his stay here ignoring her presence. Alford retraced his steps and headed up the stairs to his room.

"Ah, there you are, Burgess.'' Alford turned away from his contemplation of the ever-present mist that surrounded the house and gestured toward the fireplace. "It is beginning to be a bit cold in here. Could you light the fire?''

Burgess knelt to the task.

"How far can one see on a clear day?'' Alford asked as he returned to the window.

"Beyond Lundy,'' the man replied laconically as the fire caught.

"Still pirates out there?'' Alford asked.

"There's some that says there is and some that says there isn't,'' Burgess replied.

"Of course,'' Alford mumbled to himself and resumed his futile attempts to pick out any kind of shape in the swirling mist that lay about the house.

Until he realized that the swirling mist was inside. He whirled about. Choking, gray smoke spewed from the fireplace.

"Burgess!'' Alford exclaimed. "What in God's name?''

He fumbled with the window latch, flinging the glass panes wide. The incoming draft swept through the chamber, mingled with the sooty smoke from the fire, and sent it whirling about the room, setting both men to coughing. Rain poured through the open window in wind-driven sheets.

"Put the damn fire out," Alford called as he pulled off his coat and ineffectively flapped it at the smoke.

Burgess poked and prodded at the glowing coals without much success. Alford grabbed the washbasin and heaved the cold water on the hearth. Sizzling steam mingled with the acrid smoke, but in a few minutes the air cleared.

"Chimney must be blocked," Burgess said matter-of-factly.

"Wonderful," said Alford. "Do you suppose it could be cleaned so I can have a proper fire?"

"You be leaving tomorrow," Burgess pointed out.

"I would like to be able to sleep in a room where the temperature is somewhat above freezing," Alford said between clenched teeth as he struggled to close the window. Already he was soaked to the skin from the driving rain.

Burgess shrugged. "The sweep comes out of Bideford. You could send him this way when you reach town."

Alford held on to the last remnants of his temper. Was it impossible to get anything done on the spot in this house? "I will do just that," he snapped. "Someday there may be some other misguided soul who has the misfortune to be stranded in this God-awful place. Perhaps they would enjoy the luxury of heated rooms."

"The fireplace in the library works," Burgess pointed out.

Alford sighed. It was probably the only working fireplace in the entire house. But unless he wished to freeze slowly in his room, he would have to return there. And rejoin Miss Washburn.

A slow smile of malicious pleasure crossed his face.

"Does the fireplace in Miss Washburn's room work?" Alford asked suddenly, a wicked gleam in his eye.

Burgess shrugged noncommittally.

"I would not be in any great hurry to clean it," Alford said with a sly smile.

"It's all the same to me," Burgess said. "I'll have the missus air out your room afor bed."

Alford nodded his ungrateful thanks and went in pursuit of warmth.

Florrie looked up from her book when Alford entered the library.

"Still here? I had hoped you were well on your way by now."

"Tomorrow," he growled as he sidled closer to the fire.

Florrie sniffed. "Have you perhaps been trying to burn the house down, Alford?"

"The damn chimney in my room is plugged," he said shortly. "I suggest you forgo the pleasure of a fire in your room until the sweep can be brought out from Bideford to clean it. Wouldn't want to risk a fire. This place could go up like a tinder box."

"How unfortunate for you," she said, with cloying sweetness. "I am grateful that my fireplace worked perfectly."

Alford flopped down in the chair nearest the fire. He could swear the damp mist outside was creeping into this very room. He fought down a shiver. He'd forgotten his wet shirt when he shrugged on his sooty coat, and even he had to admit that he smelled like a chimney sweep.

Florrie eyed him smugly. The poor man was obviously freezing and had come down in search of a heated room. Well, the fire may be warm, but he shouldn't expect any warmth from her. It served him right for having brought this mess down upon their heads.

"Mrs. Burgess says dinner will be served shortly," Florrie said. "I surmise you wish to eat in your chamber—assuming the smoke has been cleared out."

"Oh, no," Alford said. "I am certain I would be much more comfortable dining here." She was not going to drive him out again. Let her retreat this time.

Florrie frowned. She had no desire to dine tête-à-tête with Alford. But neither did she wish to retreat to her room. She would not allow Alford *that* satisfaction. If he wished to stay in this room, he could, but she would do her best to pretend he did not exist. With that firmly resolved in her mind, she turned her attention back to her book of Spanish grammar.

Dinner was eaten without more than a word or two shared between them. Florrie watched with growing disdain as Alford downed glass after glass of ruby-red claret. She sipped her single glass of wine carefully. She remembered all too well what had happened the last time Alford had been foxed in her presence. He would not catch her by surprise again.

She picked experimentally at the overdone mutton. Mrs. Burgess had apologized for the plain fare, explaining that until Old Mort was back with supplies, she would not be able to prepare more elaborate meals. Anything would be an improvement over this.

Alford sat hunched over his plate, eating with a relish that disgusted Florrie. She suspected he behaved in such a boorish manner merely to annoy her, and she grew even more annoyed at herself for allowing his ploy to succeed. It was with great relief that she finished her meal and excused herself for the night.

Florrie sat before the dressing table that had been moved into her room during the day, brushing out her hair. The fire burned merrily in the grate, she was wrapped in her warmest nightrail and robe, and she felt quite smug at the thought of Alford freezing away in his unheated chamber. It served the lout right.

She had raised her hand to take another stroke, then her arm froze in midair when the door on the opposite side of the chamber slowly opened inward. Her breath caught in her throat and she felt a scream building inside her.

"I wondered where this door led." Alford peered around the edge of the door with a curious gaze.

"Get out of here!" Florrie shrieked.

Alford instinctively ducked. When no missile flew at his head, he stepped into the room. "How convenient," he drawled. "These must be the chambers of the master and mistress of the house." He nodded back toward the open door. "With a shared dressing room between. A cozy arrangement for a married couple."

"We are not a married couple," she said.

He laughed. "If we were not, neither you nor I would be here. You'd be on your way to Kit and I would be enjoying myself in London." He took a step further into the room.

Forcing herself to remain calm, Florrie prepared herself for the worst. Was she going to have to fight off a drunken Alford again? She would be certain to leave him with more than a bruised nose this time. Her fingers tightened around the handle of her silver hair brush.

Alford made a quick survey of the room, even pulling the curtains aside to peer out into the darkness beyond the window. He stopped in front of the fire, holding out his hands to the warmth.

"So this is the famous working fireplace," he said. "How fortunate you are."

Florrie watched him intently while he prowled the room in curious inspection. He did not look nearly as foxed as she thought he must be, after watching him consume so many glasses of wine at dinner. But then, an experienced drinker could often disguise his condition well.

Alford stared at the flames, unsure of why he lingered in this chamber. If ever a position was compromising . . . This was the exact thing that would bind him permanently to Florence Washburn, if word ever got out. He lowered his gaze and slanted a sidelong glance at her. She sat there tense and taut as if she expected him to attack her. The idea was laughable. Now that he knew who she was, no amount of persuasion on earth could induce him to lay a finger on her.

Still, she appeared a delectable bundle. Enveloped all in white and lace, with that honey-gold hair swirling about her shoulders, Florrie offered a tempting picture. He felt a slight pang of—regret?—at remembering how she was destined for Kit. For despite her shrewish tongue and ability to use her fists, Florence Washburn was a damnably attractive woman.

He laughed inwardly at his train of thought and glanced openly at her, his eyes sweeping her form from head to toe in an appreciative gaze.

"Are you quite finished?" she demanded acidly. "I should like to retire for the night."

"Oh, do not let me stop you," he said with a wicked grin.

She jumped to her feet and stepped toward him, a look of threatening menace on her face. "Get—out—of—my—room!"

Alford bowed. "As you wish, my dear." He turned back to the door and felt her gaze boring a hole in the spot between his shoulder blades. Turning his back on that bundle of fury was one of the hardest things he had ever done. But he dare not let her know just how much he respected her ability to cause him bodily harm. He slipped quickly into the passage and pulled the door shut behind him just in time to hear the dull thump of some weapon bouncing off the wood on the other side.

Florrie glared at the closed door. She wished she had tossed that brush a fraction of a second earlier, and caught Alford square on. The nerve of that man! There had been no mistaking that gleam in his eye—he had been ogling her as if she were Covent Garden ware. She crossed quickly to the door and examined it for some locking mechanism, groaning in frustration when she discovered no key in the lock. Turning back to her room, she went to the dressing table and half-pulled, half-pushed it across the room until it stood in front of the door. She would get the key from Mrs. Burgess in the morning; meanwhile, there would be no way Alford could make an uninvited excursion into her room during the night.

With a sigh of satisfaction, she turned down the covers and climbed into the high, wide, ancient bed, dousing the candle at her bedside. She could sleep safely now. And tomorrow, Alford would be gone.

Chapter 8

In the morning, Alford watched the incessant fall of rain with growing dismay. Except for a few short hours during the night, it had not stopped since his arrival. It grew quite apparent that he would not be able to make his way to Bideford today—at least, not without serious risk to his health. If there was any guarantee that one of the neighboring farms would have a suitable animal for him to ride, he would strike out on foot, but the thought of having to walk the entire fifteen miles to Bideford in this freezing spring rain was unpalatable. He was forced to admit that another day in Miss Washburn's company was more appealing. Barely.

His persistent nagging had goaded Burgess into unearthing what looked to be some form of medieval torture device to clean out the chimney in his room. Alford swore he would not spend another night freezing; he would sleep here in the library if necessary to keep warm. He had tossed and turned all night, restless from the cold, and every waking thought had centered on that invitingly heated chamber he knew was only a door away.

He cast a swift glance at Miss Washburn, who sat before the fire with apparent unconcern, reading her damned Spanish grammar. He did not for a moment believe she was gaining anything from her ardent perusal of the book. She flaunted the book out of spite, to remind him of where she was headed when this whole mess was resolved, and also to remind him that she would soon be his sister-in-law. He was glad he and Kit were not close; if he did not see Miss Washburn again for fifty years, it would not be long enough.

While Alford paced restlessly up and down the length of the library, Florrie watched him surreptitiously over the top of her book. The man was like one of the caged lions at the 'change. And his agitation was infectious. She had been looking at this same page for an interminable time.

"Sit down," she said irritably. "You are driving me mad."

Alford smiled. If only it were true. "Why, Miss Washburn, I had no idea you were so easily distracted from your *studies*. Perhaps you would be able to apply yourself better in the privacy of your own room."

"I find this room perfectly amenable to study," she retorted. "When I am alone."

"But as Burgess is cleaning out the chimney in my chamber, I am forced to remain here," he said.

"Then find something to do," she snapped. "Read a book. Or are you able to read anything more complex than the racing news and the betting book at White's?"

"My university tutors would be shocked to hear such aspersions cast upon my scholarship abilities," he said in a voice that was quietly mocking and yet as hard as steel.

"I had not thought your studies would have gone beyond the comparative merits of various forms of spirits and the mathematical odds at faro and hazard."

"Oh, I did much better than that," he said with a sneer. "I also mastered the art of fisticuffs, curricle racing, and pistol shooting."

"Such manly pursuits," Florrie drawled.

"Yes, indeed," he said. "But then, I do not suppose that a mere woman such as yourself can truly appreciate the skill involved. It is a slight more taxing than choosing a pair of gloves."

"Who do you prefer? Manton or Durs Egg?" Florrie's voice echoed her smug smile.

Clever chit, Alford thought. Thinking to impress him because she can rattle off the names of London gunsmiths. "It depends," he replied, "whether one is looking for accuracy at a distance, or reliability across the green."

"And, of course, the fit in one's hand and the relative ease of priming and loading," Florrie continued. "I myself feel that Manton's productions have been overrated."

"Oh, you do, do you? And you are such an expert at pistols?"

"I am reckoned a tolerable shot," she said.

Alford snorted. " 'Tis almost a pity I will be leaving so soon. For I would be tempted to challenge you to demonstrate your 'tolerable' prowess with a pistol."

It *was* a pity he was leaving, for she would dearly love to wipe that condescending smile off his face. No one who travelled the European continent in the last disruptive years dared to venture out unarmed—and mere possession of a firearm was not enough; one also needed to know how to use it. Her father had enlisted a number of willing assistants to tutor her into becoming a crack shot. She only wished she could display that skill to Alford.

Determined to ignore him, Florrie turned back to her grammar with a sigh. Learning a language from books was such a dreadful bore. It was so much easier and interesting to learn the language in conversation. But that would have to wait until she gained the Peninsula. That could not happen too soon for her.

Eager to be free from Miss Washburn's exasperating presence, Alford grabbed the brandy decanter and retreated to his room. Pouring himself a generous amount, he stared glumly into the flames of his newly cleaned fireplace, idly swirling the liquid in his glass. If it were not for that odious Washburn chit, he could almost enjoy his stay here. It was peaceful and quiet—something he realized he sorely missed in London. He half-believed he would prefer to stay and force Miss Washburn to leave instead.

He pondered the idea. She seemed adamant about staying. There must be something he could do to encourage her departure. Something so outrageous, so dreadful that she would not hesitate to set out for Bideford, even if it must be on foot.

He dismissed the idea of attempting to breach the fortress of her room. That could be too dangerous a course—for if she felt truly compromised, he would be stuck with her for

the remainder of his life. That was a fate to be avoided at
all costs. It must be something else.

Alford sat up straighter. If he did not directly compromise
Miss Washburn herself, there was another way to evoke her
disgust. What if he brought another woman into the house?
The type of woman no respectable lady like Miss Washburn
would dare to associate with. . . .

A capital idea! Although he had made no formal arrangement with that dancer before he left town, her professions
of dismay at his departure had seemed genuine enough. He
could offer her a more permanent liaison, based on her
willingness to join him in Devon. He was willing to bet Miss
Washburn would not remain under the same roof for more
than five minutes.

A masterful plan. He would have a companion to make
his stay much more pleasant, and be rid of Miss Washburn
in the bargain. It was an idea that could not go wrong. With
any luck, he would already have driven her away before
Nanette even arrived, but if not . . . Alford set down his
glass and went in search of pen and paper. He would be free
of that irksome chit and have the lovely Nanette warming
his bed in less than a fortnight.

Florrie carefully shook the beaded water from her cloak
and hung it on the peg in the passageway between the kitchen
and front hall. When the rain at last stopped earlier in the
afternoon, she seized the opportunity to enjoy a walk in the
fresh air. Although she was not certain whether it made much
difference whether it actually was raining outside or not—it
seemed to be just as wet. She frowned at her water-spotted
half-boots. They would have to be dried carefully to prevent
staining the soft leather.

Crossing the hall, she could not help but notice the letter
laying on the table. Curious, she stepped closer in an attempt
to read the addressee's name. Miss Nanette La Pierre. Florrie
wrinkled her nose in disgust. That was a most unrespectable
sounding name if she ever heard one. She noticed Alford
had signed his father's name to the missive in order to gain
free postage. Typical.

Curiosity warred within her and she reached out to grab the letter, then she jerked her hand back. Alford's letters were his own business. Weren't they? She turned to resume her journey, then halted and whirled again. No telling what interesting things she might learn. Snatching the letter, Florrie slipped it into her pocket, and turned her steps to the stairs.

In the privacy of her room, she heated her small penknife before the fire until it was hot enough to slip easily under the wax seal. Carefully unfolding the thick paper, she scanned the contents. Color rose to her cheeks as she read the lines penned by Alford.

This was outrageous! He was actually inviting his mistress to stay at this house. Florrie was speechless at his audacity. This surpassed anything she had thought him capable of. Why, the veriest scandal would descend upon her head if word of this ever reached the outside. If he thought she would remain in this house for one minute while that—

Florrie sucked in her breath in a sharp "Oh!" That was exactly what Alford intended—to drive her from this house. He must have decided to remain himself, and wanted her gone. And knew that no respectable lady would dare remain after he had dragged his *cherie amie* here.

"The bloody nerve," she exclaimed.

Actually, Florrie did have to give the man credit for his clever plot. It raised her opinion of Alford a notch or two. He was not as indolent and obtuse as he liked to appear. In fact, it was a rather crafty plan. If it had not been directed at her, she would be tempted to congratulate him on it.

But she could plot just as easily. She sat down before the dresser, tapping the letter against her chin as she thought. Her first impulse was to toss the whole thing in the fire, but Alford might notice if the letter disappeared from the table before Old Mort stopped for the mail. But she doubted Alford would examine a finished letter carefully.

Florrie set the letter aside and carefully refolded the cover sheet. She once again heated her penknife and, after warming the wax, carefully pressed the seal down until the letter was fastened close. Examining her work carefully, she expressed a satisfied sigh. All was neat and tidy, with no sign of her tampering. The pages of the letter she picked up and tossed into the fire. Let Miss La Pierre wonder at the strange missive she received. Peering around the corner of her door, Florrie made certain no one was in the corridor. She slunk down the back stairs, slipped into the hall, and deposited the empty letter in its original spot on the table.

Alford had made only one error—underestimating his enemy. Florrie chuckled as she headed for the library. Lord Alford was in for a long wait for his London lightskirt.

Cheered by his new plan to be rid of Miss Washburn, Alford was inclined to be in a generous mood that evening.

"Should you like to join me for a few hands of piquet?" he asked when the dinner dishes had been cleared away.

Florrie stared at him. Was this some devious new plot?

"You do play piquet?" he asked.

She nodded. "What stakes do you propose?"

"Stakes?" He looked surprised. "I thought this would be only a friendly game. Something to wile away the time."

"Unusual for a man with your reputation to be so unwilling to take up a challenge," she taunted. "Or do you fear that my skill will surpass yours?"

"Of course not," he said, fighting his irritation. He was only trying to be polite and here she was, snapping at him again. Lord, this chit would try the patience of a saint. "I did not know you were that interested in gambling, Miss Washburn."

"All diplomats are gamblers," she replied.

"Name your stakes, then."

"Shilling a point, ten pounds a game?"

Alford stared. She did not propose chicken stakes. "Are you prepared to lose such a sum of money?" he asked snidely.

"Are you?" she countered with a defiant stare.

Florrie had no clue as to Alford's skill at piquet; she could only assume it was tolerable, knowing his penchant for other games of chance. She was acknowledged to be a dab hand at piquet herself. It might prove an interesting match. And if not . . . well, she would make her father pay whatever she lost to Alford. He owed her that much after sending her to this abominable house. She took her seat across the table from Alford and watched while he shuffled the cards with precise skill.

The sight of his long, tapering fingers manipulating the cards was almost mesmerizing. He had very nice hands, she thought, remembering for an instant the feel of them against her body on that crazy wedding day in London. Then she hastily shook her head to dismiss the disturbing image.

Florrie picked up her cards and arranged them in suits. She glanced at Alford, who smiled at her smugly over the top of his own cards. After examining her own hand more carefully, she could see the reason for his smugness. Her cards were abominable. Two low quatorze's. If it weren't for that dratted queen and jack, she could have called carte blanche.

"Pondering your discard, Miss Washburn?"

Slapping her five worst cards on the table, she drew five more from the talon. They were equally bad. She noted with growing unease that Alford gave up nothing.

"Point?" he asked.

"Three," she said glumly.

"Five," he replied with a self-satisfied smile.

"I have a tierce," she said apprehensively.

"Two quarts and a quint," Alford said blandly. "Eighteen points."

Florrie knew now she would not even make her hand. "Quatorze."

"I have kings."

"Yours," she replied in disgust.

"That makes thirty-two," Alford replied. "Repique."

Florrie tossed down her cards. "I concede the game," she grumbled.

"You do not hesitate over things, do you Miss Washburn?" he asked, arching a supercilious brow. "Should you perhaps care to change our wager?"

"No," Florrie snapped, snatching the proffered cards from his hand. "One game does not make an evening."

"True, true," Alford said, nodding. He was quite willing to stop before further damage was done, but if Miss Washburn's stubborn pride goaded her into folly . . . well, she had only herself to blame.

Florrie was willing to concede, after several games, that she was in the presence of a master. Alford never bested her in such an insulting manner again, but he won steadily. She was forced into taking wild chances in hopes of a successful play, and her losses mounted steadily.

"You should make your living at cards," she said sarcastically, shuffling the deck.

"I do."

Florrie's eyes widened.

Alford poured himself some more brandy from the decanter at his elbow, ignoring her curious gaze. "Would you like some, Miss Washburn?"

Florrie hesitated, then nodded. "A small amount."

" 'Tis a shame to pour so little," he said, handing her the half-filled glass. "This is a fine vintage."

"I am not overly fond of brandy," Florrie said, taking a hesitant sip.

"Of what are you overly fond, then?" he asked.

"Champagne," Florrie replied.

"Of course," Alford said with a patronizing smile. "A lady's drink."

Florrie glared at him. "I will have you know many *gentlemen* prefer champagne over brandy or port," she retorted.

"Of course they do," he said sarcastically.

"Are you always so irritating, Alford, or are you making a special effort tonight?" Florrie demanded.

Alford placed a hand over his breast. "You wound me, Miss Washburn. Here I am, trying to be an amiable companion, and my efforts are flung in my face." He took a large swallow of brandy. "It is enough to drive a man to drink."

"T'would be a short drive in this instance," Florrie muttered under her breath.

"I did not ask to be sent to this God-forsaken corner of

the earth," he said with an angry scowl. "And I particularly did not ask for your 'soothing' presence, Miss Washburn. So do not expect me to act overjoyed at the situation."

"I have known cantankerous old men with better dispositions."

"They were not married to you," Alford pointed out.

"I await the news of the annulment with great eagerness," she snapped. "I would rather be wed to the Corsican himself than to you." She flung the cards onto the table. "What do I owe you?"

Alford reclined in his chair, swirling the brandy in his glass in an aimless manner that only increased Florrie's exasperation.

" 'Tis a sizeable amount," he said at last.

"I am not a pauper."

Glancing at the score paper, Alford mentally calculated her debt. "Forty-eight pounds, seven shillings," he announced. "That would buy you a few bonnets."

Florrie berated herself for having insisted on such high stakes. Her father would be most displeased.

"I might be amenable to making a few adjustments," Alford drawled, watching her closely.

"Such as?" she asked.

"I will wipe the whole debt free if you depart when Old Mort returns again," he said quickly.

Florrie drew herself up straighter in the chair. "I shall do no such thing," she stated haughtily. "It has already been decided that you shall be the one to leave."

Alford shook his head. "I begin to think I like it here."

Reaching for the paper, Florrie quickly scrawled her signature and the debt. "That should be satisfactory," she said, rising to her feet. "I bid you goodnight, Lord Alford."

He had not really thought she would rise to the bait, but Alford had to admit he admired her aplomb. She had a sense of honor worthy of a man. Too bad it meant he would have to think of some other method of driving her away.

After the thoroughly lowering evening, Florrie retired to her room. She made certain both doors to her chamber were securely locked before she stepped out of her clothing. Despite the way he had trounced her at piquet, Alford had been drinking steadily all evening, and she had thought he had begun to eye her with a bit of a leer by the end of the night. Stranded in this horrid house, she was truly at his mercy if he developed any improper ideas. And after reading that letter to his mistress, she knew he had several.

It would be useful to have her maid with her once again, she thought, as she struggled out of her gown. How long did the chicken pox last? She fully expected to have Sally arrive on the doorstep any day. But until she did, Florrie would continue to manage her own clothes. She did not feel comfortable with Mrs. Burgess.

Wrapped in her warm robe at last, Florrie crossed to the windows to draw the curtains. Across the rear lawn, the mist rose from the ground under the pale light of the half moon. It swirled about in wind-shaped wisps, growing ever thicker, almost looking like a living entity, growing, flowing, crawling across the lawn toward the house. She shuddered at the thought.

Grabbing the edge of the heavy velvet curtain, she started to pull it across the window, then stopped and peered out into the mist again. Hardly daring to believe what she saw, Florrie looked again, the curtain falling from her hand as she peered intently into the shrouded darkness.

There had been movement out there. She was certain of it. Not the mist; it was more definite and quick than that. It looked like a . . . a person, perhaps. With a trembling hand, Florrie reached up and unlatched the window.

An icy blast of air smote her as she opened it wide and leaned out. Everything grew dark as clouds scudded across the moon. There it was again! On the far side of the lawn. She stared in rapt fascination. As the figure drew closer, Florrie leaned further out the window to catch a better glimpse.

It was a woman, dressed in some flowing white garment. Her hair was long and the wind whipped it into wild disarray across her face and shoulders. Another drifting cloud momentarily blocked the light from the moon. Florrie's heart pounded; she held her breath while waiting to catch another glimpse of the mysterious figure.

As the pale moon's rays relit the lawn below, Florrie scanned it frantically for another glimpse of the white figure, but there was no sign. The woman had vanished. Completely. The moon had not been covered long enough for her to have crossed the lawn toward the house. Where had she gone?

As the cold seeped into her bones, Florrie reluctantly drew back and reached up to pull the window shut. Just as the window was within an inch of closing, an eerie wail rang out, rising and falling as if born by the wind. The hair on the back of her neck rose and Florrie stood motionless, frozen to the floor in fear. Then she tugged the window shut, fastened the latch, and jerked the curtains tight. In a quick dash, she reached the bed and crawled into it, night robe and all. Pulling the covers over her head, she huddled there until she stopped shivering from the cold—and trembling from fear.

The candle at her bedside burned brightly long after she was asleep.

Chapter 9

Florrie stretched lazily under the bedcovers, slowly allowing her body to drift into wakefulness. Through the heavy window curtains, only the faintest morning light trickled into her chamber. It was a most pleasant way to—

She sat bolt upright as she remembered the inexplicable events of the previous evening. Jumping from the bed, she ran to the window and peered out. It was a foolish action, she knew, for nothing would be there.

And indeed, the back lawn was one vast stretch of empty, verdant green, gently sloping down to the rock wall that marked the edge of the cultivated property. Beyond that, she had learned, was the rocky ledge leading to the cliffs and the sea below.

How different a sight it was this morning! The long-absent sun already had burned a hole through the early morning fog and the day promised to be pleasing. Florrie hoped she might even be able to catch her first glimpse of the sea. Even through the closed window she could hear the raucous cries of the seabirds who nested in the nooks and crannies on the cliff above the water.

Turning back toward her room, Florrie saw the burned-out stump of the candle beside her bed and grinned ruefully. She had been a royal pea-goose last evening. What she heard was the wind, nothing more. And that mysterious lady had probably been nothing more than a trick of the mist and moonlight.

Still . . . Florrie had sensed *something* odd in the air last night. Something dark and strange, and perplexing. The very thought sent a *frisson* of apprehension down her spine.

She was being silly, she chided herself while she dressed. It was like her first day, when she had half-believed Mrs.

Burgess to be a witch. Her imagination was far too active. No doubt caused by the untoward chain of events that had turned her life so topsy turvy in the last weeks. The sooner her life returned to normal, the better. And that meant getting Alford out of her life as quickly as possible.

Alford was already in the library when Florrie made her way there. He had polished off what looked to be an enormous breakfast, judging from the remnants littering his plate. She gave a disdainful sniff and rang for her own light breakfast of toast and tea.

Florrie settled herself in her chair before attempting conversation with Alford. Curiosity burned within her. How would he explain his new desire to remain at Hartland?

"It appears to be a promising day today," she said brightly. "The rain has stopped at last. No doubt you are pleased that you will finally be able to make your way to Bideford."

Alford shrugged carelessly. "I am not so certain that I will be leaving today. My father was right; the country does have a restorataive function. I have contemplated staying longer."

Florrie feigned curiosity. "Oh? Do you think that wise?"

"Whyever not?"

"We have no chaperon! Just think how it will appear to others. Why, if you continue to linger in my presence, it may be more difficult to obtain an annulment." She smiled sweetly. "You would not wish that, I am certain."

Alford laughed. "The only bar to our annulment, my dear, is for me to take you to my bed. And as pleasant as that event might prove"—he leered at her—"I am not in the slightest bit interested in leg-shackling myself to you. You need not fear for your annulment."

Florrie glared at him. How dare he even mention such a thing to her!

"Do not look at me like that," Alford protested. "You were the one to bring up the topic." He grinned wickedly. "Besides, you are soon to be a married lady. Surely you must have some knowledge of what transpires between a man and his wife."

"Of course I do," Florrie snapped. "That does not make it a proper topic for the breakfast table."

He shrugged. "If you find my conduct offensive, perhaps you should remove yourself. I am not going to put on airs in front of *you*."

Florrie fumed in exasperation. She could not allow Alford to bait her so. He took great pleasure in disconcerting her and she only played into his hands by allowing her irritation to show. She was made of sterner stuff. Composing her features, she calmly poured herself another cup of the now-tepid tea.

"I trust your fireplace is now working to your satisfaction?" she asked. It was a pity Burgess had managed to clean it. Discomfort would have been a good ally in her struggle to be rid of Lord Alford.

"Quite well," Alford replied. "I was more than cozy last evening. Slept like a babe, in fact."

Florrie thought back to her own disturbing evening. "You did not hear or see anything . . . strange?"

Alford arched one brow. "Strange?"

Florrie flushed. "Unusual is perhaps a better word. I noticed an odd sound as I was preparing for bed. It was probably nothing more than the wind."

Her remark aroused Alford's curiosity. "Just what type of noise was it?"

Florrie waved a dismissive hand. "Oh, you know, the type of sound you get with wind swooping between the chimney pots, or along the eaves. A wailing noise."

"How did it sound? Was it long and low? Or short and high-pitched?"

"Long and—oh, what does it matter? I only wondered if you had heard it as well. I probably only noticed it last night with the rain gone. It was such a relief to hear something beyond that steady drip."

"Was the sound high-pitched or low?" he persisted.

"High," she replied. "Almost . . . almost as if it were a voice."

"A voice?" Alford sat up straighter in his chair. "You thought it sounded like a voice? How odd."

Florrie nervously twined her fingers together. Last night the figure she had glimpsed seemed so vivid. But today, in the light . . . Dare she mention it to Alford?

"Well, what did it sound like?" he prompted.

"A woman's voice," she said reluctantly.

"A scream?"

"No, it was a more mournful sound, full of despair rather than fear." She laughed uneasily. "If one can say such a thing about the wind."

Alford smothered his urge to laugh. In a minute, she would be claiming to have seen a ghostly figure in white hovering in the air. "You did not see or hear anything else while this was going on, did you?" he asked.

Florrie swallowed nervously. "Well, actually . . ."

"Go on," he prompted in an eager tone.

"I was looking out the window when this all happened. It was such a pleasant night with no rain at last, and the moonlight kept filtering through the clouds. I thought I saw . . . I thought I saw a woman running across the back lawn."

"No!" Alford exclaimed, fighting back his smile. The chit was full of the night terrors! And Alford knew just the thing to fan the flames—had not old Mort bent his ear with endless tales of local ghouls and phantoms? There must be a story to match Miss Washburn's fertile imagination. "What did she look like?"

"She was dressed in white, with long hair that whipped across her face," Florrie began, then halted. "I am not even certain I saw anything. The mist was so thick . . ."

"I think it is very possible you did see something." Alford struggled to keep the excitement out of his voice. He would lead her on a merry dance! Leaning forward in his chair, he whispered in a conspiratorial voice: "The Lonely Lady of Hartland Point."

"The who?" Florrie's hazel eyes widened.

"The Lady, as the locals call her." Alford sat back in his chair again, satisfied his words were having the desired effect. Florrie's face had paled by at least two shades and her eyes were round with nervousness.

"She's real?" Florrie asked.

Alford smirked. "As real as your imagination allows. The original lady's been dead for over a hundred years." He fought against his glee at the look on Florrie's face.

"You mean she is a *ghost*?"

He shrugged indifferently. "I am no student of necromancy. The locals say she is the spirit of some poor girl with a tragic tale—a husband lost at sea or in some battle—the usual thing."

"What else did you hear about her?" Florrie asked anxiously.

"On certain nights she walks about the neighborhood, looking for her long lost love." Alford struggled to keep a straight face at his embellishment.

"Does she . . . Has she ever been seen inside the house?"

Alford shook his head. "I do not recall. Had I known the tale would fascinate you so, I would have listened closer. Why not apply to Mrs. Burgess? She is likely to know all the ghostly details."

Conscious of his scrutinizing gaze, Florrie shook her head. She did not want Alford thinking she was a pea-goose. And truly, she was not absolutely certain she wanted to know more about the woman in white. "It is of little consequence," she said hastily.

Alford beamed with joy. He had planted the seed in that fertile mind, and all he needed now was to bring the plan to fruition. He thought he had just hit upon the perfect method of persuading Miss Washburn to cut short her sojourn at Hartland. And one that would afford him much amusement in the process.

Florrie prepared for bed that evening with deliberate haste. Tonight, when she pulled the curtains across her window, she did not so much as glance out onto the lawn. If there was some strange, other-worldly creature out there, she did not want to see it. Climbing into the high bed, she settled herself under the covers and blew out the bedside candle. Tonight she would sleep with a peaceful mind.

She was nearly asleep when a sudden, unfamiliar sound

caught her attention. Lying very still, hardly daring to breathe, Florrie strained to catch another hint of the sound. There!

It was certainly not the noise that had so disturbed her the previous night. This sounded more like a distant thud. A banging shutter, perhaps. Florrie wrinkled her brow as she tried to remember if any of the windows had shutters. She thought not.

The noise sounded again, slightly louder this time. And it had more of a metallic ring to it.

Florrie sat up, clutching the covers to her chest. Should she light her candle, and go out in the corridor to investigate? It would be so cold. . . . She sank back under the blankets. Better to remain in the snug warmth of her bed. It was probably just the ever-present wind—

A loud clang sent Florrie frantically scrambling for the light box on the table by the bed. Her hands shook so hard she could barely produce a flame, let alone light the candle. Somehow, she managed and the room was bathed in its yellowish glow.

That last sound had been much, much closer than the others. Whatever made it was moving. Which meant it had to be *alive.* She shivered, and not from the cold.

Straining her ears, Florrie thought she heard a faint scraping noise, very dim and muffled, but one which sounded continuously. It grew louder, she thought, almost as if . . . as if it were coming up the stairs at the end of the corridor.

Her heart racing, Florrie sat paralyzed upon her bed, hardly daring to breathe. There was no question that whatever was making that noise was coming closer. The sound was more distinct now, the metallic tone more pronounced with each . . . step. It had reached the top of the stairs, and was slowly making its way down the corridor toward her room. Closer, closer, it came, that strange metallic clank. Florrie clapped her hands over her ears to drown out the approaching sound but it did no good. Closer, closer . . .

Then nothing. Only pure, clear silence. She drew her hands from her ears and listened, but the only sound she heard was the thudding of her heart within her chest. Florrie stared at the door, as if trying to see through the heavy wooden panels. Then her eyes widened in fear.

Slowly, very slowly, the door knob began to turn.

Chapter 10

Florrie screamed and screamed and screamed. Not until she heard Alford shouting and banging on the door connecting their rooms did she stop.

"For God's sake, what is wrong?" Alford yelled. "Unlock the door!"

Grabbing the key from the bedside table, Florrie jumped to the floor. Her hand shaking, she barely managed to unlock the door for Alford.

It was a measure of her agitation, Alford thought, that she had given no heed to the fact that she greeted him clad only in her night gown. And that gauzy creation was as ineffective as any in hiding her pleasant curves. It took some effort to turn his concentration to her distraught face.

"Good God," he said, forming his expression into a mask of concern. "You are pale as a ghost. What happened?"

Florrie pointed to the door leading into the corridor. "Someone was out there, trying to get in my room."

Alford casually crossed the chamber and tried the latch. The door was locked, as he was certain it would be. He turned and flashed her a quizzical grin.

"You lock yourself in?"

"I do not desire any unexpected visitors in my room," she snapped.

"Good idea," he said, nodding his head. "Pass me the key."

She stared at him.

"Not that anyone would have lingered, after all the noise you made. But I should like to take a look in the corridor just in case."

Florrie handed him the key.

Alford made a great production of unlocking the door,

stepping into the corridor and looking this way and that. When he stepped back into the room, he shut the door firmly behind him, locked it and placed the key in Florrie's hand.

"Not a sign of anything amiss," he said. "What exactly happened?"

Florrie sagged against the bed post and for a moment Alford thought she really might faint. He leapt to her side and half-led, half-carried her to the bed. Placing his hands about her surprisingly tiny waist, he lifted her onto the high mattress.

"There is nothing there now," he said in the most reassuring tone he could manage. "You are perfectly safe."

Florrie looked into his pale blue eyes, and saw an assurance there that gave her comfort.

"I feel . . ." she began, hesitating, " . . . I feel like a total goose, Alford. Getting so hysterical, I mean. It is not like me at all. But someone was trying to enter my room."

"Did you hear anything before that?"

"There was the oddest noise," she explained. "I swear whoever it was came up the stairs and down the hall. There was a clanking sound, as if something was being dragged along the carpet. Then . . . then the knob . . ." She shuddered at the memory.

"There, there," said Alford soothingly, patting her gently on the back. "It was probably nothing more than a strange gust of wind. In these old houses, there are drafts everywhere."

"Drafts do not go about rattling door knobs," she said curtly.

"Maybe it was Burgess, seeking to ravish you," Alford said with a sly leer.

Florrie glared at him. "I thought you were *concerned,* Alford. Now you are treating this as if it was a joke. I was frightened half out of my mind."

He immediately sobered. "That was uncalled for," he admitted. "But there are only four of us in this house. And I cannot see why either Burgess would be wandering the upstairs corridor at this hour of the night."

"Somebody was out in the hall," Florrie insisted.

"Well, it was not I," Alford said dampeningly. He gestured at his bare feet and night clothes. "I was asleep in my bed."

It came as a sudden shock of realization to Florrie that she was sitting on her bed in her night gown, talking to a man clad only in his night dress. And he looked very much like a man who had just climbed from his bed, with his tousled hair and bared legs. Florrie quickly averted her gaze from his limbs, biting her lip to regain control. They were very nice legs.

"Florrie?"

She turned her head and saw Alford watching her with genuine concern.

"Are you going to be all right?"

She nodded. "I am fine now. I am certain you are right—it was just some trick of the wind."

Alford walked to the door again and demonstrated that it was still locked. "All safe and tight," he said, then turned his eyes on her. "Lock up after me when I leave and you will be as snug as ever." He stepped toward the connecting door and made to close it behind him.

"Alford?"

He paused. "Yes?"

"I am sorry to have disturbed your sleep," Florrie said, difficult as the words were.

"That is quite all right," Alford replied with a smile. "I always welcome the chance to come to the aid of a damsel in distress." He closed the door quietly as he left.

Florrie locked the door behind him, and personally double-checked the other one before she climbed back into bed. How odd that she found such reassurance from Alford's presence. He had been soothing and comforting in his attentions, easily quelling her fears. Of course, she thought with a self-deprecating smile, it was only because she had been so badly frightened that she welcomed it so. In the normal course of things, Alford would not have created such a favorable impression.

She doubted very much that she would sleep another wink this night. If only she had a book to read. But a trip to the library to locate one was completely out of the question. She would huddle here in her bed until daylight came again.

Twenty minutes later, she was asleep.

In the morning while he dressed, Alford could not help chuckling as he recalled the picture of the near-hysterical Miss Washburn gratefully accepting his assistance. He had discovered a hole in her self-assured manner wide enough to drive a coach and four through. It was going to be laughably easy to drive her from this house. One or two nights like the last one and she would run all the way to Bideford. He snickered at the thought.

Pulling his boots on, Alford stood and surveyed his appearance in the mirror. Not bad for a stay in the country. A casually knotted scarf replaced the usual starched cravat. No need for an elaborate neckcloth out here, he thought. And once Nanette arrived, there would be little need for clothes at all. That thought brought a wicked grin to his face.

Surveying his room before leaving, Alford noticed one item out of place. With a swift kick, he pushed the errant loop of chain further under his bed. Then whistling a bawdy tune, he went down to greet the morning.

He was surprised to find Miss Washburn in the library at such an early hour. He had thought she would have slept until noon after last night. But there she sat, freshly gowned. Only a very close perusal revealed the faint lines of strain around her brown eyes. She looked damn fine for a woman who had been scared witless eight hours before. He had to admit, the chit had spirit.

"Good morning, Miss Washburn," he greeted cheerily as he helped himself to some tea. "I trust you spent an uneventful night—after the initial disturbance?"

She nodded. "I looked the veriest fool, didn't I?" she asked ruefully.

"Oh, I would not say that," he said. "I thought you looked rather fine, actually, dressed only in your night gown with your hair down."

"Alford!"

He grinned. "You asked."

"I should have known better than to try to carry on a reasonable conversation with you," she snapped. "Remember, I am practically your sister."

"I'd say a wife is a sight closer than a sister," he replied dryly.

"Oh!" Florrie scowled.

"Of course, I am not certain I would like to be married to a lady who is in the habit of luring men into her bed chamber in the middle of the night," he continued with a smirk. Between fear of ghosts and fear for her virtue, he should be able to keep her so off-balance she would leap at the chance to be free of him.

Florrie resisted the urge to fling the pot of hot tea at him. Only the thought that he deliberately goaded her stilled her hand. She could not let him win this battle of wills. She would show him who was the stronger.

Alford saw the determination in her face and laughed inwardly. She was proving to be an admirable foe. Time to stage a strategic retreat, and allow her to drop her guard again.

"Should you like to take a stroll about the grounds this morning?" he asked. "It might be just the thing to clear your head from the confusion of the night."

Florrie regarded him suspiciously. Why was he suddenly being nice? She could not imagine that Alford truly desired her company. He had some nefarious plan in mind.

"Oh, do come, Miss Washburn. I will not bite." He flashed her his most engaging smile. "You know perfectly well you are safe with me. The fresh air will do you good."

He was a rather enigmatic man, Florrie thought later, when she found herself racing along at his side, forced nearly into a run to keep up with his long strides. One moment he was leering at her like a young buck in the pit at the opera, next he was all solicitous concern and anxious friendliness. She had not decided which attitude—if not both—was a studied pose. But after intercepting that letter, she was less inclined to underestimate Alford. She suspected a great deal more went on behind that bland countenance than he let on. Lord Alford was not entirely what he pretended to be. She almost

wished he would be staying at Hartland, so she could catch
further glimpses into his puzzling nature.

"Can you slow down?" she pleaded at last, gasping for
breath.

Alford halted and grinned at her. "Too rough a pace, Miss
Washburn? You only needed to say something." He waited
patiently while she caught her breath, then struck out again
at a much slower gait.

"It is easier to observe your surroundings when you are
not galloping through them," she said acidly.

"I hardly thought the sight of the lawn warranted a close
inspection," he retorted. "I am more interested in seeing
what is on the other side of the wall."

"The sea."

He stopped and turned to her, a look of cross exasperation
upon his face. "I am trying, Miss Washburn, to be amiable
this morning. I realize you had a difficult night. But you must
recall that my sleep was disturbed as well. The least you can
do is be civil."

Florrie had the grace to look chagrined. "You are right,
Alford. I am sorry." She took a few steps toward the high
wall that protected the back lawn from the worst of the wind,
then turned back toward Alford with a questioning look.
"Are you coming?"

With a resigned shake of his head, Alford fell in behind
her.

The tall, stone wall that enclosed the back lawn rose above
even Alford's head. He examined the stonework carefully.
Overall, it was in good repair. Moss clung to many of the
rock surfaces and ivy and other twining vines roamed over
its sides. In high summer, it would be a mass of greenery.
Now, it merely hinted of what was to come with the first
budding of the new leaves.

At the far west end, a gate was set in the wall. According
to Burgess, there was a narrow path along the top of the cliff,
outside the wall. Alford was curious whether there was a
path down the cliff as well.

"You may wish to remain here," he said to Florrie as he

fumbled with the rusty gate latch. "I am not certain what the outer path is like."

"I am just as curious as you," she replied. She would not permit him to think her faint-hearted.

He shrugged. "Suit yourself."

Florrie followed him through the gate, then caught her breath at the scene that lay below them. The cliff top here was relatively wide—there was nearly ten feet of land between her feet and the edge. But to the north, she saw the path was no more than a few feet wide. And what fell off to the side fell quickly and sharply—350 feet to the ocean below.

She spotted the jumble of rocks that lay beyond the point. Watching the waves pound into them, the spray rising many feet into the air, Florrie took an involuntary step back. The area looked as dangerous and desolate as any she had ever seen. She watched nervously while Alford strode to the edge and peered eagerly down the slope.

"Is it steep?" she asked.

He laughed. "I do not think you would stop before you hit the water, if that is what you mean," he said. "If you'd put a castle on this place, you would never have worried about an attack from the sea."

Florrie stepped forward, but she could not quite force herself to get close enough to the edge to look over. Great heights made her nervous.

"I wish to walk toward the point," he said. "I shall be back in a few moments. Burgess said there was an old path down to the water and I aim to find it."

Florrie nodded. She had no desire to trace that narrow ledge, with only a few feet of dirt protecting her from the edge. "I will wait here," she agreed.

Alford set off toward the point, while Florrie more closely examined the gate set into the wall. It looked about as old as the house, its surface weathered and grayed from exposure to the harsh coastal winds. Yet incongruously, a tangle of rose vines trailed about the wall. She was surprised that something as delicate and beautiful as a rose could endure the punishment it must take. It would be a rare sight in a month's time with the wall all abloom. But she would be gone by then.

When she next glanced up the path, there was no sight of Alford. For a moment she was startled, then reasoned he must have already gone around the bend in the wall.

The wind whipping off the white-flecked sea chilled her, and it did not take long for Florrie to decide she had spent enough time outside the wall. Where was Alford? She really had no reason to wait for him—he would come back in his own time. But at the same moment, she did not want him to be out along these dangerous cliffs alone. If something happened . . .

Swallowing nervously, Florrie slowly turned her steps toward the north. She would go as far as the bend in the wall, she decided, looking ahead anxiously to judge the width of the path. It was not so dreadfully narrow. She would be fine as long as she did not look down to her left. Florrie picked her way through the scrubby plants that determinedly clung to the earth. This path was not much used, she thought, then laughed. It was hard to imagine either of the Burgesses rambling along the cliff tops. It might have been years since another person trod this walk.

She tried not to notice how the path was narrowing with each step. Where was that dratted man?

"Alford?" she called, but the wind whipped the name from her lips and carried it away. She doubted he would hear. Just to the bend, she promised herself. If he was not in sight then, she would return to the house and alert Burgess. He could go look for the foolish man.

Florrie touched the wall beside her, its solid bulk giving her a mote of comfort. She inched along more slowly now, carefully keeping her eyes averted from the cliff edge to her left. Only a few more steps and she would round the corner. Only a few more . . .

With a sigh of relief she saw how the path widened as it swept around the corner. And even better, there was Alford, heading toward her with his typical brisk stride. She took a few grateful steps toward him, still keeping her hand on the wall.

"Decided to go adventuring after all, Miss Washburn?" he greeted.

She nodded.

"Unfortunately, there is not much to see. There were a few points that look promising, but no clear path anywhere down the cliffs. They are just too steep."

"We can go back then," she said with obvious relief. She watched with indrawn breath while Alford casually brushed past her as if the path were as wide as Piccadilly. She carefully turned around and followed him.

The wind hit Alford like a slap to the face as he came around the corner of the wall. It was one thing to have it at one's back, but it was a daunting prospect when blowing in one's face. He ducked his head slightly and continued forward.

When the ground beneath his feet suddenly gave way, Alford reacted with a survivor's instincts. His feet scrabbled for purchase in the loose dirt as he flung his body forward. He landed on his chest with a thud that knocked the breath out of him.

Hearing Florrie scream, Alford staggered to his feet and whirled about, fearing she had lost her footing as well. But she stood on firm ground, her face white as talc and her hand clasped over her mouth, her eyes wide with horror.

He let out a deep breath and forced himself to smile. It had been a rather exciting moment. But he did not need a hysterical woman on his hands.

"I am all right," he said as he eyed the narrow but deep chasm that lay between them where the bank had given way. "I fear all the rain softened the earth." There was still a narrow ledge of dirt running along the base of the wall. "Give me your hand and I shall help you cross."

Florrie shook her head. "I can't."

"Of course you can," he said with encouragement.

She shook her head again, and took a step back. "I shall go around the other way."

"Do not be a fool," he said. "The path that way could be just as bad. The ledge widens out in a few more feet and we shall be perfectly safe. Give me your hand."

Florrie's arms stayed frozen at her side.

"Miss Washburn, every moment you and I stand here risks a further collapse of the bank." As if to punctuate his words, a small shower of dirt flowed down the side of the new hole. "Now, if you give me your hand, and place your foot along the wall, we can contrive to get you over the cut."

"But what—"

"Nothing is going to happen to you, Miss Washburn," he said reassuringly. "I promise."

Florrie looked at him doubtfully, but it was the second cascade of pebbles down the inside of the chasm that decided her. She inched forward toward the edge, her fingers trailing along the wall to her left.

Alford stepped as close as he dared to the chasm, afraid his greater weight would cause more earth to give way. He stretched out his arm, but it was not enough to reach her hand.

"You will have to come closer," he said. "Keep right up against the wall; the ground is safest there."

Florrie swallowed hard several times and pressed forward. She stretched out her arm as far as she could and Alford caught it in his grasp.

"Now, step to the wall with your left foot," he commanded. "Swing your right foot around and jump. I will pull you toward me and we shall have you on firm ground in a trice."

Florrie gingerly stepped forward, breathing a sigh of relief as she carefully transferred her weight to her left foot and the ground beneath it held. Closing her eyes tightly, she jumped toward Alford. Her feet landed on the edge of the bank.

Then, with a sickening lurch, she felt the ground vanish beneath her feet.

Chapter 11

Alford jerked her into his arms and staggered backward toward more solid footing. He did not stop until there was at least five feet of earth between them and the cliff edge. He leaned wearily against the wall, still clutching Miss Washburn to his chest. Relief washed over him. He had saved her, as he had promised. "Thank God," he whispered, hugging her close.

Having been exceedingly drunk the last time he had held Miss Washburn in such an intimate embrace, Alford was rather more conscious of the feel of her this time. He rather liked the way her arms were wrapped about him so tightly he could barely breathe. Her head lay against his chest and he was almost tempted to stroke the honey-gold hair that tumbled from its pins. Miss Washburn felt exceedingly nice. All those curves that had been hinted at in such a tantalizing manner last night when he viewed her in her night gown were pressed against him in a most pleasant manner. Most pleasant . . .

With a start he realized where his thoughts were drifting and he shook himself back into awareness. This would not do, he thought. It would not do at all. This was his brother's wife—or at least Kit's intended wife. The woman Alford wanted out of his life as quickly as possible. He pulled away as if he had been burned.

Florrie felt Alford stiffen and push her from him. She was suddenly conscious of how she still clung to him like a limpet to a rock—or as his precious trollop Nanette undoubtedly did. She disengaged her arms from around his waist.

"I trust we are recovered?" he said coolly.

Florrie heard the coldness in his voice and she was both angered and embarrassed. Angered, because he acted as if

99

she had been behaving foolishly. Embarrassed, because she had. She looked down and twitched her skirts into some semblance of order.

"Quite," she replied, not willing to meet his eyes.

"I should inform Burgess of the damage to the trail," Alford said, turning abruptly.

Once again, Florrie had to run to catch up to him. When safely inside the gate, she gave up the effort.

"Thank you," she yelled at his retreating back, "for saving me."

He turned and saluted her with that mocking grin of his. "Think nothing of it, Miss Washburn. It was a lovely excuse to hold you in my arms again."

Alford laughed at Florrie's scowl. She need not know just how close to the truth it was.

After informing Burgess of the landslide, Alford made his way to the library. Miss Washburn, he was certain, had retired to her room to recover from the after-effects of that rather exciting walk. He did not mind a few moments of solitude to do the same himself.

He had to get her out of here. This awkward situation simply would not do. Florence Washburn was attractive enough, enticing enough that he no longer felt confident that his aversion to her sharp tongue and her obvious dislike of him would be enough to stay his hand in a moment of weakness.

Like this morning. He had enjoyed holding her against him, grasping her so tightly he could feel her soft breasts pressed against his chest. He'd had to fight against the urge to taste her lips, to see if they were as sweet as he remembered.

It simply would not do. Florence Washburn was destined for Kit. No matter that he and Kit were not close; he would never stoop to stealing his brother's intended. And in any event, Alford had no intention of becoming leg-shackled. That was certainly the price that would be demanded before any dalliance.

Yet Miss Washburn was quite correct when she had said yesterday that their situation had great potential for creating a scandal. And if he compromised the chit, he would be honor bound to continue this unintended marriage. That was something he had no desire to do. He would contrive to drive Miss Washburn from this house for her own good. And his.

Florrie took luncheon in her room. She had no desire to speak to Alford now.

That experience on the cliff had been shattering. She still recalled the sickening lurch in her stomach when she had watched the path crumble beneath Alford's feet, saw him fall. She had been frightened out of her wits. And then to be forced to cross that chasm . . . But Alford promised she would be all right and she had been. An inane sense of relief and security had washed over her when she clung to him, the thudding of his heart beneath her ear sounding a reassuring litany. For a moment she had forgotten all else and relaxed in his comforting arms.

Florrie tossed her head at the thought. It was ridiculous to think she was attracted to Alford. He was spoiled and arrogant, an idler and a wastrel. He had none of the ambitions she so admired in his brother. Alford would make an abominable husband. He would reel home at all hours from some gambling house or drunken party. Or his mistress's. It would not do. She may not be marrying Kit for love, but she did respect him. Alford had not done anything to earn her respect.

Even that dramatic rescue on the cliff had been turned into something else with his flippant response. How could she possibly have enjoyed being held in the arms of such a boor? She wished he would leave, and let her remain in peace. He owed her that much. This whole intolerable situation was his fault, after all.

Florrie remained in her room until dinner, when she finally joined Alford in the library. They ate without much conversation, only a few polite remarks on the flavor of the savory soup and the excellence of the wine. But she could not bring herself to retire upstairs when the meal was finished. Even Alford's annoying presence was better than solitude. She drew out her Spanish grammar and took a seat before the fire.

Alford leaned over her shoulder. "I thought you might be growing bored with your lessons," he said with a hint of a smile.

Florrie turned to him with a haughty gaze. "Oh, you did?"

"Yes," he said. "I took the opportunity of searching the library this afternoon for some more suitable reading. Not that there was much." He gestured at the shelves. "A more boring collection of tomes I have yet to see. But," he continued, bringing out the book he held from behind his back, "I discovered that Mrs. Burgess is an avid reader and has her own private collection."

Florrie smiled weakly. She could only imagine what Mrs. Burgess would read. Probably improving tales from Maria Edgeworth.

"Her tastes are rather dramatic, I fear," Alford continued, holding the slim volume in such a way as she could not see the title. "Popular novels and the like. I was not sure if you approved of novels."

"There is nothing wrong with novels," Florrie said with exasperation. "I find I quite enjoy a well-written one."

"Still, her likes may not be elevated enough for your tastes."

"Alford, quit dilly-dallying and tell me what you have."

He brandished the book before her. "*The Castle of Otranto,*" he said.

"I've read it," she replied casually.

Alford grinned. He had suspected Miss Washburn was fond of gothic novels. "But I have not. Perhaps you would consider reading it to me."

"Why should I read to you?"

"With your talent for the dramatic, Miss Washburn, I imagine you will be able to do it justice. Besides," he added impishly, "you recall I am not fond of reading anything more complex than the sporting results. I fear an entire book is beyond my capabilities."

Florrie considered. She enjoyed reading aloud—her father and she had done it often. And she was growing thoroughly sick of her Spanish grammar. At this point in time, anything looked more appealing.

"All right," she agreed. Alford was obviously in one of his good moods and she wished to take advantage of it. He could be pleasing company when he tried.

Alford smiled, handing her the book. If all went as planned, it would be more fuel for the fire. He settled in his chair, a look of expectant eagerness on his face.

" 'Manfred, Prince of Otranto, had one son and one daughter; the latter, a most beautiful virgin, aged eighteen, was called Matilda. Conrad, the son was three years younger—' " Florrie paused. "Are you really certain you wish to hear this, Alford?"

"Oh, certainly," he said from his chair opposite hers in front of the fire. "I love frightening tales. Someday you shall have to get Kit to tell you his. The lad has a fiendish bent for the occult."

Florrie stared at him. That was something she did not know about Kit. It struck her that Alford could tell her a great deal about his younger brother. But that was almost a form of spying, she told herself. She turned her attention back to the book.

" '—a homely youth, sickly, and of no promising disposition . . .' "

Alford sipped his brandy, watching her more intently than he pretended. He had to admit, she was easy on the eyes. The firelight glinting off her hair turned it the hue of burnished gold. And those lips . . . he watched their movement in rapt fascination.

After a few minutes, Alford uttered a deep sigh, and closed his eyes. There was no harm in looking; still . . . He leaned back and listened to her low, melodious voice. She read well, injecting a bit of the dramatic into the dry words on the page. He was of the opinion that gothic novels were so much claptrap, but there would not be such a hue and cry against them if women were not susceptible to their eerie tales. And he wanted Miss Washburn to be in the most susceptible of moods. She had already shown how impressionable she was. Mrs. Burgess had an immense stock of gothic novels. Horrifying novels by day, strange noises by night. He would have Miss Washburn fleeing the house in terror in no time.

And then he could have some peace—until Nanette arrived.

Florrie read on, through the horrors of the giant helmet crushing poor Conrad, Manfred's mad ravings, and the terrified Isabella's flight. Periodically she glanced over to Alford, who sat calmly sipping his brandy. He had hardly moved all evening, except to refill his glass, which she noticed he emptied at a steady rate.

She halted at the end of the first chapter.

"Finished already?" Alford inquired. "What a shocking tale. No wonder good fathers keep their daughters away from novels."

"There is nothing wrong with novels," she retorted. "For those with minds mature enough to appreciate them."

"You do not think that your education was ruined because of your novel reading?" he taunted gently.

"Of course not," she snapped, suspecting it was the brandy that made him so surly. "I have an excellent education. It is those poor women who have nothing beyond the smattering of knowledge that passes for a young lady's education these days who have problems. Ignorance is never a useful skill."

"But you precisely point out the dangers of too much education," he said. "If you were not educated, you would not know what had been kept from you. And you would be content."

"Why would I be content to live in ignorance?"

"You cannot be ignorant of what you do not know," he said.

"I would be ignorant compared to you, or Kit, or my father. Can you honestly say you would care to have a wife with whom you could not discuss the slightest issue?"

"Women are to be looked at and admired, not listened to."

Florrie snorted her derision. "Coming from you, that is not an unexpected attitude. Thank God, Kit is more sensible."

"Ah, but I wager one day he will regret that he has taken one such as you to wife," Alford said, the brandy making his tongue unguarded. "He will wish he had taken one who was more biddable, more conformable. A termagant like you will be a constant thorn in his side."

"You call me a termagant? When you are the most arrogant, insufferable man I have ever known?" Her eyes flashed dangerously.

"Is it arrogance to know that men are superior to women in every way? Look at that little incident this morning. You would still be standing on that crumbling path, paralyzed with fear, if I had not pulled you across."

"I would not," Florrie retorted. "I would have made my own way across. Or found another route. I did not need your help."

"And you did not need me last night, when you were so frightened in your bed?"

"I do not recall calling for you by name," she said.

"I suppose you expected Burgess to come rushing up from the kitchen? Face it, Miss Washburn, despite your protestations, you are very dependent upon male protection."

"I am not!"

"It is nothing to be embarrassed about," he continued. "It is merely the way of the world."

"I am perfectly capable of taking care of myself."

"Then why is your father so eager to see you wed? I heard him say himself that he was relieved to have a husband's protection for you."

"He meant that in the broadest sense," Florrie explained. "The protection of a name, the status of a married woman. He did not mean a husband who would keep me under lock and key."

"The world would be safer," Alford muttered. "You could use a strong hand."

"I would never marry a man who sought to dominate me," Florrie said. "I wish for a man who will heed my opinion and be guided by my ideas."

"You mean one who is content to be led around by the nose," he retorted. "Do you think Kit is going to stand for that?"

"I do not want to lead anybody," she protested. "I only wish to have my views consulted and considered. In a marriage of equals, that would happen."

"If you are so equal to Kit, Miss Washburn, why are you not shouldering a gun on the Peninsula?"

"Kit is not over there to fight," she snapped. "He is a staff officer. He is there to think."

"And can you think as well as he when you are covered with mud, cold, wet, and starving?"

"I am used to hardship as well as the next person," she retorted. "Try spending a winter in St. Petersburg!"

"A frightening prospect, I am sure," he said with a mock shudder.

Florrie slapped the book shut. "This conversation is pointless, Alford. Your mind is as closed to new ideas as it is to literature."

"I never said I did not like literature," he protested. "Was I not a willing listener?"

"Your steady consumption of brandy did not imply an interested response," she said, standing. "But I suppose even a novel such as this is too taxing for your limited capacities."

He was on his feet in an instant and roughly grabbed her wrist. "I would not be so quick to pass judgment on others, Miss Washburn," he said in a voice that was as icy as it was rough. "You do not know a damn thing about me."

"I know quite enough to judge that you will never be half the man Kit is."

Florrie was appalled at her words before they were even out of her mouth. She watched icy rage flit over Alford's face, and she would have taken a step back if he had not held her wrist in his grasp.

"I . . . I should not have said that," she said quietly. "It was uncalled for."

Alford released her wrist. "Oh, no doubt you are quite correct, Miss Washburn." He grabbed the brandy glass from the table and tossed the remaining liquid down his throat. "After all, I would much rather drink, and game, and wench than involve myself in the affairs of state."

The bitterness in his voice puzzled Florrie. Was he not

happy with his life? She shook her head. The thought was absurd. She set the book down and grabbed her shawl off the chair back. ''I shall see you on the morrow, Lord Alford,'' she said.

He nodded curtly and turned toward the fire, pointedly ignoring her departure.

He did not need some slip of a girl to tell him what a waste his life was. He knew it already. But what good was all his university scholarship, or his interest in architecture, or reform legislation when he could do nothing about any of them? He had an income that allowed him to live a life of relative ease when supplemented with his gaming-table winnings. He owned no property beyond his horses and carriage. His ideas for the improvement of the ancestral hall fell on his father's deaf ears. His avid desire to stand for parliament had been met with derision by those same paternal ears. There would be plenty of time for that when he took his seat in the House of Lords, Alford had been told. Leave the Commons to the professional men. The heir to an earldom would not want to sully his hands with a common political campaign. And with his father's hands on the purse-strings, he could do nothing on his own.

Alford scowled. His father denigrated his ambitions. Florence Washburn thought him a wastrel. And Kit . . . he did not know what Kit thought about him, if ever he thought of his brother at all. But he most likely would fall in at Miss Washburn's side. And Alford suddenly realized that he would like her to have a somewhat better opinion of him, although he was not certain why.

He reached for the brandy decanter and poured himself a generous glass.

Chapter 12

Alford stared bleary-eyed at the plate of cold toast on the library table. The lavish butter spread upon the pieces had congealed into great globs of pale yellow grease and the resulting picture looked revolting. He turned away from the table with a shudder and focused his eyes on the brandy decanter instead. That looked much more the thing. He poured himself a glass and downed it in two swallows. Much more the thing.

"Rather early for brandy, is it not?" Florrie had slipped into the room while Alford was eagerly—a bit too eagerly in her eyes—downing his morning restorative.

"And what business is it of yours?" he responded sourly.

"Oh, dear, we are a bit grumpy this morning." She smiled sweetly and sat down at the table, where she eyed the cold toast with much the same lack of enthusiasm as Alford. "Did you ring for breakfast?"

He shook his head. Florrie frowned and walked over to the bell rope, which she pulled with clear enthusiasm. "I, for one, would like to have something a little more substantial for my morning meal." She returned to the table and sat down. Upon inspecting the teapot, she found the water tepid at best. She saw Alford pour himself another glass and wander to the windows.

"Do you always drink your breakfast?" she asked crisply.

"No," he said.

"My, we are touchy. I suggest a walk, Alford. Fresh air can work wonders with even the surliest disposition."

"There are times," he said, turning to face her, "when I find it impossible to believe that you have lived to such a ripe old age, Miss Washburn. Certainly, someone was tempted to strangle you long ago."

"Many times," she replied sweetly. "My father has proposed that remedy more than once."

"A pity he never followed through."

"He must have saved me for you," she said. She leaned back, baring her neck. "Here, Alford, my throat. Do your best."

He snorted derisively and turned again to the window. Florrie sat back in her chair, a smug smile on her face. If Alford was willing to enter into this war of nerves to see who would first leave the house, she would give him a spirited battle. She only wished she could reveal how she had already foiled his main plan. It was a pity that he could not expect any sort of reply for several days. She wanted to watch him wait, and squirm when he heard nothing from his precious Nanette.

"Likely to rain again today," Mrs. Burgess announced as she bustled in with breakfast.

"Nothing unusual," muttered Alford, still staring out the window.

Florrie eyed the slices of ham, hot buttered toast, and jam pots with enthusiasm. Let Alford drink his breakfast. She was hungry. She eagerly spread marmalade on her toast.

What did she care if it chose to rain again? It was not as if it would deprive her of any special outdoor activity. Walking across the lawn seemed to be the best this place had to offer in terms of outside recreation. It would not differ much from the long Russian winter. The warmth and sunlight of Portugal sounded more appealing than ever. She prayed the annulment would be procured soon.

"This has to be the wettest place on earth," Alford pronounced as he flopped into a chair by the table. He forked two gigantic slabs of ham onto his plate and dug into them with a relish that astounded Florrie.

"I imagine you must find it dreadfully dull," she said, smiling sweetly. "It must make you greatly miss all the diversions of London."

"That it does," he said rudely, with a mouth full of ham.

"Perhaps you should reconsider your return," Florrie said.

"You could be back there easily in four days. Think of what you must be missing!"

Alford eyed her warily. "So could you," he pointed out. "And since you have spent so little time in London of late, Miss Washburn, it would be boorish of me to deprive you of that pleasure. Please, consider yourself free to go. Anytime."

"Certainly, you cannot expect me to travel alone?" Florrie tried to look aghast. "Whatever would people say?"

"You arrived here alone," Alford pointed out.

"That was necessity," Florrie reminded him. "And 'twas only for a short time. My father would not be pleased if I arrived in London without a companion."

"You could always take Mrs. Burgess with you."

Florrie laughed without mirth. "I assure you, Alford, that will not be necessary. My maid will arrive eventually. Then perhaps this conversation will have some purpose."

Alford scowled. He had bungled things last evening, first arguing with the chit, then staying down here and drinking into the late hours, when he should have been upstairs carrying out his tactics of terror. He firmly pushed from his mind any memory of how delectable she had felt clasped in his arms on the cliff walk. His letter to Nanette should be reaching London soon; it was conceivable she could arrive by early the following week. He wanted to make quite certain Miss Washburn would be eager to leave by then—if she had not already departed.

He would have to swallow his irritation and ask her to read again tonight. And he must make very certain that she did not sleep well afterward. Perhaps the "Lady in White" should reappear, in a form a slight more substantial than wavering sea-mist. The thought cheered him. He would seek out an accomplice immediately.

"Why would I be wantin' to dress up in a bed sheet and go running about the back lawn?" Mrs. Burgess stared at Alford in puzzlement.

"Because I would like you to, Mrs. Burgess," he replied patiently. "It is merely a little joke I wish to play on Miss

Washburn. I would do it myself, but then I would not be there to judge her reaction."

Mrs. Burgess shook her head. "Can't see as there's any good reason."

"Think of it as aristocratic eccentricity," Alford said. "Ghosts and such are all the rage in London. Miss Washburn will be able to dine out for weeks on this tale. It will increase her popularity immensely."

The housekeeper still looked doubtful. "What if it rains?"

"Then we will have to contrive another such scenario in the house," Alford said. He thought for a moment. "In fact, that may be a better idea altogether, Mrs. Burgess. It will pose less inconvenience for you. All you need to do is be seen for a brief moment at the end of the upstairs corridor, then you can return to your quarters." He smiled his most winsome smile. "Please?"

Still shaking her head, Mrs. Burgess muttered her acquiescence.

"Capital!" Alford exclaimed. "I will come get you when Miss Washburn retires—I will do my best to encourage her in an early evening. Be waiting with your sheet and the whole matter will be over in a matter of minutes." He bowed low. "I thank you from the bottom of my heart, Mrs. Burgess."

Alford exited the kitchen, whistling a cheery martial air.

Now all he had to do was create the proper mood this evening. He would have to put on his most charming manner in order to get Miss Washburn to read again. But on a dark and stormy night, with only a few candles, and an eerie story . . . he thought she would be quite impressed by his little plan.

Florrie prepared for bed that night with little dallying. Why she felt more safe and secure when tucked under the covers, she did not know, but unquestionably she did.

It had nothing to do with that foolish book, of course. She had read it before and not found it particularly frightening. She had read much worse. But somehow tonight, a disquiet crept upon her. It seemed as if the whole house was creeping up around her, pressing inward.

It was only the rain raging outside, she reasoned. With

the curtains drawn and a fire blazing in the hearth, the library had been decidedly cozy. Alford had even listened attentively, sprawled in his chair with brandy in hand.

It was easier to be swept up into a story of that kind when one was reading, she thought. Her attention could not be diverted by a flickering flame, or a spot on the carpet. That was why Alford appeared so unaffected. Tomorrow, despite his protestations, she would insist he read. She would feign a sore and tired throat if he demurred.

Nestled under the covers, Florrie lay back against the pillows and pulled the blankets up to her chin. She heard the sheets of rain lashing against the windows, blown by the gusts of wind that danced and whistled under the eaves. On occasion, a particularly hard blast of wind hit the house, and she imagined that even its stone walls shook from the force. She could not imagine what winter would be like here.

She had almost drifted off to sleep when a particularly strong wind rattled the windows, shocking her into wakefulness. Florrie listened carefully, but discerned no other odd sound. She put her head back on her pillow, starting when she heard another noise. That had not sounded like the wind, it had sounded like—

An eerie wail scattered her thoughts. Florrie lay there in the dark, her heart pounding inside her chest. It was like the sound she had heard the night . . . the night she saw the lady on the lawn.

Swallowing hard, Florrie tried to calm her racing pulse. It was just the wind, she reminded herself. Lord knows, there was enough of it on a night such as this.

The noise sounded again, and she could have sworn it was closer. And inside.

She shivered, remembering the horrible noise in the hall the other night. Thank goodness, she always locked her door. She would be safe, no matter what lurked outside in the corridor.

As long as whatever made the noise was human. But Alford had labeled the lady a ghost. Did a locked door have any effect on a ghost?

Florrie clenched her fists until her nails dug into her palms.

There had to be a simple, rational explanation for all of this. There had to—

She sat upright as she heard the wailing voice again. There was no question it came from the corridor.

Florrie was too frightened to even light the candle at her bedside. Only the faintest of glows issued from the fireplace on the far wall, lighting her room just enough to make out the shadowy bulk of the furniture against the walls. Florrie was grateful she could not see the door. She did not want to know if anyone was trying the knob again. As long as it was locked, she was safe. As long as it . . .

A silent scream tore from her throat as the door slowly opened inward.

Chapter 13

In the shadowed light, Florrie saw a flash of white outside the door. A high pitched wail sent her diving under the covers, pulling them over her head to hide the hideous scene from her sight.

She lay there for what seemed an eternity, hardly daring to breathe, her heart beating as if it would leap from her chest. Stiffening in anticipation of what would come next, Florrie braced herself for some horrible fate.

When nothing occurred for several minutes, Florrie cautiously stuck her head out and glanced to the door. It was still open, the gap clearly illuminated by the dim light in the corridor. Slowly, cautiously, Florrie crept from her bed. She grabbed the silver candlestick from the table beside her, clutching it tightly in her fingers. It would make a tolerable weapon. With hesitant steps, she inched toward the open door.

Peering cautiously around the frame, Florrie saw nothing amiss at the north end of the hall. She looked the other way. For a moment, she thought she saw something white. Then an eerie wail echoed down the hall and the candle holder fell from her fingers with a resounding crash. Florrie tried to scream but no sound came from her throat.

"What the deuce?" Alford came barreling out of his chamber. Even in the dim light, he could see that Miss Washburn's face looked as white as her night gown. "What is going on here?"

Florrie tried to speak, but she could not find her voice. She shuddered instead.

Alford was all solicitous concern. He picked up the dropped candle holder and took her hand, drawing her back into the chamber.

"Your hands are like ice," he said, chafing them to bring back some vestige of warmth. "For God's sake, Miss Washburn, what happened? I heard the strangest noise."

"It was the Lady," she whispered in a harsh voice. "The one I saw on the lawn the other night. Except this time, she was in the house."

"You saw her?"

She nodded. "At the end of the hall." She flung herself into his arms and buried her face against his chest. "Oh Alford, it was awful. That same horrible wailing. And she actually started to come into my room!"

"My God!" He patted her in a comforting manner while a self-satisfied smile flitted over his face.

It was some minutes before Florrie regained her composure.

"How in the devil did your door come open?" he asked. "Did you forget to lock it?"

"No! I always check it the last thing before I get into bed."

"And this figure in white actually opened your door?"

Florrie nodded. "I heard a noise in the hall—that horrible wailing—so I was looking right at the door. When it opened I caught a glimpse of something white and . . ."

"Then what happened?"

"I pulled the covers over my head so I would not see any more."

"I see." He struggled to keep the grin from his face. "So you finally conquered your fear and went into the hall to investigate?"

She nodded. "I saw nothing and was ready to turn back into my room when I saw a flash of white at the far end of the hall. Then she wailed again and you came out."

"Most mysterious. I heard the noise myself, but I was too late to see anything."

"What does it mean, Alford?"

He shook his head. "I do not know. As a rational man, I cannot help but think there is some explanation for all this— some natural phenomenon, or some strange construction in this hosue that contrives these odd occurrences. But on the other hand . . . There are too many tales of the supernatural to make me a total disbeliever. Why, last year, Seb Cole swore he had seen a haunt at a country house.''

Florrie shuddered at the thought. ''I heard many strange tales in Europe, of ghostly creatures and haunted castles. From perfectly sane people. It does make one wonder.''

''What wonderful luck, to find ourselves amidst such an experience.'' Alford smiled.

''I find nothing enjoyable about it,'' she said curtly.

''Oh, come now, Miss Washburn, do not say you are frightened of ghosts?''

''I am not afraid of ghosts,'' she snapped. ''I merely resent these intrusions upon my sleep.''

''Understandable,'' he said, a slow smile spreading over his face. ''Although I find I do not mind it at all, when it means I can be continually invited into your chamber.'' He reached out and straightened an edge of the lace at her throat. ''Particularly when you are in such enticing disarray.''

Florrie's cheeks flamed. ''You are appalling!''

He grinned. ''Because I can appreciate the sight of an attractive woman? Come now, Miss Washburn, you are quite familiar with my reputation. How could you expect anything less from me?''

''I could hope that you would behave with decorum and respect toward your prospective sister-in-law!''

''Ah, but you are not yet my sister-in-law,'' he pointed out. ''You are my wife.'' He took a step closer and delighted in her retreat. Ghosts and lechery. The two things most designed to send her fleeing from this house.

''Are you afraid of me as well?'' he asked.

''No. I merely find you as bothersome as that misguided spirit who stalks the halls. Neither of you are welcome.''

''Old Mort is due back in a day,'' he said. ''He would be most willing to transport you to Bideford, and set you on the stage for London.''

''You would like that, wouldn't you?'' She faced him angrily, feet apart and hands on hips. ''Well, I will not allow you to chase me off, Lord Alford. I am perfectly capable of defending myself against your lechery. And I find I am most intrigued by the thought of investigating these ghostly happenings. I will not leave.''

Alford swallowed hard. She could have no idea of how enticing she looked, standing so defiantly before him. Her night gown was pulled taut over her breasts and he could clearly see their hardened tips pressed against the fabric. He clenched his fists against the unbidden desire that rose within him. How could such an aggravating chit have such an enticing body? He needed Nanette here. Soon. Or he was likely to make the most horrible mistake of his life.

Florrie smiled inwardly when Alford refused to hold her gaze. She had shown him she was determined to remain here. She no longer felt threatened by his outrageous, suggestive remarks. One word from her, and he would find himself her husband for life. And she knew that he wished to avoid that fate at any cost. No, she had nothing to fear from him.

She was less certain about the ghost—if there was such a thing. Her rational mind told her it was impossible. Alford was probably right, it was some strange trick of the house that led to such eerie happenings. She could not allow herself to be upset over such a thing. It made her appear weak and silly. That she could not abide.

''Do you have anything more to say?'' she demanded. ''Otherwise, I think you could leave now.''

''Are you certain you shall feel safe, Miss Washburn? If a locked door can open by itself . . .''

''I am certain I must have failed to lock it properly. In these drafty corridors, it could easily blow open. I will be certain to lock it most carefully next time.''

He nodded. Now that her initial terror had subsided, she was back to being the acerbic, practical Miss Washburn again. He rather liked her better when she was scared witless. She was much more soft and vulnerable.

''Then I will say goodnight,'' he said, ostentatiously bowing his way out the door. She slammed it behind him, and he clearly heard the key turning in the lock.

Alford grinned. Oiling the lock to Miss Washburn's door this afternoon had been a masterstroke. It had been as easy as child's play to unlock it with the housekeeper's key. And Mrs. Burgess had played her part to perfection. Despite Miss Washburn's protestations to the contrary, he knew she had been badly frightened tonight. His plan was progressing with admirable success. He doubted the "Lady" would need many repeat performances before Miss Washburn was ready to decamp.

In the morning, Florrie refused to dwell upon the frightening events of the previous night. In the brilliant spring sunshine, the idea of ghosts and mysterious ladies in white seemed absurd. There had to be a logical explanation for all of this.

And to find it, Florrie determined to explore the house. She undoubtedly would discover some strange architectural oddity that created freak drafts of wind, which could easily produce the odd noises she had heard. And it *was* possible that she might have mis-locked the door. The wind could have pushed it open as well. She was less successful at coming up with a rational explanation for the white-clad form she thought she had glimpsed, but there was undoubtedly something that would account for that as well. A trick of the candlelight, perhaps.

Following breakfast, Florrie slipped out of the library without telling Alford her plan. He would probably insist on accompanying her, and she wanted to solve this mystery on her own.

Plus, she could not help but remember how she had cast herself so gratefully into his arms last night. Why did he always have to be present during her moments of weakness, when a sturdy male chest offered comfort and security? He would label her a vaporish female, when she was nothing of the sort. She was strong, confident, sure of herself. She did not need a male shoulder to lean on. She wanted to be a partner, not a dependent. And Alford had the horrible knack of always seeing her in the latter role.

She would show him. He would not be able to hide his admiration when she solved the mystery by herself.

Florrie began her exploration in the long gallery that lay

across the end of the house opposite her room. It was a dull and gloomy room, illuminated only from the windows at either end. Whatever paintings had once hung here were long gone, and the dark wood paneling only increased the darkness. The room was devoid of furniture, even curtains, and Florrie's steps echoed loudly as she walked across the inlaid wood floor.

She examined the windows at either end of the chamber. Both were latched securely and did not rattle in their frames. She doubted even the strongest storm would ring a sound from them. Frowning, she examined the walls more closely, but did not see any obvious cracks or holes that would allow air to enter from the outside. The doors hung securely on their hinges and the latch was not broken or bent. This room was not the source of her problem.

Florrie undertook a similar examination of all the other rooms on the first floor, but discovered nothing to support the theory that strange house-drafts were responsible for the odd occurrences. With a resigned sigh, she mounted the stairs to investigate the upper floor. Drafts could easily blow down the stairwells.

The upper floor showed ample signs of disuse. Dust lay thick upon the furniture covers in the first chamber she examined. It was obvious nothing had disturbed this room in years. She shut the door and went into the next chamber, which was in a similar condition.

This was getting her nowhere, she thought, as each and every room revealed the same undisturbed state. Any wind strong enough to blow open a door would have disturbed the dust. Some rooms looked to have been ignored since George III's accession.

Florrie pulled open the final door with a sense of frustration. But once she stepped through the door frame, a very different sight met her eyes.

The room was still dusty, and what little furniture it held was securely under cover. But a table and chair stood in the middle of the chamber, and they were both free of dust and dirt. Someone had been in this room recently.

She took a cautious step toward the table. A few crumbs

were scattered across the top. Florrie leaned over and inspected them closely. Bread and cheese. And decidedly fresh. She straightened and made to move, then froze at a sudden sound.

The faint noise of footsteps echoed in the corridor. And whoever they belonged to was taking great pains to walk quietly. Florrie looked around the room in panic for a place to hide, but there was nothing that offered much security. Only a large chest of drawers and a few chairs pushed against the wall.

She heard the faint sound of a door latch catching, and realized the person in the hall was looking into the other rooms on the floor. But it was done in such a stealthy manner that Florrie had no doubt of the person's aim. He was looking for her.

Her only hope was the element of surprise. If she stayed pressed against the wall alongside the door, she might pass unnoticed for the moment it would take her to dart into the hall when the intruder entered.

If only she had a weapon. But the room offered nothing more deadly than a chair cushion. Surprise was her main chance.

Florrie tip-toed across the room, the squeak of the floor-boards beneath her feet sounding ominously loud in the silence. She paused halfway to the door, listening. No sound came from outside. Had the person heard her movement; was he waiting to hear another sound, just as she did?

Her heart thudded in her chest and she struggled for breath, not daring to draw too much air into her lungs. She took another cautious step forward and cringed at the unmistakable noise as she shifted her weight to that foot. Not wanting to prolong the agony, she quickly covered the last few feet to the doorway and pressed herself against the wall.

Biting her lip to keep from making any sound, Florrie strained her ears to listen for the sound of approaching footfalls. She heard them again, not loud, but clearly headed in this direction. Florrie raised her arms, in preparation to ward off a blow if necessary. She planned her escape carefully. She would run to the near stairs and hurtle down them,

praying she did not trip and break her neck in the bargain.
Once she reached the ground floor she could yell for help—
surely one of the Burgesses would be in the kitchen at the
rear. Alford, who was probably still in the library at the other
end of the house, would be no help to her now.

With a pang of regret, she wished she had enlisted his help
in her search. He would offer her a measure of protection
against whoever sought her out.

The footfalls were closer now; Florrie heard the latch click
on the room across the hall. It would only be seconds . . .
She took a deep breath and tensed, prepared to move at the
first opportunity, fighting against the overwhelming urge to
shut her eyes. She listened in aching awareness as she heard ·
each slow, deliberate step crossing the hall. First one, then
another. Closer, closer, closer they came . . .

Chapter 14

Alford peered cautiously around the door frame and found himself staring into the wild-eyed gaze of Miss Washburn, who was backed up against the wall as if she wanted to become part of it.

"Playing hide-and-seek, are we? You might have clued me in earlier."

"Alford." Florrie nearly collapsed with relief at the sight of him, then her emotions quickly shifted to anger. "How dare you give me such a fright!"

"My apologies," he said with a mocking smirk.

"What are you doing up here?" she demanded.

"Looking for you."

"I don't see why you have to do it in such a skulking manner," Florrie snapped.

Alford placed a denying hand on his breast. "I? Skulking? I would rather say you are the one guilty of that action. You don't see me hiding in corners."

"I was hiding from you!"

"Oh." He grinned. "Thought the Lady was coming to carry you off, did you?"

"No," she said with irritation. "I thought that whoever had breakfasted in this room might be coming back."

He was instantly alert. "How do you know someone was eating here?"

"Look at the table." She waved her hand toward it.

Alford inspected the surface, picking up one of the crumbs and twirling it between his fingers, a calculating look upon his face. "You are right, this is fresh." He casually glanced about the chamber. "It certainly does not look as if the room has been used for anything else."

"What do you suppose it means?" Florrie asked.

He shrugged. "Perhaps this is Burgess's refuge from his wife. God knows, if I were he, I would not mind such a place."

"But why would he bother to come all the way up here?" Florrie asked. "There must be plenty of other rooms that are cleaner."

"And cleaner means that Mrs. Burgess visits them," Alford explained. "It is obvious she does not spend any time up here."

"But what if it isn't Burgess?" Florrie asked. "What if there is a . . . a stranger in the house?"

"Really, Miss Washburn, I think you have been reading too many novels. What possible reason would anyone have for being in this house?" Alford walked to the window and peered out. "Even if a burglar wished something, there would be no way to carry off any booty. And the house is so isolated that no casual wanderer is likely to happen by. It must be Burgess."

Florrie had her doubts, but she held her tongue. Let Alford think what he will. There was a mystery here and she was determined to learn more about it.

"Why were you looking for me?" she asked.

"Old Mort is here," he replied. "He is amenable to taking you to Bideford if you can ready your bags quickly."

"I have no intention of leaving," she said, glaring at him. "I thought it was you who planned to leave."

"Ah, but I have changed my mind, remember? I find the peace and isolation of the country far too soothing to exchange for the noise and disruption of London."

"Well, I am not leaving until my father sends for me," she said with determination.

"Suit yourself. But do not complain that you were not given the opportunity. Old Mort will be back again in a few days. Maybe you will change your mind by then." He turned to go.

Florrie hastily fell in behind him. She did not want to remain alone on this floor.

"What were you doing up here?" Alford asked.

"I was trying to determine how a draft could have blown my door open last night."

"Find anything?" he asked with an amused half-smile.

"No," she said slowly. "But that does not mean it could not have happened. I may have missed some architectural oddity that caused it."

"Undoubtedly."

"It makes much more sense than believing there really is a ghost walking the corridors," she argued as they started down the stairs.

"Ah, but think how much more romantic a thought that is." Alford turned to her. "You are a romantic, Miss Washburn, are you not?"

"I am a realist, Alford. And I find it hard to believe that there really is a ghost in this house."

But you did not think that last night, he thought. *Your current display of bravado is merely a product of the sunlight. Once it grows dark again . . .* He smiled in anticipation. He would plan something very special for tonight.

Alford had made light of the matter with Florrie, but the discovery that someone was making use of that isolated room upstairs did not sit well with him. Something mysterious was going on here at Hartland, and he was determined to come to the bottom of it. Starting with a thorough exploration of that room upstairs.

To avert suspicion, he slipped outside right after lunch. With a casual air, he made a circuit of the house, quickly noting the location of all the doors and any windows that might be used to gain entry. Fortunately, in a house this old there were few. No flimsy, glass-paned doors led out onto the terrace, no modern double-hung windows afforded an easy entrance. No, if one entered this house, it would be through the doors. He made a mental note to query Burgess about his locking habits.

Entering the house through the door at the gallery end, Alford crept quietly up the rear stairs. He hesitated at the first floor landing. Would it be of any use to examine this floor? He shook his head in decision. He knew very well who had caused all the disturbances on *this* floor. With determination, he gripped the banister and continued upwards.

Like Florrie, he had glanced into every room on this floor in his search for her this morning. Alford grinned again in remembrance of the look on her face when he had peered around the door at her. She looked like a cross between a frightened hare and Boadecia preparing to do battle. He was lucky she had not popped him on the nose again.

He did not exactly tip-toe down the corridor, but he found himself deliberately stepping lightly. Not that he expected to find some stranger lurking behind the door. It was half possible that his hastily concocted tale of Burgess seeking refuge from his wife was true.

The door was still ajar from their departure earlier. Cautiously pushing inward, Alford stepped into the room. Everything looked as it had in the morning, the dust covered cloths shrouding the furniture and the lone table and chair near the center of the room.

Why, or more important, who would choose to have their meal in this isolated roost? Alford pondered the question while he stared out the window. Like his and Florrie's rooms, this one overlooked the back lawn and the sea beyond. Was that in itself significant? Was the person who had been in the room waiting and watching for something?

With a sigh, he turned away from the view. There was little further to be learned here. Perhaps another visit, during the night, might prove more productive. With his hand on the door latch, Alford turned once more to see if he had missed anything.

By late afternoon, Florrie decided she had endured enough studying for one afternoon. She looked up from the grammar book she held in her lap for the hundredth time. Why was it so deucedly difficult to concentrate on these dratted Spanish verbs?

She was bored, of course. Despite the rather dramatic events that occurred after dark, the days here at Hartland were not filled with excitement. There was no lively conversation sprinkled with diplomatic gossip, no political intrigue, nothing, in fact, that so much as hinted of her usual pastimes. There were not even newspapers to keep her informed of the latest doings.

Her restlessness this afternoon certainly had nothing to do with Alford's absence. The man was free to come and go as he pleased. Although what he could have found to occupy himself with since luncheon, she could not guess. Perhaps he was making a lengthy inspection of the grounds, or had walked to the nearest farm. Or . . .

The thought froze her in the chair. He had been so interested in finding a path down the cliff face. Perhaps he had gone in search of it again, and attempted a descent on his own, and . . . The image of a broken and bleeding Alford lying crumpled at the bottom of the cliff brought the sting of tears to her eyes.

She shook her head. It was absurd of her to worry about Alford's whereabouts. He was a grown man, and he did not need her worrying like a nurserymaid. If he was foolish enough to attempt some treacherous seaside path, and injured himself in the process, well, he would only have himself to blame.

Florrie reminded herself how pleasant the afternoon had been without his irksome presence. Even when he was being his most amiable, she had the unnerving feeling that Alford was laughing at her—and why that was, she did not know. He seemed to take great enjoyment in baiting her; unfortunately, she only encouraged him by rising to the bait. She would have to be most careful in the future to avoid responding. Resolutely, she forced her mind back to her Spanish grammar.

Lost at last in her reading, Florrie did not look up again until the shadows of impending night were creeping up the library walls. She looked to the mantel clock and noted it was almost time for dinner. Alford had yet to make an appearance, and Florrie grew genuinely concerned.

Then she remembered what he had said this morning—Old Mort had come today. Had Alford, despite his protestations of enjoying the peace of the country, decided to take his leave after all? It would be just like him to do so without telling her. Florrie tossed down her book with a flare of anger and strode toward the door.

She raced up the stairs and came to a breathless halt in front of Alford's room. She tapped quietly, then more forcefully when no response came. When there was still no answer, she carefully tried the knob.

It was locked. What did that mean? Florrie chewed her lower lip while she thought.

If Alford had left without informing her, she had every right to be angry. And, logically, she had a right to know if he had left. This lengthy absence was quite unlike him; it justified her worries—and her plan of action.

With a nod of assent, she fished in her pocket for the key and unlocked her own room. Then she went to the connecting door that linked her chambers with Alford's and unlocked it as well.

Stepping through the doorway, she found herself in a smallish chamber, obviously intended as a dressing room. Had it been for the master or the mistress, she wondered? It was bare of furniture and gave no clue.

Another door led into what was Alford's chamber, and Florrie was grateful to find it unlocked.

A quick glance around the room told her that if Alford had traveled with Old Mort, he had not taken any possessions with him. A dressing gown was thrown over the foot of the bed; a traveling case sat neatly atop the chest of drawers. He had not left Hartland, then. But where was he?

She could not resist the opportunity to peer about. Of course, there would be little of his personality reflected in this guest chamber. How much more she could learn from his own rooms! But she could already tell that Alford was neat in his habits. It pleased her to find that he was not a slave to his valet.

Realizing she would learn nothing more of Alford's whereabouts looking around in his room, she made a move to the door, but halted as she caught a glimpse of what lay upon the bedside table. Scarcely believing what she saw, she stepped closer.

A partially burned candle stood in its silver candle holder. An undramatic sight; her bedside sported the same item. Next to it lay a book—so he did read on occasion! But what caught her attention were the spectacles that lay atop the book.

Alford? In spectacles?

Florrie walked around the bed to look more carefully. Gingerly she picked up the gold frames and peered through them. They made her vision blurry. But if Alford's eyes were bad . . . She bent over to see the title of the book Alford was reading with his spectacles in the secrecy of his room. *Improved Field Cultivation Techniques.* Florrie's jaw dropped in disbelief. Alford had an interest in agriculture?

Perhaps he only used it to lull himself into sleep. But the bookmark was placed nearly two-thirds of the way through the book. He must be reading it—for pleasure?

Florrie saw the corner of a paper peeking out from under the book, and temptation was too strong. Sliding the book to one side, she twisted her head to read what was written on it. "Swinton Hall—North Field—new rotation plan." What followed was a list of crops and dates.

She put things back as they had been, carefully restoring the spectacles to their previous position while she pondered this new information. Alford had definitely been keeping things from her. He did read items more weighty than the sporting news! And gave a thought to more than the odds at faro.

Florrie cringed, remembering the many times she had scornfully derided Alford for being a fribble, with no interests outside of the fanciful pursuits of a young lord. No wonder she had angered him so!

She felt a twinge of guilt at discovering the two things Alford had obviously been at great pains to conceal, and crept silently from the room. Could it be she would have to make amends? The thought of apologizing to Alford did not sit well. But if she had misjudged him . . . She carefully locked her two room doors and went down the stairs.

If Alford had not left with Old Mort, she was back to her original worry, only exacerbated now that she was looking upon Alford in a more charitable light. It would be dark within the half hour; if something had happened to him outside, there was no time to lose. She hastened to the kitchen.

"Have you seen Alford?" she asked Mrs. Burgess, who was busily stirring a pot on the stove.

"No."

"I am becoming concerned," Florrie said. "I have not seen him since luncheon. Did he by chance tell you his plans?"

"No."

The woman was a fountain of information. "Is Mr. Burgess about? Alford was looking for a path down the cliff the other day and I fear he may have continued his explorations today. Something may have happened."

Mrs. Burgess jerked her head toward the door. "In back."

Florrie smiled thinly and entered the back pantry. She never quite felt comfortable in Mrs. Burgess's presence.

Burgess was polishing the silver.

"Mr. Burgess, have you spoken with Lord Alford today?"

He shook his head.

Florrie frowned. "He has not been here since lunch," she explained. "I fear he may have gone out to explore the cliff path again. Did he mention any plan to you?"

Burgess again shook his head.

Florrie fought against her rising frustration. "It is very close to the dinner hour and Lord Alford has not been seen for some time. I am concerned he may have met with an accident."

"And what do you wish me to do?" Burgess asked blandly.

"I thought that it might be advantageous to make use of what little daylight is left to look for him," Florrie said with exasperation.

"He could be miles away if he took it in his mind to go walking."

"Well, since he has done nothing like that since he first arrived here, I doubt that was his intention today," she snapped. "It is more likely he went out to the cliff path. He said he was looking for some way down when we were there the other day."

Burguess turned toward her with a sigh of resignation. "I will go look," he said in a tone that indicated he wished to do no such thing.

"Thank you," Florrie said curtly.

Upon returning to the library, she watched out the windows in growing apprehension as the last rays of the sun swept across the lawn. Where had that dratted man gone?

A sudden idea leaped into her head. Alford had laughed at her fears that a stranger had slipped into the house and was using the second floor room as a haven. But what if her idea was true? The stranger could have crept up on Alford somewhere in the house and caused him harm. The man could be anywhere now, waiting for another victim to come his way.

She swallowed hard. These last nights had been bad enough, even with the strangely comforting presence of Alford. Without him . . .

Florrie shook herself. She was becoming as goosish as Alford had accused her of being. She *had* read too many novels. There was a rational explanation for the strange happenings near her room, just as there would be a perfectly reasonable explanation from Alford as to his whereabouts today.

But when Burgess returned from the cliffs, saying he had seen no sign of Alford, Florrie's fears grew. The sun sank below the horizon and Mrs. Burgess brought dinner. Florrie was so distracted she could barely eat. Something had happened to him, she knew it.

Well, even if the Burgesses thought nothing amiss at one of the guests disappearing, Florrie did. She was not prepared to go haring off outside into the dark night. But she felt quite capable of investigating within the house.

Arming herself with a heavy silver candle holder and her chamber candle, Florrie went first to the gallery. The door creaked ominously in a fashion she did not recall from her earlier visit. The dim light from one candle was not enough to illuminate such a large chamber, so she was forced to walk nearly the entire length of the room before satisfying herself that there was no sign of Alford here. Her steps echoed loudly in the empty room.

She looked into each of the other chambers on that floor without result, although she had not expected any. If someone was up to a nefarious plot, they would not risk discovery with the comings and goings of the household. No, they would be upstairs. . . .

Florrie's courage faltered and she could not bring herself to head up those dark stairs alone. Mr. Burgess would probably be as pleased about this as he had been about going outside, but Florrie was adamant. She wanted to satisfy herself that Alford was not in this house.

"Can't see why Lord Alford'd be bothering himself about what's up the stairs," Burgess grumbled as he climbed with what seemed excruciating slowness. "Nobody's been up here in years."

"Oh, but they have, Mr. Burgess. I myself was up here this morning."

He grunted.

"And there was evidence someone else had been there recently. One table was all cleaned of dust, and there were food crumbs left upon it."

If she had expected this revelation to elicit some response from Burgess, she was disappointed. He showed no outward reaction to the news.

"Here we be," he said when they reached the landing. "Now what's it you wish me to look for?"

"Alford," Florrie said curtly. She brushed past Burgess and went to the first door.

All the chambers looked as they had in the morning—empty and full of dust. Florrie thought she must be searching for a mare's nest after all when they reached the last room—the one where Alford had given her such a scare this morning. Florrie reached out to push the partially ajar door open, but it only moved a few inches before it hit something.

"How strange!" she exclaimed.

Curiosity getting the better of her caution, she wriggled

through the narrow gap between door and frame. Lifting her candle, she looked down with growing horror at the inert body laying upon the floor.

"Alford!"

Chapter 15

Florrie knelt beside Alford's crumpled form as Burgess struggled through the doorway.

"What's he doing sleeping up here?"

"He is not sleeping," Florrie snapped. She gingerly touched her fingers to the dark patch on Alford's head and her fingers came away red. "It appears he has hit his head. Run and get Mrs. Burgess. We shall need a basin of water, and some cloths to bind the wound. And scissors."

She glared at the man, who stood staring at her. "Go! Now!"

Not until she heard Burgess's footsteps grow fainter did she realize that she was now alone on the upper floor. Florrie swallowed hard and lifted her candle to glance apprehensively around the room. All looked as it had before. At least she knew that no one could be hiding anywhere in the chamber, having tried to do so herself. She turned her attention back to Alford.

He lay on his side, facing away from the door. Had he tripped and hit his head? She saw nothing on the floor that could have impeded his path. And he was too far from the table to have fallen and hit his head against it. Although, perhaps he had managed to move a few inches before succumbing to unconsciousness.

How long had he lain here, alone, hurt? Fighting the urge to cradle his head in her lap, she reached out and gingerly traced her fingers down his cheek. He looked so dreadfully pale. But his breathing was even, and Florrie prayed he was not seriously injured.

The Burgesses returned in what seemed an age to Florrie. She grabbed the cloths from Mrs. Burgess and directed her to hold the candle.

Gingerly drawing back Alford's hair, Florrie closely inspected the cut on his head. It was not deep, and for that she was thankful.

"Scissors?" she asked Mrs. Burgess. With them, Florrie clipped the matted hairs from around the wound.

As Florrie tore one cloth into a long strip, Alford began to stir. Florrie leaned down to hear what he mumbled. She was nearly nose to nose with Alford when his eyes flicked open and stared dazedly into hers.

"An angel," he whispered, his eyes fluttering shut again.

"Alford, you clunch, it is I. Florence. Miss Washburn." She resisted the urge to shake him into consciousness again.

He groaned and opened one eye. "You're not an angel?" he asked hopefully.

Florrie smiled in relief, and shook her head.

"That must be why my head hurts like the devil," he moaned. "If I were dead, I would feel better."

He raised his hand to his head, but Florrie batted it away.

"Let me get this bandage on first," she said. She pressed a neatly folded wad of cloth on the wound, then bound it tightly by wrapping the long strips around Alford's head.

Alford gingerly sat up. He took a few deep breaths to steady himself, keeping his eyes tightly closed until his dizziness passed.

"What happened?" Florrie asked, when he opened his eyes again.

He made a wry smile. "I suspect your mysterious diner coshed me over the head," he said.

Florrie's eyes widened. "Did you see anyone?"

Alford fractionally shook his head. "Caught me completely by surprise, from the back."

"How terrible!" Florrie whirled on the Burgesses. "What do you know of this?" She watched Burgess glance uneasily at his wife.

"Nothing."

"You mean there are strangers roaming through the house and you do not even know?" Florrie shivered. "We could be murdered in our beds."

"Might be Silly Willy," Mrs. Burgess said quickly.

"Silly Willy?"

"Willy. He don't have any other name. He's harmless enough. Lives out in the open mostly, 'cept when the weather's bad. He comes by for food sometimes. But he never hurt nobody afor."

"Have you seen this Willy recently?" Florrie asked.

Both Burgesses shook their heads.

"I think, for everyone's safety, that all the doors in this house should be locked." Florrie looked pointedly at Mrs. Burgess. "I think Willy has been hiding up here, for the table is cleared off and someone has eaten here recently. If all the chambers are locked, he will not have a refuge. And the doors and windows leading into the house should be locked, as well. Of course, this will be after you have thoroughly searched every inch of this house for an intruder."

Mrs. Burgess looked at her husbasnd, who nodded his assent.

Florrie kneeled again by Alford. "Do you think you can walk to your chamber if Burgess helps you?"

"Maybe," he said. "Let me try getting to my feet first."

With Burgess assisting, Alford struggled to his feet. He immediately reached for the table to keep from toppling over. His head ached abominably, and his eyes were not focusing well. And his stomach felt as if—

"Give me the basin," he gasped, sinking to his knees. Florrie snatched up the basin and placed it before him just in time.

Alford almost wished that Silly Willy or whoever his attacker was *had* hit him a trifle harder. Death sounded like an infinitely more pleasing prospect than what he was feeling right now. A new spasm shook him and he retched again.

Someone wiped his face with a cool, damp cloth while he knelt trembling over the basin. He heard footsteps scurrying about, but he dared not open his eyes. It was much better in the dark. He took several large breaths, shuddering with the effort.

"As soon as you feel ready, we should get you to your room," Florrie said quietly. "You will be much more comfortable there."

Alford nodded. Slowly, carefully, he sat back on his haunches. Nausea rose within him again, but he fought it back successfully this time. Still keeping his eyes screwed shut, he hung his head down. Somehow, it made the painful thobbing in his head less intense.

After several minutes, he finally dared to open his eyes. This time, the room did not dance about before him, but stood still and steady. One small improvement.

He carefully turned his head to the side and saw Florrie sitting beside him on the floor, concern etched in her face.

"I think I may live," he said with a shaky laugh. "You will not be a widow after all."

"You wouldn't dare die," she said, a smile flitting across her face. "Else I could not marry Kit."

Forgetting his condition, he attempted to grin but it turned into a wince as a shooting pain stabbed through his head.

Florrie rose and dragged the chair from the table. "Perhaps it will be better if you sat before trying to stand," she suggested. "I imagine it would be best if we could carry you downstairs, but I fear that is a task beyond the three of us."

"Why don't you just bring me a blanket and pillow and I can sleep here?" he asked wearily.

"Someone will have to sit with you through the night," Florrie said, "and you cannot sentence them to such discomfort. You will have to walk to your room."

Alford rested one elbow on the chair seat while Burgess grasped the other. Alford rose to his knees, then to one foot. With a final burst of effort, he shifted his weight and slid onto the chair.

The wave of dizziness was smaller this time, and he only needed to keep his eyes shut for a short while. Finally, he nodded to Burgess. Best to get it over with quickly. Grasping Burgess's arm, Alford cautiously stood up.

Leaning heavily against Burgess, with Florrie grasping his other arm, Alford slowly shuffled across the floor to the door and into the corridor.

"It looks a deucedly long way to the stairs," he sighed.

Florrie squeezed his arm in encouragement. "Take your

time," she said. "We have naught else to do this evening."

He shot her what he hoped was a lowering look, then concentrated on putting one foot before the other. Only once, on the stairs, did he stumble, and both Burgess and Florrie were quick to catch him.

"We shall need your key," Florrie said when they at last neared his room.

"Waistcoat." He grimaced at the effort needed to keep upright. Only a few more steps . . . He breathed in sharply as he felt Florrie's fingers fumbling in his pockets.

"Were you afraid of the Lady, too?" she asked him archly as she put the key in the lock. "Was that why you went back upstairs?"

"All ladies terrify me," he replied with a wan smile. Burgess and Florrie led him across the chamber and he sank down gratefully upon the bed.

"Do you think you could eat something?" Florrie asked as Burgess drew off Alford's boots.

Alford made a face. "Not immediately, if you please. My stomach is still none too steady."

Florrie nodded in agreement. "Weak tea may be best, then. I will have Mrs. Burgess see to it. Burgess can assist you into bed."

"You do not wish to help?" Alford raised a lop-sided brow.

His impertinence elated Florrie. It meant he was feeling more himself. "I shall return when you are comfortably settled, Alford."

By the time Florrie reached the confines of her own room, she was as weak-kneed as Alford had been.

Something was terribly, terribly wrong in this house. No ghost had struck Alford on the head. There was a stranger here, a stranger who meant them harm. She shivered. Once Alford was settled, and Mrs. Burgess brought tea, Florrie fully intended to lock herself and Alford into their rooms and bar both doors with furniture. She did not wish to take any chances tonight, when Alford would be of little assistance if something happened.

She heard Mrs. Burgess arrive with the tea, so Florrie unlocked the door to the connecting dressing room and knocked on the door at Alford's side.

"Come in," he said.

He looked better already, Florrie thought, eyeing him critically. He sat propped up against the pillows, sipping the steaming tea. His face had regained some color, and except for the stark white bandage wrapped about his head, he did not look as if he had undergone such a terrible ordeal.

"Feeling better?"

Alford nodded.

"I will sit with you for a while," Florrie announced. She looked at the Burgesses. "I suppose it is too much to hope that there is a doctor closer than Bideford?"

"I do not need a doctor," Alford protested.

"Clovelly," Burgess replied.

"Perhaps in the morning we should send for him. Is there some nearby farm lad who could take a message?"

Mrs. Burgess nodded. "Jemmy Swittle will be here in the morning with the eggs. I can send the lad off."

"I do not need a doctor," Alford reiterated.

"Yes, you do," Florrie retorted. "Injuries to the head are very peculiar things." She turned back to Burgess. "Who is the magistrate for this district?"

"What you be needing the magistrate for?"

"Someone attacked Lord Alford in this house," Florrie said evenly. "Had we not found him, he might have died. That is attempted murder. The authorities must be notified."

Burgess opened his mouth to speak, but his wife jabbed him sharply with her elbow. "The lad can see to that as well."

"Thank you," said Florrie. "You may go now. I believe Lord Alford will be all right. Thank you for your assistance tonight."

Burgess led his wife out of the chamber, muttering to her in a low undertone.

Florrie pulled a chair over to the side of Alford's bed.

"You need not make yourself so comfortable," he

protested. "As you said, I am all right. I do not need a nurse-maid."

Florrie ignored his comments. "What do you think happened?"

"Someone hit me over the head."

"And unfortunately, it did little to improve your faculties. Do you believe that story about Silly Willy?"

"It makes as much sense as any. The Burgesses have probably been slipping him food, and he's retreated upstairs to eat it. When he found me in his lair, he panicked."

"Do you think it has been he wandering the halls at night?"

"You would prefer it to be a human, rather than a ghost? I do not think it likely. It is understandable he wished to protect his hideaway. But what aim would he have in trying to frighten us?"

"I don't know," Florrie admitted.

"How did you happen to find me?" he asked, keeping his voice deliberately casual.

"You were gone for so long, I grew concerned. I even made Burgess go out and look along the cliff path." Florrie reddened. "I knew when you missed dinner that something was terribly wrong."

"Today it was your turn to play knight in shining armor," he said with a smile. "I . . . I am grateful, Miss Washburn."

"Call me Florrie," she said impulsively.

"You will not think me too forward?" he asked with a trace of a grin.

"As my future brother-in-law, I think I can allow such a lapse in formality."

His grin faded. "Is that what Kit calls you?"

"All my close friends do," she said quickly.

"Then I am honored, Florrie, that you count me among their number."

Both fell silent for a moment. Florrie did not wish to leave him alone—she knew that it was important to keep a close eye upon one suffering from a head wound—yet she knew Alford would not wish to be babied.

"Should you like me to read?" she asked, brightening.

"I am not certain I am up for the high drama of *Otranto*," he said.

She took a deep breath. "I could read from *Improved Field Cultivation.*"

He looked startled, then eyed her suspiciously. "What makes you think I should be interested in such a thing?"

She gestured to the table, where the book and the spectacles lay. "I was in here earlier," she confessed. "When I was searching for you. I thought that perhaps you had decided to go with Old Mort after all, and I was—"

"Snooping?"

"I merely wanted to see if you had left without telling me," she protested.

"Do you make it a habit of invading other people's rooms?" he asked coldly.

"You are known to have done so," she retorted.

He leaned his head back against the pillow and shut his eyes. "You are right, of course."

"Alford?"

"Yes?"

"Do you need your spectacles to read? Is that why you never read downstairs in the library?"

"Yes, Florrie, I need my spectacles to read."

"Then whyever do you not use them?" she asked, then realized the obvious answer. "You are embarrassed!"

His eyes flicked open. "I am never embarrassed," he said coldly.

"Yes, you are," she said, her voice triumphant. "You certainly did not want me to know about them, else you would have worn them long ago."

"I assure you, I am no more embarrassed about wearing spectacles than you are about wearing half-boots. There has not been any occasion to wear them since your arrival."

A monstrous thought dawned in Florrie's mind. "Is that why you missigned the marriage papers?" she asked suspiciously. "Because you were too vain to be seen with your glasses on?"

"I am not vain," Alford snapped.

"It is true!" she chortled with glee. "I can not believe you are such a clunch, Alford. You created this whole, horrible mess because you were too full of vanity to put on your spectacles and read what you were signing."

Alford sat up. "I think, *Miss Washburn,* that you have worn out your welcome. Feel free to leave at any time."

"Oh, I would not think of leaving an invalid alone. Tell me, what other dreadful mistakes have you made while refusing to wear your spectacles?"

Alford flung the covers back. "Leave. Now. Or I will personally escort you to the door."

Florrie stood up. She was not going to let him think he intimidated her.

"I will lock your door for the night," she said calmly. "In case your friend Silly Willy is lurking about in the halls tonight." She did as she said, then walked over and plopped the key into Alford's lap. "Sweet dreams." Back rigid, she walked to the connecting door and pulled it shut behind her.

Alford set the key on the bedside table and pulled the covers back up to his chin. It was cold. He lay his head back on the pillow and closed his eyes.

Damn that nosy girl. He could not deny her charge—of course he did not want to be seen wearing his spectacles. He'd be laughed out of every club in London. Why did she, of all people, have to discover his secret? She was liable to tell everyone she knew, particularly in light of the disaster with the marriage papers.

He felt as if he had been stripped bare in front of her, and he did not much like the sensation. First, she had been witness to that impressive performance over the wash-basin upstairs. Then he'd had to rely on her and Burgess to get back to his room, as though he were an invalid. He was only lucky she had not insisted on undressing him for bed! Thank God she had enough sensibility to spare him that indignity.

Yet Florrie's actions tonight surprised him. Despite her protestations, he had thought her an eminently silly widgeon. But in a crisis, she had ably taken charge. There was no sign of the trembling, terrified woman he held in his arms on the sea-cliff path, or frightened out of bed the previous evening. A rather complex bundle of contradictions, he thought, beginning to feel drowsy in spite of the throbbing pain in his head. Florrie was full of surprises. What else had he to learn about her?

Chapter 16

Florrie dressed for bed, but she was determined to stay awake through the night. Someone had to watch Alford until the doctor came on the morrow and declared him fit.

Florrie was not exactly certain why she needed to watch Alford; she only remembered that it was recommended practice for one with a head wound. But was she only to watch? Or was she to examine the patient for signs of—what? She desperately wished they were closer to town, and the doctor could be summoned at once. If Alford's condition worsened because of the delay . . .

He would resent her presence, she was certain. Alford was the type of man who hated to show any sign of weakness. And tonight he had demonstrated several. She had no doubt he would find some way to place the blame on her. It was her exploration that lured him upstairs, her discovery of the occupied room that led to his own investigation. And her visit to his room had revealed the truth about his eyesight.

Men were so vain. They constantly derided women for their interest in fashion and ornament, when they were all peacocks themselves. Why else would so many men stuff themselves into creaking corsets, use false calves under their stockings, and display the most colorful and elaborate waistcoats? Alford's refusal to be seen wearing his spectacles was a perfect example. Better to stumble around blindly than appear less than perfect. Men were such fools!

Florrie carefully traversed the empty dressing room and put her ear to Alford's door. Was he asleep yet? Or would he be able to sleep? His head must hurt dreadfully. But she did not hear any sounds that would indicate he was thrashing about in his bed. He was not moaning in pain. Perhaps all was well. She placed her hand on the latch and carefully opened the door.

The candle still burned on the dresser. Tip-toeing quietly, she crossed to the bed and peered down at Alford. He was sleeping like a babe, thank goodness. She reached out and briefly touched her hand to his forehead. He was cool; no signs of fever.

Florrie desperately wished she could remember what one was supposed to do for patients with head wounds. The memories hung tantalizingly on the edge of her mind. There had been a member of the embassy staff in St. Petersburg who had slipped on an icy step and taken a severe blow to the head. She remembered discussing the injury with the other ladies, but not what the doctors did about it. She bit her lip in frustration. If anything horrible happened to Alford, she would not forgive herself.

She was momentarily stung by the thought that she cared for Alford. Then reason regained the upper hand. Of course she cared what happened to him—he was family, after all. It had nothing to do with any personal feelings for Alford— which were quite sisterly, she hastened to reassure herself.

It was her fault, after all, that he had been hurt. If she hadn't been snooping around like a silly goose, looking for a ghost, she never would have found that room upstairs. And Alford would never have set off to search it himself. He could have spent his afternoon in the library, his spectacles perched upon his nose, reading away about modern agricultural techniques.

She sighed. There was little she could do about it now. For penance, she would keep herself awake all night, to watch over him. He would not need to know she was here. She wrapped her robe closer and curled up in the chair.

Alford awoke with an excruciating headache, which confused him for a moment. Too much brandy again? He didn't remember a lengthy conversation with the brandy decanter last night. And this pain felt different, more one-sided, more . . .

A confusion of images flooded his brain. His stealthy investigation upstairs, the sudden attack, the descending blackness. He remembered Florrie, and the Burgesses and . . .

Reluctantly, Alford opened his eyes, adjusting them to the dim morning light that crept around the curtains. He gingerly felt the bandage wrapped about his head, wincing when his fingers reached the padding over the wound. It had been no dream then, and this headache was not the product of over-consumption. Someone had deliberately hurt him.

It was a disturbing thought. He did not particularly want to have to walk around always keeping an eye on his back. The mystery would have to be solved quickly, before something worse occurred.

He recalled the Burgesses' talk of some local vagrant. Alford could not quite believe a total stranger had taken up residence inside the hall. Granted, the house was a rabbit warren, with its odd-sized rooms and ancient architecture, and it was certainly old enough to have something along the lines of a priest's hole or similar device that may have been used during Cromwellian times. But why would such a man wish to damage his position by hurting a benefactor? It did not make sense.

Of course, there was always the possibility that the Burgesses had more to do with this than they claimed. Alford thought he remembered seeing a wary glance pass between them. He had sensed last night that they were hiding something. A son on the run from the law or the military? A man like that might be desperate enough to kill whoever came into his path. If that were the case, Alford would have to be very, very careful.

Which meant what he needed was a weapon. He cursed himself for not having brought his pistols, but he had never considered that he would actually need them for protection in a house owned by his own family. And he could only imagine the age of whatever weapons were on hand in this house. Yet anything was better than his bare hands.

The first thing he wished to do was get Florrie out of the

house. A sharp pain stabbed at him at the mere thought of her being in any real danger. Neither his father nor hers would forgive him if anything happened to her. Nor would Kit. He had caused his brother enough grief with the botched proxy. How would he ever explain any injury to Florrie? He would send her back to Bideford with the doctor.

Might it be better if he left today with Florrie as well—and brought back the sheriff or magistrate to investigate? If the Burgesses were involved in some manner, Alford did not like the idea of being at their mercy. It would be far too easy to arrange some sort of accident for him. They could put some drug in the food, haul him out to the cliff and toss him over, with no one the wiser. Florrie would testify to his fascination with the cliff walk. It would all look like a tragic accident. Alford shuddered at the thought.

Except for one thing. If the Burgesses had wanted to be rid of either him or Florrie, they could have done it ages ago. Why now? Because he and Florrie had discovered someone was using the room upstairs?

It did not make sense. The use of the room meant nothing. He would have been perfectly willing to accept his own suggestion that Burgess hid out there from his wife. But after being knocked over the head, Alford's suspicions were now aroused. It was obvious he and Florrie had seen something they were not meant to. But what?

The effort of concentrating only made his headache worse. Alford closed his eyes and tried to let his mind drift. Perhaps he could discuss matters with the doctor when he arrived.

He felt dreadfully thirsty and looked with longing at the pitcher of water at the bedside. He had vague recollections that he had been of little use last night, knew that it had taken Burgess and Florrie to get him back to his room. Could he handle something as simple as sitting up?

Gritting his teeth, Alford slowly raised his head from the pillow. The pain did not become any worse, he noted with relief. Moving cautiously, he managed to sit up without mishap. Encouraged by his success, he swung his legs around until he sat on the edge of the bed. From this position he could not quite reach the water pitcher and glass. With trembling resolve, using the edge of the bedside table to steady himself, Alford stood up.

And did not fall. Or even waver. He smiled at his success. If it weren't for the blasted headache . . . He poured himself a tall glass of water and drained it thirstily.

Alford turned his head to one side and his eyes widened in surprise as he saw a familiar form huddled and asleep in the chair across the room. Had she been here all night?

Sitting back on the edge of the bed again, Alford contemplated the sleeping girl. Florrie, he corrected himself. He remembered she had given him leave to call her that. But as he remembered more of what had transpired last night, a frown formed on his face. She had twitted him about his need for spectacles, and his vanity in refusing to wear them. She had not been gracious about it. In fact, she had been downright rude.

Should he wake her or let her continue to sleep in that contorted pose? She would probably awake with an unpleasant crick in her neck. He smiled at the thought. T'would serve her right for her verbal attack of last night. But as he watched her, seeing the steady rise and fall of her chest as she slumbered on, he took pity upon her.

He again rose to his feet, feeling much steadier this time, and slowly crossed the room.

"Florrie," he said, gently shaking her shoulder. "Time to wake up."

"Come back later," she mumbled and curled up into an even tighter ball.

Alford shook her harder this time. "Florrie. Wake up."

Her eyes fluttered open, then grew wider as she took in the sight of him. She sat up straighter, glancing about her as if uncertain where she was.

"I fear you fell asleep in the chair," Alford explained.

"What are you doing out of bed?" she demanded, fully awake now.

"Except for a raging headache, I feel perfectly fine," Alford said. He spun around. "See? Steady as a rock."

"I insist you remain in bed until the doctor arrives," said Florrie, scrambling to her feet. "Head wounds are very serious things, Alford. They are not to be trifled with.''

"I do not need a doctor.''

"Yes, you do,'' she insisted. "I am sure Burgess has already sent for the man and he will likely be here before noon. Climb back into bed like a good boy and wait to hear what he has to say.''

"I won't,'' said Alford, more out of a desire to irritate Florrie than out of any strong conviction. He was not going to let this chit manage him any more than she already had. Last night, he needed her help. Today he did not.

Florrie put her hands on her hips and glared at Alford. "If you do not get back into that bed right now, I will march into my room and send letters off to everyone I know in London, telling them that you wear spectacles.''

"That is blackmail,'' he protested.

"The doctor will be able to take the letters to the post,'' she said.

Alford scowled. He did not think she would really carry out her threat, but he did not want to call her bluff just yet. Then a wide grin of triumph spread over his face.

"I fear that under the circumstances, I would then be forced to write some letters of my own,'' he said. "Telling how a certain Florence Washburn spent the night in my room.''

Florrie gasped aloud. "You would not dare!''

"I think we are both at point-non-plus,'' he said. "If you desist from brow-beating me, I will not say a word about where I found you this morning.''

"You do not play fair, Alford,'' she charged.

He laughed. "A case of the pot calling the kettle black, I fear. Truce?''

"You really should rest,'' she said, deliberately ignoring the offer. "It would be the best thing for you.''

"Only on the condition that you do the same,'' he countered. "I am certain you did not sleep well in that chair. Did you spend the entire night there?''

"No,'' she said. For she did not want him to know just how concerned she had been. Florrie was angry with herself for having fallen asleep; much goold she would have been to Alford if the need had arisen.

"Then," he said, taking her by the shoulders and steering her toward the connecting door, "you go back to your own room and try to get some sleep. I promise I will hop back into bed the moment you are gone."

"All right," she agreed reluctantly.

The doctor, when he arrived, made Alford think twice about divulging confidences. He barely looked capable of practicing medicine. One button hung by a string from the man's waistcoat, while another had totally disappeared. His linen was none too clean, and there were suspicious stains on his breeches.

"So, bumped our head on something did we?" An overpowering odor of garlic emanated from the doctor as he began to unwrap the bandages around Alford's head.

"Something like that," Alford replied.

"And probably hurts like the devil today."

Alford nodded, then winced as the doctor pulled the bandage away from the wound.

"Well?" Alford asked when the doctor said nothing.

"Looks fine to me," the doctor replied. "Not worth stitching. A little sticking plaster ought to do the trick. Any dizziness today? Blurred vision? Vomiting?"

"I was sicker than a dog yesterday, but I feel fine today," Alford replied.

"No signs of fever?"

"None."

"Stand up," the doctor commanded. "Now, walk across the room. Turn around, and walk back toward me. Slowly."

Alford did as the doctor commanded.

"Now," the doctor continued. "Close your eyes and stand on one leg."

Feeling exceedingly foolish, Alford did as he was directed.

"What's your mother's maiden name?"

"Brooke."

"What year did Nelson die?"

"1805."

"How old are you? What year were you born?"

"Twenty-seven. 1784."

"Brains don't seem addled to me," the doctor said, reaching into his bag. "I'll leave some powders for the headache. If it isn't better within the week, send for me again."

He put the powders on the dresser. "Mix one of these in a glass of water. No more than three a day." He turned and looked at Alford. "Don't suppose you want to settle your bill today?"

"Talk to Burgess," Alford said. "He can take it out of the household account."

"Good man, Burgess. He keeps a good eye on things here."

Alford was tempted to add "not good enough," but he did not. Until he was certain about the Burgesses's involvement—or lack thereof—he did not wish to raise any suspicions.

"Remember, send for me if there are any changes. You've got a hard head there." The doctor waved vaguely as he left the room.

Had Alford been better convinced of the doctor's competence, he would have been well-pleased with his pronouncement of good health. But at least he had something for the headache. Alford grabbed a packet off the dresser, catching a glimpse of himself in the mirror. He drew back with a start. What in God's name had been done to him?

The blob of sticking plaster looked more amusing than frightening. But his hair! It looked as if it had been lopped off with a mowing scythe.

Florrie! He remembered the cool touch of her hands as she had bandaged his head. She had done this to him—on purpose, no doubt. He stormed through the connecting door.

"What did you mean by butchering my hair in such a man—Good God!"

Florrie was clad only in a thin lawn chemise—much sheerer than her night wear—and in the few seconds before

she reacted to the intrusion, Alford had the opportunity to
see a great deal more than she would have wished. An
appreciative smile lit his face.

"Get out of here!" she screeched, diving for the bed and
her robe.

Alford could not tear his eyes away. Every curvaceous line
of her body showed under the diaphanous fabric and he felt
an unexpected heat rise within him. He watched in stunned
dismay as she threw on her robe and hastily pulled it closed.

"How dare you burst in here unannounced," she yelled.
"You have no right. Get out! Now!"

"I had not intended . . ." he stammered. His fingers ached
to reach out and wrap themselves in the honey-gold hair that
spilled over her shoulders. He wanted to pull the robe from
her shoulders so he could feast his eyes again on what lay
beneath.

"I do not care what you intended, Alford." Florrie glared
at him. "Please get out of my room."

He suddenly recalled his purpose. He gestured to his head.
"I suppose you did this as a joke," he said.

"Did what?"

"Hacked off my hair with whatever blunt instrument you
managed to put your hands on," he snapped.

"It was Mrs. Burgess's shears and, no, I did not do it as
a joke. I did it so I could bandage your head properly."

"I look like some freak at the country fair."

"No, you don't. What you do look like is an arrogant
aristocrat who does not have any sense of propriety or
gratitude."

"I am supposed to be grateful because I will be forced
to shave my head in order to have some semblance of
symmetry there?"

"Stop being such a dandy, Alford. No one is going to see
you out here except me. And I could not possibly think worse
of you than I already do."

Alford continued to glare at her, but without any real
vehemence. She was right, of course. It was ridiculous of
him to complain about such a paltry matter. He was suddenly

aware that she had twisted him around in circles. She had an uncanny knack for doing that.

"I am sorry," he said stiffly. "I know you were trying to help. I am rather grumpy today because my head hurts."

"As it well should," she said, the anger leaving her voice. "That was a nasty cut and a heavy blow to have knocked you unconscious, Alford. Do not treat it lightly."

"The doctor pronounced me healthy enough."

"The doctor was here? Whyever did you not tell me?"

"I did not think he needed to see you." Alford grinned. "I am the one with the injury."

"I wanted to speak to him about your care," Florrie said. "I am certain he would wish you in bed right now."

"He said nothing of the sort," Alford said. "Gave me powders for the ache and said I was fine."

Florrie sniffed. "I would not place too much trust in the pronouncements of a country doctor."

"Quite true," Alford said. "While you, on the other hand, are more than qualified to pass judgment on all manner of medical conditions."

"I never said that," Florrie retorted.

"Then stop ordering me about. I am not a child. I am perfectly capable of taking care of myself."

Florrie frowned but held her tongue.

"I am being a rotten patient, aren't I?" He smiled wryly.

"Yes, you are," she said, with an answering smile. "But I find men usually are. Papa is a veritable dragon when he becomes ill. It is just a weakness in the male character, I think."

"Florrie . . ." Alford's voice held a hint of warning.

"Back to bed," she said, waving her hands at him. "Shoo. Scat."

He retreated before her onslaught, backing through the doorway while he tried to keep from laughing. Florrie grabbed the door and prepared to close it behind him.

"Florrie," he said, before he ducked into his own room.

"What?"

"I envy Kit," he said, recalling what he had seen earlier. "He will have a lovely wife."

Florrie slammed the door shut with a resounding thud.

Chapter 17

Florrie assumed Alford would remain in bed for the remainder of the day, and was therefore surprised when he entered the library shortly before dinner.

"Should you be up?" she asked.

"I feel quite fit, *Doctor* Washburn. And famished."

Florrie's cheeks reddened. Let him ignore her advice. She would wash her hands of the matter.

Alford settled himself into the other chair before the fire while Florrie poured him a cup of tea. "I suppose it is too much to hope that Burgess found some sign of the intruder?"

"I did not ask him," Florrie said, handing him his tea. "But certainly, whoever it was must surely be gone by now."

Alford shrugged. "One would hope so."

"You are feeling better?" Florrie asked with an uneasy look.

"My head still hurts. But not as badly as before."

"I do wish you had called me when the doctor arrived." She studied him carefully. "You are certain he said you were fine?"

"There is probably little he could have done if I wasn't," Alford observed. He smiled. "Relax, Florrie. I promise not to die until the annulment is obtained."

She gave him an exasperated stare. "Really, Alford. My major concern is for you."

He patted the ragged ends of his hair. "That *must* have been the reason for your excellent job of barbering."

Florrie grinned. He must be feeling better if he was still harping about the way she had trimmed his hair. "It gives you a more countrified look, Alford. Somewhat bucolic, in fact."

"Exactly what I was looking for," he said glumly.

"Alford?"

"What?"

"Do you think there is any connection between this attack on you and the person who tried to get in my room?"

A sudden coughing fit overtook Alford.

"Do not drink your tea so fast," Florrie admonished him. She looked at him expectantly. "Well? Do you?"

Alford carefully schooled his features into an expression of innocence. "I had not thought about it," he said, quite truthfully. "But none of the stories I have heard about the Lady indicated she brought harm to anyone. And it was no ghost that banged me over the head."

"We still do not know if what I saw was a ghost," Florrie said, then laughed at the thought. "Alford, the idea is absurd. This is the nineteenth century. We are long past the age of primitive superstition."

A mischievous gleam crept into his eye. "You firmly disbelieve in the idea of ghosts, then?" He could not resist the impulse to twit her. "You certainly gave some very convincing demonstrations that you thought otherwise."

Florrie glared at him indignantly. "One is scarcely a rational creature when one's sleep is disrupted in the most alarming manner," she protested. "Now that we know there is—or was—some stranger in the house, it makes much more sense that he was the cause of it all."

"That does not explain the woman you saw on the lawn. Or the one you said you saw in the hall."

"I do not know what I saw," Florrie admitted. "The first could easily have been the sea-mist. The second might have been a trick of my imagination, or the shadows."

Alford sat back in his chair, as if considering the matter. He felt rather foolish about his attempts to frighten Florrie, now that real danger lurked within the house. He only wished he had succeeded in driving her away for her own safety.

"You are probably right," he said, and laughed. "It is absurd to think we even considered the idea of a ghost. We can only blame the influence of that dreadful novel."

Florrie's eyes narrowed. "You were the one who first mentioned this wandering lady."

"I was only repeating the tale I had heard," Alford said. "I never once, if you will recall, made any claim to the truth of the story."

"Oh, it does not matter." Florrie shook her head. "Now that you have been injured, we have a much more exciting mystery to solve."

He shrugged with calculated indifference. He did not want Florrie aware of his concerns. She would probably insist upon launching a new exploration of the house. He must keep her out of harm's way. "I think there is little mystery. Silly Willy is probably the culprit and I doubt he will make another appearance for a while."

"But what if the tale is truly exciting?" Florrie asked, her eyes aglow with excitement. "What if it is an escaped French prisoner, making his way to the coast where he will be picked up by a French vessel?"

"I highly doubt it," Alford said dryly.

Florrie pouted. "Dartmoor is not so dreadfully far from here."

"Any Frenchman in his right mind would go south, rather than north," Alford pointed out. "We are in the opposite direction from France, Florrie."

"But that is precisely why he would come north," Florrie said with mounting excitement. "No one would think to look for him here. Why, this could be the major escape route for every prisoner in England."

"And exactly how many French prisoners have escaped in the last year?" Alford asked.

Florrie's face fell. "I do not know."

"I am certain the number is tiny," Alford said. "Else a hue and cry would have been raised."

"What makes you think you would have noticed?" she asked sarcastically. "I doubt it was included in the racing news."

"I read the papers, Florrie," he said with exasperation. "The *Times*, the *Post* and the *Chronicle*. So I can vouch for the matter."

"Whyever do you read all three?"

"Each paper takes a slightly different view of the political situation. The truth is usually somewhere in between."

"You read the parliamentary news?" Florrie stared at him in amazement.

"Yes, I read the parliamentary news," Alford said crossly. "Little use that it is."

"You are interested in politics?" Florrie asked in surprise. He gave her a suspicious look, then relaxed. "Yes, I am."

"Tory or Whig?"

He smiled. "Whig, of course. My father's a Tory."

"Alford, I can truly say that you have amazed me," Florrie said.

"But not to the point of speechlessness," he teased.

"That," she announced archly, "takes a great deal. If you are so interested in politics, why are you not more involved?"

"How can I be?" he asked bitterly. "I cannot take a seat in the Lords until I inherit the title."

"There is always the Commons."

"Do you have any idea of the cost of an election campaign?" he asked. "Not to mention the difficulty of finding an available seat. Without help, it is impossible."

"Have you asked your father?"

"Many times. He refuses."

"There might be others who would be willing to promote your candidacy," Florrie suggested. Her brain whirled with these new revelations. Alford had built up a completely false facade—for what reason? Why would a man who was possessed of a great deal of intelligence, an interest in politics and agricultural matters, hide behind the image of an indolent rakehell?

Alford sighed. "There are few who would support a Whig candidate," he said sadly. "Far too many seats are held by landowners who want no part of change. It is precisely why the election system needs to be reformed—but it cannot be done from the outside. And there are many who are determined to keep the reformers out."

"But with the Prince now Regent, will that not help your cause?"

Alford's face grew bitter. "The Tories are as deeply entrenched as ever. The Regent turned his back on the Whig cause the moment the Regency was proclaimed."

"It must be dreadfully frustrating for you," Florrie said in sympathy, suddenly realizing just how much impact that frustration had on his life. It explained so much about him— his determined pursuit of excess was an escape, not a vocation.

"It is," he acknowledged, with the sudden realization that he had never discussed this with anyone—outside of the ongoing arguments with his father. Why was he baring his soul to Florrie, of all people? He regretted his candor. It would matter little to her. "But certainly no more frustrating than waiting for dinner to arrive. Are you sure Mrs. Burgess is cooking tonight?"

Florrie was taken aback by the abrupt switch in the conversation, but shrewdly guessed that Alford had regretted his uncharacteristic loquaciousness. She smiled sweetly. "Have another cup of tea. I am sure dinner will be here momentarily."

The prompt arrival of dinner stilled Alford's tongue, and Florrie was unable to get more than the most innocuous remarks from him for the remainder of the evening. It was not long before he pleaded tiredness, and a headache, and her offer to read more about the mysterious castle of Otranto did not elicit a favorable response.

Although Florrie insisted she was far too awake to take to her own bed, Alford insisted she could not remain in the library alone. Florrie had to agree the prospect did not much appeal to her. Not that she feared any attack. It was, actually, that without Alford it would be deucedly boring to remain downstairs. Alford escorted her upstairs, and Florrie smiled at his insistence upon locking her door himself.

She had not realized until the past two days just how much she enjoyed his company. His wit could be acidic at times, but never dull. Life was decidedly flat without the opportunity to trade barbs with him. And she was eager to pry more secrets from him.

Alford's professed interest in politics had come as a great

surprise. So few members of the Lords actually enjoyed the work. It was a pity someone like Alford, who welcomed the challenge, could not be allowed to take his seat now, supplanting his father, who sounded as if he had far too many old and fusty ideas.

Florrie began to wonder, for the first time, whether Alford and Kit were really so dissimilar. She had always assumed so. But as she thought about it, she realized that impression had been fostered more by the earl, and his tales of Alford's behavior, than any observations on her part. She and Kit had never really talked about his brother. Was Kit as unaware of Alford's interests as his father?

It was a sudden shock to realize she had sadly misjudged Alford. She had relied entirely on hearsay for her opinions. Granted, Alford had done little to dispel the image, but since it was an image he had carefully cultivated, that could be expected. Florrie was chagrined to find she had not the perception to see beyond that image to the real man underneath. It bespoke a sad want of understanding on her part.

For the first time she considered the plight of an elder son. They rarely entered the army, for the succession must not be endangered. They did not work with the foreign office, for what was the point of training them for a diplomatic career they would abandon when they took on the title? Politics was closed, for it was highly unusual for a future lord to take a seat in the Commons. They really were not allowed any useful pursuits. All they could do was wait and watch.

Certainly, that was the case with Alford. He could only sit back and watch other men—men like Kit—pursue their own dreams and ambitions, while his remained stillborn. Yet, she argued with herself, Alford could have rebelled against his father, if he had wanted something badly enough. It was a pity he had not set his heart on the military, for he could have snapped his fingers at the earl and purchased a commission. But the political arena was a different animal. One did not enter it without backing, and a man at odds with his father would have a difficult time. A pity Alford had not cultivated Tory leanings. . . .

Florrie realized she had been thinking on Alford's situation for far too long. When all was said and done, it was of little concern to her. After all, once this farcical marriage was annulled, they would have little contact. Alford's future did not affect her.

She was still not of a mind to retire, so she walked to the window. Below, the lawn looked to be almost in daylight from the light of the full moon. But the wall along the cliff loomed like a dark, shadowy form, and beyond it lay the blackness of the sea.

Suddenly a light punctuated that inky blackness. It winked out as quickly as it had appeared, and for a moment Florrie thought she had imagined it. But as she peered harder, it appeared again, for only a moment.

It must be a boat rounding the point nad and heading up the channel, she thought. A common enough occurrence. She was almost ready to draw the curtains and prepare for bed when she saw another light flare briefly. This one looked as if it was on top of the cliff wall.

Florrie stared intently at the spot where the light had first appeared, but it did not reappear. Had it only been some trick of the moonlight? Was there something atop the cliff wall that would reflect light? What reason would anyone have for shining a light on the cliff wall?

Then she remembered her conversation with Alford before dinner, and her theory that his mysterious attacker had been an escaped French prisoner. He could be out there now, signaling his compatriots in the boat—which would account for the light she had seen on the sea! Florrie tensed with excitement. There *was* something going on here at Hartland.

Florrie hastily pulled the heavy draperies closed to block out the light from her window, then crawled under them so she could watch the drama being played out below. She frowned when there was no further sign of any lights, either on the sea or the wall. Disappointment grew within her. Was nothing else going to happen?

Then, as she watched with growing horror, a thin, white-robed figure drifted across the lawn.

The Lady!

In sick fascination, Florrie watched the mysterious figure

progress as it drew closer and closer to the wall. She was heading directly for the spot where Florrie had seen the light! Then, in the blink of an eye, she simply vanished.

"Oh!" Florrie exclaimed in both frustration and fear. The figure had disappeared into thin air. It was not possible.

Florrie's eyes remained glued to the scene outside for many long minutes, but there was no further sign of any activity on land or sea. Puzzled, she at last climbed from beneath the curtain and sat down before the dressing table.

It was all so confusing. Escaped prisoners were flesh and blood and very real. But the white-robed figure? Ghosts could not possibly exist. There had to be some other explanation. But the more Florrie thought on it, the more logical became a ghostly solution. Each time Florrie had seen the Lady, she had vanished as quickly as she had come, in a very unhuman manner. Yet someone had attempted to enter Florrie's room two times. Someone had taken a meal in the room upstairs. And someone had hit Alford over the head in that same room. How did it all fit together? Or did it?

She shivered. There was something very strange and mysterious going on in this house, and she was not certain she really wanted to know what it was. Perhaps it was a good idea to leave, after all. There might be danger here for everyone.

But she did not like the idea of leaving before the mystery was laid to rest. And despite Alford's current amiability, she did not want him to think she had been driven away by fear, of all things. She would remain as long as he did. Perhaps they could solve the mystery in the meantime.

Chapter 18

In the morning, Florrie hesitated upon telling Alford what she had seen the previous evening, fearing he would belittle her experience. Why was it that she was the only one to see these baffling occurrences? Alford would be less sanguine if the mysterious lady in white were traipsing through *his* bedchamber. But at last Florrie decided to speak with him. Perhaps he could come up with a logical explanation.

"I saw a rather strange sight from my window last night," she said casually while she buttered her breakfast toast.

"Oh?" Alford raised a curious brow.

"I saw lights. Both on the water and on the cliff wall."

"Lights?" Alford regarded her quizzically.

"Like a lantern, or some such thing. I know you thought it silly yesterday, but do you think there is some truth to my theory that your attacker was an escaped Frenchman? He could have been signaling his countrymen to pick him up."

Alford kept his face carefully neutral, but inside he fought down his excitement. Florrie may just have stumbled across something very close to the truth.

"Did you see anything more than the lights?" he asked casually.

Florrie studied the table cover. "I thought I saw a white figure again," she said at last.

"The Lady?"

"I don't know. I saw someone—or thing—dressed in white, crossing the lawn. When it reached the wall, it disappeared."

"Interesting." A hint of a grin touched his face.

"Alford, what is going on? Do you think there are French prisoners escaping?" Florrie paused. "Or are we really being haunted by the ghost of a woman who's been dead for ages?"

He smiled. "I am sure there is some rational explanation."

Florrie eyed him with skepticism.

"Would you feel better if we went outside and looked around?" Alford asked genially. "Perhaps your French spies will have dropped a tricolor in their haste."

Florrie wished they had. It would explain much. "I would love to go outside," she said with feigned sweetness. She would dearly love to prove to Alford that what she had seen last night was not all in her imagination.

Once free of the house, Florrie tried to hasten Alford across the lawn, but he would have none of it.

"I sustained a serious injury two days ago," he protested mockingly. "I am nearly an invalid. Have some consideration."

"If you were wounded so severely, you should be in bed," Florrie countered. "Besides, I saw how much you ate for breakfast. No invalid would dare put away that much food. It won't wash, Alford."

He put up his hands defensively. "Caught out again," he said, laughing. "I should have known I could not pull the wool over your eyes, Florrie."

Florrie colored slightly at hearing her name from him, still unaccustomed to his use of it. Yet she felt strangely elated by it as well. Somehow, it sounded oddly different on his lips, formed in his lazy drawl. More personal. More intimate.

She hastily turned away.

Alford saw the momentary confusion in her face, and it engendered the same emotion in him as well. Confusion over exactly what he felt for this snippy, outspoken miss who was never loath to point out his numerous faults—yet he could recall the tender touch of her hands as she carefully ministered to him after his injury, and her concern as she had watched over him during the night. He wanted to see more of that gentle, caring side of her, the side she would show to her friends—or those she held in affection.

"I think this is where I saw the light," Florrie called.

Alford looked up, startled. While he stood lost in thought, Florrie had reached the garden wall. He hastened to her side.

"You said the light was on top?" he asked as he casually surveyed the ground for any suspicious signs.

"It would have to be, wouldn't it, in order to be seen from the sea?" Florrie answered sarcastically.

"If they were signaling to the sea."

"I told you there was a boat on the water. It had a light as well."

Alford looked at the wall, and then examined the ground at his feet more carefully.

"Well," he said at last, "if there was a light atop the wall, there is little we can do to check. Unless you have a ladder handy."

Florrie peered intently at the irregular stone surface. "I think I can get a toe-hold here if you can lift me up," she said.

"I don't think that at all wise," Alford said. "Perhaps Burgess has a ladder."

"It will only take a moment this way," Florrie pleaded.

"All right," said Alford reluctantly. He had seen all he needed to, and doubted Florrie would discover any new evidence on top of the wall. But if she was so determined . . . He locked his fingers together and held them out for her foot.

Florrie stepped into his outstretched hands. Placing one hand on his shoulder, to steady herself, she grabbed for a handhold on the irregular wall surface as Alford boosted her up. She was able to get one booted toe into a crevice, but her position was precarious.

"See anything?" Alford asked.

"I need to go higher," Florrie replied. "Can you boost me up more?"

Alford obligingly lifted her higher. Florrie found another toe-hold and pulled herself up until she could peer over the top of the wall. To her disappointment, she saw nothing out of the ordinary. No candle stubs, or spills, or any sign that anything had been atop the wall. She glanced out to the sea, knowing no boat would be there, but feeling compelled to look anyway.

"I hate to be rude, but this is becoming a trifle difficult," Alford warned.

Florrie glanced over her shoulder at Alford, who did indeed look awkward holding up her foot at near shoulder level.

"Oh," she said, startled, and immediately moved to step down. She stuck the tip of her boot in what seemed to be a safe recess in the rock wall, but the instant she put her weight on it, the stone crumbled. Her fingers slipped from their tenuous grip and she fell backward . . . into Alford's arms.

"Oof!" he cried as they tumbled to the ground.

"Oh, Alford, your head!" Florrie twisted in his grasp until she faced him. "Are you all right?"

His eyes fluttered open. "An angel," he murmured.

"Alford!" Florrie did not know whether to be relieved or angry at his teasing.

He opened one eye. "Most women I know would find it a compliment to be compared to an angel," he complained.

Florrie grinned, then her face grew serious. "Are you really all right? I didn't mean to fall on you. You did not hit your head again, did you?"

"How could I possibly complain about a minor tumble that ended with you laying on top of me, clasped in my arms?" He grinned wickedly, tightening his grip about her waist. "I would say it was a fortuitous event."

She should be struggling to free herself, but Florrie suddenly wondered what Alford would do next. He had leered, intimidated, and threatened her with his attentions ever since she arrived. But he had never actually attempted anything. Would he now? Florrie raised up on her forearms and looked down into his face.

"You would?" she inquired, trying to read the thoughts in his clear blue eyes.

It would be so easy, Alford thought, to bridge those few inches that separated them. To place his lips on her own full, slightly pouting ones. To see if she had passions equal to the ones of anger and fear he had already seen. So easy . . .

He watched her watching him, saw the varied emotions that played across her face and shone in those soft hazel eyes. Amusement, curiosity, apprehension, and . . . invitation?

He mentally shook his head. Not Florrie. Not Kit's intended.

"I think," Florrie said at last, surprised at the disappointment she felt at his inaction, "that you are a fraud, Alford."

He grinned, relieved she had granted him an easy escape. "Caught me out at last. My reputation will be in tatters now." He relaxed his hold on her and she rolled off him.

"Oh, your secret will be safe with me," she said, with a faint smile. "Just think how lowering it would be to confess that I could not inspire you to new levels of lasciviousness."

But you shall not know to what degree I was tempted. Alford laughed lightly. "Kit will thank me, I am certain."

Florrie scrambled to her feet, disconcerted by his mention of Kit. Of course he would think of that. A true gentleman would. And Alford, she was discovering, was much more a gentleman than he pretended.

"You never did say whether you saw anything atop the wall," he said casually, falling in step beside her as they returned to the house.

She shook her head. "No sign of anything. Perhaps I did imagine it after all. Some strange trick of the moonlight, I suppose."

Alford nodded in feigned agreement. He had his own ideas about what was going on, but he did not wish to enumerate them to Florrie. She was safer in her ignorance. If what he suspected was true, they would not be bothered for a while. Plenty of time to get her out of the house and back to London, where she would be safe.

Florrie found Alford strangely subdued for the rest of the day, which she credited to the lingering effects of his sore head and that unexpected tumble. She was relieved when he chose to retire early.

The more time she spent in his company, the more confused she grew. It had been much neater, and simpler, when she had thought him a shallow pleasure-seeker. It was easy to dismiss him then.

But the new Alford, the *real* Alford, was not so easily dismissed. He was intelligent, witty, and informed. With no outlet for any of those talents. Florrie could understand his frustration. Was it not akin to what she often felt, as a woman? Her aspirations would all be tied to her husband's; her diplomatic successes would be in the drawing room and not the halls of power. Despite her grasp of European politics and personalities, she would only be a consultant, never a player.

She had placed all her hopes and plans on this marriage with Kit. He was being groomed for a diplomatic career; their marriage would put her in the only position of power she could hold. It had seemed the best opportunity for her. But was it really? Dare she wish for more? Like a husband who sent the blood singing in her veins with a look, or whose slow, widening smile sent shivers up her spine?

Sighing quietly, Florrie began her preparations for bed. Right now, she felt so confused that she no longer knew what she wanted. Except a good night's sleep. In the morning, things might be clearer. Perhaps.

She had been asleep for some length of time when her eyes blinked open at the sound of a strange noise. Florrie shut them again and rolled over, seeking sleep, then froze at a new noise.

Someone was in her room.

Hardly daring to breath, she lay there listening. She heard nothing but sensed a foreign presence. Dare she roll over again and try to look through half-closed eyes? Or should she yell for Alford now? Even if he awoke immediately, he might arrive too late. Better to feign sleep, and pray that whoever it was would go away.

With her ears straining to catch the faintest sound, Florrie lay there, trying to remember to breathe normally so the intruder would not know she was awake. She almost began to think she had imagined everything, when she heard a faint sound that could only be a cautious footstep on the ancient floorboards. Florrie peered through her barely opened lids and caught the clear outline of a person standing between her and the fire.

Caution be damned. Florrie leaped from her bed with a

shriek and raced to the connecting door, not daring to look behind her. "Alford! Alford!" she cried as she raced through the dressing chamber.

Alford was in the midst of a very pleasant dream that involved himself, an intimately lit setting, and a woman who bore a remarkable resemblance to Florrie. "Go away," he mumbled sleepily.

"Alford, wake up," Florrie said, tugging at his arm. "Someone is in my room."

He sat up instantly, shaking the cobwebs from his brain. Damn. He had thought there would be no further problems. Quickly he looked around his dimly lit chamber for some sort of weapon.

"You stay here," he said to Florrie as he climbed out of bed. Pouring the contents of the water pitcher into the basin, he hefted the pitcher and headed toward the dressing room.

"Be careful," Florrie pleaded.

Alford stepped cautiously through the doorway and toward the half-opened door to Florrie's room. He wished he had more light. But he could not carry this damned pitcher and a candle and expect to protect himself. Slowly, carefully, he pushed the door into Florrie's room open inch by inch.

The glowing coals in the fireplace gave off enough light for Alford to see that no one was in the room. Unless he or she was hiding. Raising the pitcher in preparation, Alford slipped into the room and peered behind the door. No one. He walked around the end of the bed, finding no one crouched on the other side. The room was unoccupied.

"Florrie," he called. "Bring a candle."

She must have been standing in the dressing chamber, for she was at his side in an instant.

"No one is here," he said.

"But someone was, I swear it, Alford. He must have slipped out the door."

Alford walked to the door and turned the knob. It was securely locked. "What exactly did you *think* you saw?" he asked her.

"I saw a *person,* standing between the bed and the

fireplace, so there was a clear outline,'' she said with a trace of anger. He did not believe her.

"Are you certain you were not dreaming?" he asked, remembering his own lost dream with regret.

"I was not." Florrie stamped her foot with irritation. "Someone was in this room." She glared at Alford. "Did you look under the bed?"

He quickly did so, but no one was there.

"I think you must have had a very vivid dream," he said soothingly. Nearly as vivid as his own. He eyed Florrie with an approving gaze. The woman in his dreams had worn her hair down around her shoulders in just such a manner.

Florrie whirled about, looking all around her room for a sign of something amiss. There had been someone here, she was certain of it. But where had he gone?

"Look, over on that wall!" She pointed to the paneling near her dressing table. "There is something odd about the wall."

Taking the candle from her, Alford crossed the room. Setting the light on the table, he knelt and examined the wall.

Florrie was right; something was strange. This section of panel was out of line with the others. Almost as if . . .

Alford sucked in his breath with a rapid "oh." After all his poking and probing, the panel was no longer flush with the wall. There was a definite gap. A movable panel. Was it a door? He carefully felt all around the edge with his fingers. If he could only get a grip on the side and pull, he could . . .

Alford sat back on his haunches in amazement as the panel in his hands slowly swung inward. The faint odor of musty damp wafted into the chamber.

"A secret passage!" breathed Florrie as she peered over his shoulder. "I wonder where it leads?"

Chapter 19

"I don't know, but I mean to find out," said Alford, rising to his feet. He started back to his room.

"Where are you going?" Florrie asked anxiously.

"I plan to explore that passage," Alford said over his shoulder.

"But what if there is danger?" Florrie asked, scurrying behind him. She drew up short in the doorway to his room when he waved his breeches to her.

"I am going to get dressed," he said. "You can stay if you wish," he flashed her his best leer, "or you can quietly return to your room."

"I'm going with you," Florrie said.

"No, you are not," Alford replied as he sat down on the edge of the bed to pull on his socks. That task complete, he stood again. "If you are going to linger about while I dress, the least you could do is get me my boots."

"Oh," said Florrie with an exasperated sigh, and she returned to her room.

She had absolutely no desire to head down that dark passageway with Alford. Or with anyone. But she did not want to remain here alone, either. And she did not want Alford off exploring on his own. His head was by no means healed and he should not venture anywhere unaccompanied. What was she to do?

Steeling herself for the ordeal, Florrie rummaged under the bed for her slippers. She would go with him, whether he wished her to or not.

She was still deciding which dress would be best to wear when Alford came striding through the room, pulling on his coat.

"Wait," she said, "I am going with you."

"I told you before, you are not." He glared at her. "Look at you. You cannot go traipsing around in the middle of the night in some dark and dank tunnel in your night clothes. What would your father say?"

"I can be dressed in a few minutes."

"Florrie, stay here. I will be back soon." Alford knelt before the opening in the wall and placed his candle inside.

Florrie frantically tied up her slippers and threw on her warm robe. "I am ready," she announced.

"No."

"Yes. It is my passageway," she insisted. "It leads to my room. I was the one who was frightened out of my wits by whoever used it. I have a right to know what is going on."

Alford shook his head. Impetuous female. Yet he admired her willfulness. "Come along if you wish," he said. "But I will not be responsible if anything happens to you."

Florrie snatched up her candle and crouched beside Alford, peering into the dark cavity. At its opening, the passageway was little more than three feet high. But after a yard, the ceiling rose to a man's height, and the floor dropped down into a series of spiraling stairs. She watched anxiously while Alford crawled to look down the stairs. Then he straightened and held his candle high, watching the flame carefully.

"I do not see any signs of a draft," he told Florrie. "I think we will be safe with these open candles. Bring your lightbox just in case."

Florrie grabbed it and some spills and followed Alford into the passageway.

"The drop is steep and these steps are narrow, so be careful," he warned when she was at his side. "If you trip, I do not want you taking me down as well."

"Perhaps you should follow me," she said sarcastically.

They carefully followed the narrow, wooden steps, which circled downward for a fair distance. Alford judged they must be at the depth of the cellars, at least, when the steps stopped and the floor leveled out. The tunnel was not cut to a great height here, and it was all Alford could do to refrain from ducking his head as they slowly followed the passageway.

"Are we under the house?" Florrie whispered.

"I judge we are at the right depth," said Alford, "but I cannot see the use of a passage under the house. More likely we are moving away from it."

"Why is this here?"

"I don't know," Alford snapped. "Perhaps it is a remnant from the Tudor religious squabbles. Or Cromwell's time."

"Has this house really been here that long?"

"Florrie, I am not an expert on the history of Hartland. I never even knew it belonged to the family until my father mentioned it. But yes, I think it is old enough to have been here for Cromwell, at least."

"Perhaps it was used to hide Royalists," Florrie suggested eagerly. "Maybe even Charles himself!"

"If it had, this house would be in every guide book in the country," Alford replied dryly. "I suspect the purpose was more private."

"Like smuggling French prisoners out of the country?"

Alford turned to her in exasperation. "I do not for one minute believe that is what is going on here, Florrie. I hate to discount your theory, but it simply won't wash."

"Then what is *your* theory?"

"Time will tell," he said enigmatically.

Florrie scowled. He probably had no idea at all of what was occurring.

After a short distance, the passageway began to narrow. Florrie, trailing Alford, grabbed hold of his coat tail. It gave her a small mote of comfort. She wished she had not been so insistent on coming along. It was altogether too dark and dirty down here. There were probably spiders. Or worse. She glanced apprehensively over her shoulder. What had become of the peson in her room, who had certainly escaped down this way? What if they ran into him?

"Alford?" she asked weakly.

"What?"

"Are we going to follow this passage to its end?"

He stopped and turned toward her, his face shadowy in faint candlelight. "Regretting your impulsiveness, Florrie? Wishing you were back in your snug, warm bed?"

"Yes," she retorted. "I am."

He laughed. "This does go on much farther than I thought it would." He glanced at the candle in his hand. "And we will not have light for that much longer. It would not be a bad idea to turn back. I can wait until morning and explore it more properly. I own I would feel more comfortable carrying a lantern. A freak blast of air could throw us into total darkness."

"It could?" Florrie moved one hand protectively around the flame of her candle and stepped a pace closer to Alford.

"Yes, it is best that we turn around." He looked at her expectantly. "Lead on, Miss Washburn."

Florrie was not at all certain that she wished to lead, but it was comforting to know that Alford was directly behind her. Now no one would be able to creep up on her in the dark. She walked with an increasingly fast pace until they reached the bottom of the stairs.

Alford gestured to the steps. "Ladies first."

Florrie awkwardly gathered up her skirts in one hand and started up the narrow steps, holding her candle high before her. It had been so much easier going down!

Alford waited until she was nearly out of sight around the curve until he started after her. This managed to put him at eye level with her ankles, which were quite enticingly revealed beneath her raised skirts. Her hips swayed in a most alluring manner as she trod up the stairs. Alford sighed, knowing the futility of his thoughts.

As Florrie neared the top of the stairs, she grew puzzled. Had they not left the secret door open? No light from the room shone through the opening. Had the candle burned out? Or . . .

"Alford," she said in a quavery voice. "I think someone has shut the opening."

He stepped up behind her. "Are you sure?"

"No." She flattened herself against the wall to let him pass. "But I cannot see any light from my room."

Alford squeezed past her, dropping to a squat as he reached the low-ceilinged entry. The panel was definitely closed against them. Holding his candle closer, he peered at the inside wall, looking for some sign of a latch or lever that would open the section of panel. Seeing none, he set the candle down and began tapping along what he thought was the outline of the door. Nothing happened.

"Why don't you just pull on it?" Florrie suggested. "Perhaps a draft blew it shut."

"There are mighty powerful 'drafts' in this house," Alford muttered under his breath. "They can open and shut doors with regular frequency. And there is no handle of any sort on this side." He rose to a half-squat and examined the top of the panel.

"There must be some way to open it," Florrie said, fighting down her rising panic. "What is the point of having a secret passageway that you cannot get out of?"

"Would you like to try?" Alford asked curtly.

"Yes," she snapped. Alford moved aside for her.

Florrie examined the wall as carefully as he had, but she saw no sign of any opening device.

"Perhaps it takes a magic password," Alford quipped.

Florrie shot him a withering stare. "Open Sesame?"

Alford sat down on the top step. "I think we have two options," he said quietly. He saw the growing nervousness in Florrie's eyes, and wished suddenly that he had not tormented her so in past nights. She was already on edge and he did not want a hysterical woman on his hands just now. "We can stay here and wait for someone to come into the room, then call for help."

"Mrs. Burgess rarely comes to my room," Florrie pointed out. "And in any event, my door is locked. As is yours."

"Surely Mrs. Burgess has a key?"

"What is our other option?" Florrie asked, even though she knew what it would be.

"We go back down the passage and find out where it leads," he explained. "It is bound to exit somewhere, probably on the estate grounds."

"Will our candles last long enough for that?"

He shook his head. "I do not know, Florrie. All we can do is try. If we douse yours, that will give us all that more light."

Florrie shivered. Neither course was very appealing. "What do you suggest?"

Alford debated. If it was only he, alone, he would take the second course and discover where this passageway led. But with Florrie . . . Which course made rescue, or escape, more likely? He must make certain Florrie was safe.

There was the mysterious intruder to consider. Had he hidden in some unseen alcove while he and Florrie explored the passageway, then escaped through her room, shutting the exit behind him? Or was he still below, waiting for them in the darkness? Where would Florrie be safest?

"I think we should try to find the way out," he said at last. "There will be an end to this somewhere. We shall have to go along until we find it."

Florrie swallowed hard. Standing here, they were only inches away from the secure comfort of her bedroom. But what now appeared to be a solid wall lay between them and sanctuary. The ceiling over her head and the walls seemed to close in on her, shrinking as she cowered beneath them. Why, oh why, had she insisted on accompanying Alford? She clenched her fists until her nails dug into her palms, willing herself to calm.

"I will go along with whatever you suggest," she said, with a show of false bravado.

Alford smiled with an encouragement he did not completely feel. "Brave girl. Let us keep both candles while we negotiate these stairs. You go first this time."

Florrie nodded and headed back down the stairs again.

"Alford?"

"Yes, Florrie?"

"How many miles have we walked?"

"Five or six at least," he joked. "Are you growing tired?"

She nodded, then realized how foolish a gesture it was in the inky blackness that surrounded her. "I am."

Alford looked at the candle he held. It was their last one, and it would not last much longer. How far could this blasted tunnel continue? The floor had been tilted at a downward

incline for some time now. His head began to throb from
the effort of concentrating, and the lack of sleep. He was
not certain what time Florrie had dashed into his room, but
it must have been past midnight. What time was it now? Two?
Three? It was easy to lose all track of time, and distance,
in this dark hole.

"I would let you rest," he said gently, "but we need to
keep going, Florrie. The candle . . ."

Peering around his shoulder, Florrie saw how little wax
remained. She looked to Alford for some comfort.

"We will find a way out, won't we?" Her wide eyes
implored him.

"Of course we will," he reassured her. "And the quicker
we walk, the quicker it will be." He hated to drive either
of them so hard, but he did not relish the idea of being in
here in the pitch black darkness any more than he suspected
Florrie would.

They proceeded onward, walking as fast as they dared over
the increasingly rough floor. Alford stumbled more than once
over some rock in his path, passing a warning on to Florrie.

The candle was beginning to sputter when Alford called
a halt.

"I am afraid we are out of light, Florrie," he said. "Hang
tightly onto my coat and I will lead on." He felt her take
hold of him with what was close to a death grip.

He continued to walk as quickly as he could, ducking now
and again to miss some dangling spider web or low spot in
the ceiling. Then the flame flickered, and sputtered, and
winked out. They were left in the darkness.

"Florrie?"

"Yes?"

"I am going to have to walk much slower now," he said,
praying that she would remain calm. "Shuffle along behind
me. I will tell you if there are any rocks underfoot so you
will not stumble."

"Thank you," she said in a voice so quiet he could bearly
hear.

It was a totally new experience, he discovered, to walk
surrounded by total darkness. Discarding the useless candle

holder, he kept one hand along the wall, and the other stretched out before him. That would work adequately enough as a warning unless he stumbled over something underfoot. And at the pace he was going, even stumbling would not be much of a danger.

"Alford?" Florrie asked after they had walked along in the darkness for a while. "Can we stop and rest?"

There was little reason not to, now. "That sounds like a good idea." He stopped and turned toward her in the dark. Taking her hand, he gently guided her to the ground. The tunnel, while dark and dusty, was not damp or intolerably cold. He sat beside her, their backs against the rock wall.

"Not exactly the adventure you expected, I wager."

Florrie made a wry face in the dark. "Not quite." She shivered.

"Cold?"

"A little," she confessed. "More nervous than anything. I do not like the dark."

"Pretend you are in your bedroom, with the drapes drawn and the candles out," he suggested. "Very little difference."

"Ah!" she shrieked.

"What?"

"Something brushed my cheek! It was a spider, I know it was." She buried her face in Alford's shoulder.

"Don't like spiders, do you?"

"I hate them," she said, her voice muffled. "As you should well know."

"Why should I—good Lord!" He had completely forgotten that long-ago incident from childhood. How monstrous he had been!

Memory flooded through him. He must have been—what—ten, eleven? It was the first time Florrie had spent any time at Swinton Hall and she had insisted on accompanying Kit and him *everywhere*. She had been, in fact, a regular pest. Determined to be rid of her presence, Alford had lured her into the wine cellar and locked the door, then spent the afternoon fishing with his brother. Florrie spent hours in her dark prison before Alford was forced to confess his crime.

His punishment had been severe, and well-deserved. He tightened his arms protectively around her.

"It was an abominable thing to have done," he said at last. He looked at the darkness surrounding them. "I suppose you can call this poetic justice. 'Tis only a pity you are here as well."

"It is not so bad this time," she said in a quiet voice. "I am not alone."

She was silent for a moment. "Alford?"

"Hmm?"

"We will get out of here, won't we?"

"Of course we will," he said with more conviction than he felt at the moment. "I will personally see to it."

"Promise?"

"Promise."

"Thank you," she said, snuggling closer against him.

He heard the trust in her voice and winced. Much good he would do her. He berated himself for not insisting that she remain in her room. Neither of them would be in this fix now if she had. Then a thought chilled him. Had that panel really shut on its own accord? Or had someone deliberately closed it behind them? If so, and Florrie had remained behind . . . Perhaps it was better she was with him. This way, he was in a position to protect her from any danger.

Not that he would be able to do much, with no weapon beyond his fists. He had no way of knowing what lay ahead and they could be walking into a highly dangerous situation. He had no fears for himself, but Florrie . . . He dared not allow anything to happen to her. She had been placed in his care, and he was obligated to keep her safe. For Kit.

For Kit. The very words cut deeply through Alford. He did not want to keep Florrie safe for his brother. With sudden realization, Alford acknowledged he wanted her for . . . for himself.

What a damnable coil! The situation would be laughable if it were not so complicated. It would make a glorious farce. Here he was, married by accident to his brother's betrothed. Alford was bound by honor to free her from the bonds, but now he was not so certain he wanted to. And Florrie . . .

Florrie probably still wished him to the devil, if all was told. He had brought her nothing but trouble, locking her in cellars when she was a child, ruining her wedding, then tormenting her nights with his staged hauntings. She had every reason in the world to look upon him with disfavor.

Sadly, he knew he could not offer her half of what Kit could. There was no glorious diplomatic career in Alford's future. Only a life of idleness and dissipation. Even if he managed to convince his father to allow him free rein at Swinton Hall, what would that mean to Florrie? Diplomatic hostesses did not practice their trade in Sussex. The very least she would settle for was London. And there was nothing for him there. She would grow as bored as he with a life of endless waiting.

As he listened to Florrie's slow, even breathing, he realized she had fallen asleep. Alford smiled. He liked the feeling of her asleep in his arms, huddled against him for protection and security. It was a pity he could not offer her either.

For a lady he was supposed to keep his hands off, Florrie was too damn attractive. It was not fair. It would try the patience of a saint to be in such close proximity to her and not be tempted—and he was by no means a saint. If she was anyone else . . .

But she was not.

With a sigh, Alford planted a gentle kiss atop her head. Now, in the darkness, he could at least pretend she was his. For a short while.

Chapter 20

Alford must have drifted off to sleep, for he awoke with a start. The total darkness disoriented him and it took a moment to remember where he was. Trapped in the tunnel. With Florrie.

He could not see her in the total darkness that surrounded them, but he did not need to. She was still snuggled up against him, her breathing slow and even. Alford realized with a pang how much trust the simple act of sleeping implied. She had total reliance on his ability to keep her safe.

Yet what was he doing now to achieve that aim? Sitting on his backside in a narrow tunnel? They had to continue onward if they were ever to find the way out. But he had not the heart to wake her. Her sleep had been interrupted once tonight. That was enough.

But he was awake and impatient to get them away from this dark cavern. They had to be close to the exit. The passage had already gone on much longer than he would have guessed; they were probably only a few twists and turns from the end. He could quickly investigate on his own, and with any luck be back before Florrie awoke. He could greet her with the good news. Alford found he liked the idea of appearing a hero in her eyes.

Carefully, so as not to disturb her, he sidled away. Cradling her head on his leg, he shrugged out of his coat. Alford folded it neatly and slipped it under her, pillowing her head. Then he rose to his feet and stretched his cramped muscles. Thank God his head felt better.

He would have to hurry. If Florrie awoke while he was gone, she would be frightened. He must not go too far; he had to be able to hear her if she called. With one hand at the wall at his side, Alford slowly moved down the tunnel.

He had only gone what he judged to be twenty or thirty paces when he saw a faint gleam up ahead. The end? He quickened his pace eagerly.

The tunnel branched, he discovered, as the wall beneath his hand abruptly vanished. Peering down that path, he saw a definite glimmer of hope—light. He hastened forward. The light grew stronger, increasing in brightness until Alford was certain it was an opening of some sort.

He reached it at last, the prickly brambles that had over-grown—or deliberately covered—the opening allowing in only filtered slivers of daylight. But there was no doubt he had found the exit. He turned to hasten back to Florrie, then halted. What lay outside the exit? Visions of the sheer cliffs that fell from the point danced through his brain. Would this be a cruel joke—an opening half way up the cliff side, an exit but not an escape?

Grimacing, Alford tore at the brambles with his bare hands, trying to create an opening big enough to allow a glimpse of what lay outside. His hands were scratched and bleeding when he was finished, but it had been worth the effort. The tunnel opened out onto a sloping, grass-covered hill. Nary a cliff in sight.

Alford sped as fast as he dared back through the tunnel. He would have Florrie out of here in a trice. A thrill of relief raced through him. He had lived up to her expectations; he had saved her.

In his excitement, Alford neglected to keep his hand before him, and he walked straight into the far wall of the tunnel when he reached the fork. "Oof!" he groaned.

Florrie opened her eyes to utter blackness and she was not certain whether she was really awake or not. But when she felt the hard stone floor beneath her, the memories of the past evening flooded over her.

"Alford?" she whispered. "Alford?"

But no reply came. Crawling on her hands and knees, Florrie blindly reached out, groping for his form. The first beginnings of panic rose within her. She was alone.

All those long-buried memories of that horrible day at

Swinton Hall came tumbling through her head and she was reduced once again to a tearful five-year-old, whimpering in the corner. Gulping in air, Florrie clenched her fists, gritting her teeth with the effort. *I will not behave foolishly,* she chided herself.

She carefully felt about the floor again, locating Alford's coat at once. She hugged it tightly to her chest, seeking security from it.

He must have gone on, looking for a way out. He would not have left her here alone, on purpose. Not again. She brushed away a trickling tear with the back of her hand.

Should she stay and wait? Or follow after him? The latter would get her out of this nasty tunnel sooner. With determination Florrie rose to her feet and took a few halting steps.

Until she realized she had no idea which way to go. In her mad scramblings, she had become all twisted about. When they had stopped, the tunnel continued to her left, but was it now her left, or her right? With a low moan of frustration, Florrie sank down to the floor again. She had been foolish, and stupid, and now could not do anything until Alford came back for her.

If he ever did.

No, no, he would come back, he would. He had promised to get her out of here, hadn't he? A gentleman's promise was like an oath, it could not be broken. He would come back.

Florrie jumped at the faint sound that reached her ears. She listened carefully, but heard nothing else.

"Alford?" she asked doubtfully. She raised her voice. "Alford?"

"I am coming," he called back, hearing the panic in her voice. He raced up the tunnel toward her.

"Alford? Where are you?"

"I am here, I am here," he said, reaching out with both arms. "Reach out your hand."

Florrie did as he said and he caught it in his. She latched on with a grip of iron and he pulled her into his arms.

"Where were you?" she demanded. "I woke up and you were gone and I was so frightened!"

"It is all right, I am here," he said, crushing her against his chest, stroking her back as he sought to calm her. "I found the way out."

"What?"

He released her from his arms, keeping hold of her hand. "We were laughably close," he explained as he led her along the passage to where the first faint glimmers of light could be seen. They quickly reached the exit and Florrie blinked in the unaccustomed brightness.

"Damn!" Alford exclaimed. "We left my coat. It would have been good protection against those thorns."

"Don't go back for it," Florrie said quickly. She did not wish to be left alone again, even in the light.

"I will go first," Alford offered. "I can make a bigger hole for you to follow."

Florrie winced as Alford, on his hands and knees, began tearing his way through the tangled vines. In one moment his sleeve would get caught, in another, the back of his shirt. The vicious brambles seemed to have a mind of their own, reaching out and grabbing him as if they wished to keep them imprisoned in this dark cavern forever.

"I've cleared a path," he called at last, from outside. "Keep low and you should be all right."

Hunching over, Florrie carefully kneeled in the opening Alford had forged. But the hem of her robe caught almost immediately, and as she turned to free herself her hair snagged on another branch.

"Damnation!" She jerked at her robe and ripped it free. Wrapping her skirts around her legs as closely as she could, Florrie inched forward. Her knee caught on the bunched fabric and she heard another loud tearing noise. Tears of frustration welled in her eyes. She pulled her skirts loose, one knee at a time, moving forward as far as she could, then repeated the procedure. Every other shift forward managed to tangle her hair in another branch.

She glanced up, seeing Alford peering in at her.

"It's these skirts," she gasped. "I swear, the next time I go crawling through bramble bushes I am wearing breeches!"

Alford grinned and moved back from the opening. Florrie finally managed to crawl the last foot and collapsed in a heap on the grass.

"Are you all right?" Alford asked, leaning over her.

Florrie looked up and thought she had never seen a more pleasant sight than his face silhouetted against the brilliant blue sky above. She nodded, tears of relief streaming down her face.

"Don't cry," Alford said soothingly, wiping away a trickling tear with a finger. He lowered himself to lay beside her, propped up on one elbow. "You are a very brave lady."

She daubed at her eyes with the sleeve of her gown. "No, I am not," she protested. "I was horribly frightened."

"But you did not show it," he said, staring at her lips in rapt fascination. They looked fuller, redder than he remembered. Lips that begged to be kissed.

Florrie managed a wan smile. "I had to put up a brave front for you, Alford."

"Thomas," he whispered as he inched closer until his mouth hovered above hers. "My name is Thomas." He saw her wide-eyed, startled, gaze, saw the curiosity in it as well. She knew what he was going to do next—and wondered about it. This time, they would both find out.

"A very brave lady," he repeated, then lowered his mouth onto hers.

Those lips were as soft and warm as he imagined, pliant, and to his delighted surprise, not at all resistant. Alford wrapped one hand in her honey-colored locks, cradling the back of her head as his lips explored hers with soft, gentle kisses.

He felt her fingers lightly caress his cheek and he groaned with delight at her touch. He pulled her to him, molding her body against his, allowing his kisses to grow more demanding. He felt the heat rising in him and groaned again, this time in frustration.

He could not, he dared not. Florrie was not his. With a sigh of dismay he wrenched his mouth from hers and rolled to one side.

Florrie struggled to catch her breath while she struggled against her . . . disappointment? Those kisses had shaken her beyond belief, as had her response to them. And there was no mistaking the keen regret she felt when Alford withdrew. It was over so quickly, she had not even had time to . . .

"Florrie?"

She kept her gaze directed at the sky overhead.

"Florrie, look at me."

Reluctantly, she turned her head. Alford was gazing at her, his pale blue eyes reflecting mingled guilt and—what? Desire? Longing? And sadness, as well.

"I should not have done that," he said quickly.

She laughed shakily. "Neither should I. But I daresay we have both done a lot of things we should not have."

"It was only . . ." His voice dropped. "I was only so pleased we were safe. At last."

Florrie shut her eyes, surprised at the tears that stung her lids. What had she expected him to say? That he had been consumed by overwhelming passion? More likely he had been motivated by curiosity. It had been part of her motivation. The other part she was not certain she wanted to think about right now.

She had never kissed Kit, so there was no way to compare the two brothers. But she had kissed and been kissed enough times to know that it had never been like this before. Exciting, exhilarating, and oh-so-tempting. She found that frightening. It made her feel so dangerously out of control.

"We had best return to the house," Alford said at last.

"You are right." Florrie sat up, ruefully examining her torn clothing. She tried to run a hand through her tangled hair, and finally dared a glance at Alford. "I must look a fright," she said, then quickly looked away as she saw the answer in his eyes.

Alford scrambled self-consciously to his feet, reaching down a hand to help Florrie up. The sooner they returned to normality, the better.

"Where exactly are we?" she asked as she looked about the hillside.

"I think we are northeast of the house," he replied. "The land flattens out at the top of this slope and the house should be there, just beyond those trees."

"Oh." There was nothing else to say. Alford kept her hand in his and they slowly trudged up the slope.

"What do you suppose the Burgesses will say to all of this?" Florrie asked as they reached the crest and the house came into view. "Do you think they were the ones who shut the panel?"

Alford shook his head. "I cannot be certain, but I do not think so. I think they know some of what is going on here, but are not actively involved themselves."

"What is going on?" Florrie asked.

"I want to explore that tunnel more thoroughly before I answer that," he said. "I think it will answer all our questions."

"You are going to go back down?" Florrie stopped and stared at him, aghast.

"Better prepared, this time," he said with a laugh. "I shall take a dozen candles."

They had reached the front lawn, and Florrie thought suddenly of the image they presented, if anyone was watching. She, in her torn and dirty robe and gown, Alford in his equally disheveled shirtsleeves. Hand-in-hand, like two grubby children. The very picture made her laugh.

"And what do you find so amusing?" he asked, relieved she could find something to laugh at.

"Our appearance," she said.

"Ah, well, it was a more enthusiastic morning stroll than we had anticipated," he said. "But quite in keeping with our country setting, don't you think?"

"Undoubtedly."

Mrs. Burgess greeted them with a look of surprise, but did not inquire into the cause of their uncommon appearance. Florrie acted as though it was an everyday occurrence for her to appear at the front door in her torn and dirty night clothing. Even Florrie's request for the key to her room raised not an eyebow from the dour housekeeper.

Alford followed Florrie into her chamber, firmly shutting

and locking the door behind him. "I want to examine the panel more closely," he said. "If there is no latch on the inside, the opening mechanism must be in this room."

The panel was so firmly shut that it took him a moment to find its exact location. He carefully examined the surrounding wood, tapping and pressing it with his fingers.

The latch was hidden simply in a strip of molding. When Alford pressed against the exact spot, the panel popped open.

"Laughably simple," he said as he examined the mechanism on the panel.

"But why would they have a panel that only opened from this room?" Florrie asked.

"It would be easy enough to make one's escape down the tunnel," Alford replied. "And this way you do not risk strange intruders coming into the house."

"But that means . . ." Florrie's voice trailed off.

"That whoever left the panel ajar *was* in your room last night," Alford finished for her. And if that person had not come through the passage, he had come through her locked door. And that was all his fault. If he had not oiled the lock so well, no one could have made such a silent entrance.

Alford hastily closed the panel. "Once the door is shut, we know no one can come through that way. If you shove the chair against your door, you would have plenty of warning if someone tried to enter from the corridor."

"Alford, what is going on?"

He avoided her troubled gaze. "I expect we will find some answers today," he said, wearily rubbing the back of his neck. "But if I don't get some sleep right now, I fear I will not be able to do anything later."

"Promise me you will not go anywhere on your own?"

Alford grinned. "Unless you think I can make it through your room and into the passage while you sleep, I think you have nothing to fear."

Florrie nodded and walked with Alford to the dressing room door.

"Thank you," she said. "For keeping your promise."

He looked at her with a puzzled expression.

"You found a way out."

"I had a personal interest in the outcome," he joked, uncomfortable with her gratitude. After that improper kiss, she had every right to be angry with him. That she was not, he reckoned a miracle. "Sleep well now."

"I shall."

Florrie insisted upon bathing before she attempted sleep. Refreshed from her bath, she sat in front of the fire, drying her hair in the reflected heat. Now, she had time to sit and think. But she was not at all certain she wished to.

What had happened this morning with Alford had been quite an accident, she was confident. And it most surely meant very little. It had been sheer relief that had prompted Alford's kiss. He had admitted that himself. There was nothing more to it than that.

Which was just as well. Alford was not a part of her plan. She would marry Kit, cultivate useful acquaintances on the Peninsula, and be prepared to go with him to wherever he was sent once he undertook his diplomatic career. That was what she had always planned for herself. It was what she wanted—wasn't it?

Once, the friendship she had shared with Kit would have been enough. Now, she was no longer certain. And that made it difficult to ignore her confusing reactions to Alford. If she had only kissed Kit, been held in his arms . . . then she would know how to deal with these conflicting emotions. She would be able to prove that it was just opportunity, not desire, that made Alford so captivating.

Because he was certainly not at all the kind of man she wished for herself. Granted, he was not the brainless gamester she had initially labeled him, but that did not make him any more respectable or responsible. He still had done nothing with himself. Surely, if he really wanted to, he could have overcome his father's oppositions and done *something*. Just because he had held her close when she was frightened, and kissed her when they were safe, did not mean he would be a suitable partner.

But a tiny voice inside her head told her she was lying to herself. Told her that she would experience more passion in a week with Alford than she would in a lifetime with the amiable Kit. But passion did not a marriage make, she argued back. She wanted dependability, security, and success. When had Alford ever demonstrated any of those qualities?

When had he ever been given a chance, that persistent voice asked. He'd been hemmed in by his father, society's conventions, and limited opportunities. No one expected him to do anything with himself. Why criticize him then, for behaving as he did?

Florrie stopped her brushing and stared into the flames. She did not like the way all her neat, orderly plans were coming apart. She should be in Spain with Kit right now, not in Devon with his brother.

Alford—Thomas—upset all her plans, set her senses whirling, and made her wonder exactly what it was she wanted from life. He was dangerous. Uncontrolled. Disconcerting.

A part of her wanted to leave Hartland today, now, before it was too late. Another part wished to stay, to play out these strange circumstances to the end, to discover what would happen. And it was that part she wished to listen to.

She yawned. Maybe it would all make more sense after she slept. But she doubted it. Nothing had made very good sense ever since Alford had mistakenly scrawled his signature on the wrong line of the proxy papers. And she was dreadfully afraid that it would take more than a simple annulment to chase him from her thoughts.

Chapter 21

Alford lay upon his bed, desperate for sleep, but unable to free his brain of its swirling thoughts. What he had done was unbelievable. Unconscionable. It was far, far worse than that simple kiss. He had fallen in love with his brother's wife-to-be.

It was a contemptible action. One that even he, with his rather misspent life, could not tolerate. He had already created enough grief for those two. Had it not been for his lamentable, drunken mistake, Florrie would be with Kit now, married and forever beyond his reach.

Alford knew it was foolish to even think that his feelings would matter to her. He had no illusions about how she viewed him. There was nothing in his past that would win the smallest crumb of approbation from her. He had wasted his time and his life quite effectively up to this point. Even if Kit was not involved, the outcome would be no different. Alford had nothing to offer Florrie.

He thought briefly that if given the opportunity, he might be able to win her respect and admiration. Lord knows, he would try. To gain Florrie's approval, he would tackle anything, take any risks to prove himself. He smiled sadly. How awkward to be finally fired with ambition, only to no purpose. A perverse twist of fate had placed the one woman he wanted totally out of his reach.

There was only one solution. He had to leave Hartland, as quickly as possible. Once he had explored that bother-some tunnel, and made certain Florrie would be safe from any intruders, he would pack his bags and leave. It was the best thing for both of them. He would not succumb to temptation if he removed himself from it. And if she ever suspected his depth of feeling . . . well, he did not wish to become a source of future amusement for Kit and Florrie. It would only create awkwardness at family gatherings.

If only he had not kissed her! That had been an act beyond foolishness. For it had been a shattering experience, for him at least. He only hoped his glib apology had sufficed to stifle her curiosity, praying she would quickly forget the incident.

Alford struggled with mixed guilt and longing as exhaustion crept up on him. Later, when he was rested . . .

He sat up suddenly with a groan of dismay. Nanette. He had forgotten about her completely. She could arrive at any moment! He could only imagine Florrie's reaction. Jumping from bed, Alford frantically searched for pen and paper. If he was lucky, she had not left London. And in the event she had, he would pen a note to Old Mort, telling him under no circumstances to bring any lady to Hartland. Nanette's arrival would only put a seal on Florrie's contempt for him. He had to spare her the humiliation of that situation. God, what a coil he had wound about himself.

Alford felt less than rested when he awoke in late afternoon. His sleep had been a twisted jumble of images: Nanette creating havoc, Florrie, pliant in his arms, kissing him with wild abandon, juxtaposed against the harsh and condemning face of his brother as he jerked her from Alford's clasp. He winced at the image.

Pacing his room, Alford thought he would drive himself mad with his regrets and longings. He needed something— anything—to take his mind off Florrie. Descending into the tunnel again would be exactly the thing. He ignored his promise to her. It was his responsibility to keep her safe— for Kit. And the sooner he could resolve the mystery, the sooner he could flee from temptation.

Alford walked boldly into the kitchen, unafraid of a confrontation with the Burgesses. Whatever their involvement, he suspected they were only passive players. He thought he had little to fear from them.

"I need a lantern," he said to Burgess. "Two, in fact, if you have them."

flame is too dangerous—might set the house on fire.''

Burgess eyed him dubiously. ''Mightn't you be better doing such a thing outside the house?''

Alford shook his head. ''Too much wind. Don't worry, it's safe enough if arranged properly.'' He looked at Burgess expectantly. ''The lanterns?''

Shaking his head, Burgess went in search of the desired objects.

Armed with his lanterns, an ample supply of candles and lighters, and a stout kitchen knife he had purloined from beneath the unobservant eyes of Mrs. Burgess, Alford hesitated in the dressing room, outside Florrie's door. He pressed his ear to the wood, wondering if she was still asleep. No sound issued from the other room.

She would be angry with him when she discovered what he had done, but he did not care. She would be far safer in her room. And Florrie's safety was his major concern. Hopefully, after today he could guarantee it. Then he could leave her, knowing he had done all he could.

He cautiously tried the knob, which to his relief was unlocked. Now, if he could only slip through her room, open the panel, pass his supplies through and close it again without waking her. A not inconsiderable task . . .

Slowly he eased the door open. Peering cautiously around the door frame, he saw Florrie's sleeping form upon the bed. So far, so good. Carrying a lantern in each hand, he tip-toed as silently as he could manage across the floor. One or two boards squeaked ominously underfoot as he passed, but the figure on the bed did not stir.

The panel opened with laughable ease this time. Alford set both lanterns inside. He started to climb into the opening, then hesitated. It was foolish, but there was no way to be certain of what lay ahead of him. He wanted one last look at Florrie—just in case. Carefully retracing his steps, he stood beside the bed. Her soft hair lay gently tumbled on the pillow, her face formed in a peaceful expression. It hurt just to look at her, when he knew how ridiculous his longings were. He bent down, intending to plant a whisper of a kiss on her brow.

Instead, he found himself staring into her suddenly opened eyes.

"Alford?" she asked sleepily.

Damnation! He stepped back.

Florrie struggled to sit up, her gaze taking in the opening in the wall, instantly wide awake. "You were going down the tunnel without me!" she said accusingly.

Alford nodded.

"Well, I won't have it," she said.

"But if you remain here, you can let me back in," he countered. "I don't want to crawl through those brambles again."

"We could just as easily prop the door open with a chair," she said, grabbing her robe from the foot of the bed. She hastily pulled it on and clambered from the bed. "Now, if you don't mind, I should like to dress."

Alford's fingers clenched at the thought. He recalled the day he surprised Florrie in her chemise and a stab of physical longing pulsed through him. How he wished to assist her.

Noting Florrie's look of exasperation, a wide grin spread over his face. He could not resist the urge to tease her once again. And perhaps he could yet dissuade her from accompanying him. "Do not let me stop you," he said, arms folded across his chest as he leaned in a negligent pose against the bedpost.

That cheeky grin sent shivers of remembrance down Florrie's spine. That kiss—those kisses—this morning. What had they meant? Had they been just another part of his incessant teasing? Or had they meant more? She had almost begun to take Alford's brazen remarks in stride—until today. Now . . . how serious was he? Did he truly desire her?

Alford saw the confusion on her face and his grin faded. He did not want to increase her disquiet. He had caused her enough trouble already.

"Call me when you are ready," he said, and escaped to the dressing room, pulling the door shut behind him with more violence than he planned.

"What you be wanting a lantern for?" Burgess asked.

"Scientific experiment," Alford replied blandly. "Open

Florrie sat down on the edge of the bed with a sigh. What was Alford doing to her? Her thoughts were all in a jumble. This was so unlike her! She was always in control of herself, her thoughts, her emotions. But with Alford . . . He created the most chaotic sensations.

Mechanically, she drew out her serviceable traveling dress from the wardrobe and fastened herself into it. She laced up her sturdy half-boots, and laid out her heavy cloak. If she had to scramble through the brambles again, she wanted some protection against their grasping branches.

Florrie jerked open the door to the dressing room, stepping back in surprise as she came face-to-face with Alford.

"You're ready?"

"Yes," she said, turning quickly before he could study her carefully. She schooled her features into a semblance of normality.

"If we move the chair," Alford pointed, "we can prop the panel open. That way, we can have at least two exits."

Alford dragged the piece of furniture across the room while Florrie retrieved the lanterns and lit the candles in each.

"Ready?" Alford asked.

She nodded.

It was not so bad this time, Florrie thought, as she followed him down those narrow, twisting steps. "Do you think these stairs were originally built into the house?" she asked Alford when they reached the bottom.

"Highly likely," he said, peering around the small chamber. He had not bothered to explore last night, but he wished to be more thorough this time. Under the curve of the stairs, he discovered the faint outline of another doorway, set into the wall.

"Where do you suppose it leads?" Florrie asked.

"Probably to the cellars," Alford replied. He wished he had thought to explore that part of the house earlier. It might have saved both of them endless trouble.

"Do you think these are the only set of hidden stairs in the house?"

He shrugged. "It is difficult to tell. The house could be riddled with them. Perhaps they all lead to the cellars, and then join up to the main tunnel here."

Florrie wondered at the type of person who would build such things into his house—or the times that would make such building a necessity.

The brighter light from the lantern only served to illuminate the spider-webs that hung at crazy angles from the sides of the tunnel. Florrie grimaced at the sight. It had been better in the dark, when she could not see them. She was glad Alford was in the lead.

Florrie's arm ached from the weight of the lantern when they arrived at the side passage that had been their escape. Alford peered ahead into the darkness, then turned to Florrie.

"I would feel better if you would remain here."

"Alone?" she squeaked. "No!"

"I am not certain what we shall find at the end of the main tunnel," he said quietly.

"You must suspect, if you are worried," she said. "Tell me."

Alford scowled, but knew she would not agree to remain unless he told her his guess. "I could not put my finger on it until the night you saw the lights."

Florrie's face brightened. "You mean someone *is* helping French prisoners escape?"

"Rather the opposite, I suspect."

She stared at him in alarm. "French spies are coming to England?"

"More likely French contraband," he said with a wry smile. "Like the fine brandy in the library."

"Smugglers?" she asked incredulously.

He nodded. "It makes sense. It was full moon the night you saw the lights. An isolated area of the coast . . . a nearly abandoned house. I would not be surprised to find they have been using Hartland as their headquarters."

"Why did you not tell me you suspected smugglers?" she demanded. "I have been terrified."

Alford smirked. "Thought it really was ghosts, did you?"

"No!" she retorted. "But I certainly would have been

more comfortable knowing what specific threat we faced.''

"My pardon," Alford said, sketching a bow. "Next time, I assure you, I shall share my suspicions with you.''

"Do you think it was one of them who was using that room, and who knocked you on the head?''

"Probably. And that is why I wish you to stay here," Alford insisted. "If they are using this tunnel, they might not appreciate our explorations.''

"I feel safer with you than I would alone," she said.

There it was. Her blind trust in him to keep her safe. And right now he wanted her admiration and approval more than anything in this world. Alford considered. It had been two nights since the cargo was unloaded; it may have already been dispersed around the neighborhood. It was unlikely any of the smugglers would still be around; they would not try to move any remaining goods until after dark. And he did feel better having Florrie in sight.

"All right," he agreed. "Follow me.''

The tunnel bore straight for a short while, then turned abruptly and descended down steep stairs hewn in the rock. Alford was grateful they had not come this far in the dark earlier. He most likely would have gone hurtling down them.

The stairs continued for a considerable distance. Alford began to hope there was an exit here; he did not relish the thought of climbing back up again. But he should have expected it—they would end up at the bottom of the cliff. He could already smell the sea in the air, and thought he felt a slight breeze.

Indeed, in only a few more steps, the ceiling opened up over their heads and they looked into a goodly-sized cave. The floor was covered with sand and barrels and chunks of wood.

"You were right," Florrie breathed.

Motioning for her to remain on the steps, Alford dropped to the cave floor. He lifted the lid from one of the whole barrels, but it was empty. The last shipment must have been moved already. Crossing the sandy floor, he walked to the narrow cave entrance. It opened out onto a small strip of sand between two towering rock formations.

They must row the cache in from the boats, he mused, store it in the cave, then row it back out to transport it along the coast. He could not imagine any number of men lugging the heavy casks of brandy up those stairs. It was a clever setup. The cave was nearly inaccessible from the sea. And no one would ever find the tunnel entry within the house. In an emergency, the smugglers could move the cache out through the house or the tunnel.

The house was the key, of course. The smugglers used it as their headquarters to signal the incoming boat that it was safe—the lights Florrie had seen the other night. Alford was now certain it had been one of the smugglers who knocked him over the head. Surely, the Burgesses were involved in some manner. He breathed a sigh of relief. At least the mystery was now solved, and once the smugglers were convinced he and Florrie posed no danger ot their little enterprise, they would likely be left in peace.

"What do you find?" Florrie asked impatiently from her vantage point on the stairs.

"Nothing, I am afraid," Alford replied. "They probably moved all the cargo out the last few nights."

"Do you think . . . was it one of them who entered my room last night?"

"I suspect so."

Florrie shivered. "How can I ever sleep again? What if they try to murder us in our beds?"

"I do not think they will bother," Alford said. "I think a word or two dropped to the Burgesses will end any danger."

"You think the Burgesses are involved?"

"Think about it, Florrie. A house with a secret passageway leading to the beach, a house that has been unoccupied for years? It is the ideal location for a group of smugglers." He grinned. "The Burgesses must have been aghast when we showed up."

"Will talking to them keep us safe?" Florrie asked doubtfully.

"Smugglers, on the whole, are not a bad lot," Alford said.

"Oh?" Florrie eyed him reproachfully. "You are intimately acquainted with them, I suppose?"

Alford laughed. "Not quite. But if they know they have nothing to fear from us, I doubt they will pay us any more heed. I'll request a sizeable order of brandy from the next shipment. That should lay their fears at rest."

"But if all that was caused by the smugglers . . . what about the Lady?" Florrie asked.

Alford cringed. If Florrie ever found out about his attempts to frighten her away . . . "That was probably them as well," he said hastily. "Not nearly so romantic as a ghost, but more believable."

Florrie felt oddly disappointed to have such a prosaic explanation for matters. Not that smugglers were exactly ordinary, but they were not as exciting as a ghost. Despite her denials, she had been half-disposed to believe they existed.

"It is a long climb back," she said, casting a rueful glance up the stairs.

"And an even longer swim," Alford pointed out. "I think there is little choice. Upwards it is."

Florrie gathered up her skirts and trailed Alford up the stairs. She said little during the return to the house. Not because she wished to conserve her breath, but because she needed time to absorb all the new discoveries she had made today. Finding the smugglers cave was the least of them.

She tried to objectively assess her deepening feelings for Alford, but had little success. There was no logical reason for them. He was not at all the kind of man she wished for a husband. He had no standing in diplomatic circles or the political arena. He was intelligent but lazy, bored but indifferent to any cure. Florrie still believed that had he really wished to, he could have found something useful to do with himself.

Yet, how would she have reacted to a similar situation? Her father had encouraged and nurtured her interests, not stifled them. Would she have fought against him if he had? Alford had not totally accepted defeat—he had his new plan for agricultural improvements. All he really needed was a chance to prove to his father—and to himself—that he *could* do something.

Florrie brightened at the thought. Surely, with her father's contacts, she could find someone willing to lend Alford assistance. If Barstow vetoed the agricultural improvements at Swinton, there were many more landowners who would welcome them. There were men in the Foreign Office who owed their position only to connections, and not skill. They needed bright, decisive assistants. There even might be the possibility of a seat in the Commons, Florrie mused. How much could one election cost? She had a good deal of money of her own. Enough to finance a campaign for Alford?

She would have to sound him out very carefully, to ascertain which prospect held the most appeal. But she thought with some judicious prodding, he might be persuaded to take something on. And any of those prospects would make a good start. In short time, Alford could be well-established. It was a promising solution.

Except, of course, she had no idea of Alford's feelings for her. She placed far too much importance on that kiss. Had he himself not apologized for his actions? She always suspected Alford saw her in a slightly contemptuous light, and a few innocent embraces did not mean he thought differently.

Even worse, there was the matter of Kit. Florrie was betrothed to him. They both knew it was not a grand passion, but that did not obviate her obligation to take his feelings into consideration. She knew that Kit would not hold her to her promise. He was too much her friend. But could she toss Kit over on the mere hope that Alford's feelings for her had warmed?

Chapter 22

After helping Florrie from the tunnel, and settling her in the library, Alford went in search of Burgess. If they could not reach some accommodation with the smugglers, Alford was determined to get Florrie out of the house today, if he had to carry her all the way to Clovelly himself.

"So, Burgess," Alford began, when he had run the man to ground in the pantry, "do you get paid for your role in this smuggling operation, or do you take your cut in goods?"

The man cast a hesitant look at Alford. "I beg your pardon, sir?"

"The smuggling ring that operates out of the cave below the cliff—are you the ringleader, or only the watchman?" Alford saw the fear in the man's eyes, and laughed. "Good Lord, Burgess, I do not want to turn you over to the magistrate. I only wanted to order some brandy. If it's the same thing you've been serving in the library, I'll take a cask or two."

Burgess visibly relaxed. "I think that could be arranged, sir."

"I trust there will be no more incidents like the other day?" Alford touched the healing wound on his head. "I do not give a damn what sort of illicit activities are going on in the neighborhood. But I do take exception to physical attacks."

"T'were an accident," Burgess said. "No one meant you any harm."

"Good, good," said Alford, turning to go. He paused, and looked back. "And Burgess, I think that it might be a nice gesture if some lace or silks were presented to Miss Washburn. She has had an unpleasant time of it, what with people wandering through her room and being shut up half the night in a dark and dusty tunnel. It would make amends."

Burgess nodded.

Alford felt a thrill of satisfaction. There was nothing to fear from that quarter anymore. They could smuggle in the entire brandy production of France, for all he cared. Just so Florrie was safe.

His steps slowed as he neared the library. He had done what he set out to accomplish, which was to assure her safety. That had been easy. But now there was no longer any reason for him to stay. Remaining in her presence would only serve to remind him of what he could not have. Yet a perverse desire to torture himself further led him to the door.

Florrie looked up with apprehension as Alford entered the room. "You were gone for so long, I began to be frightened," she said quickly. "Did you talk with the Burgesses?"

"Everything is taken care of," he said. "I think we have nothing more to fear from the smugglers."

"The Burgesses were working with them?"

Alford nodded. "But I convinced Burgess my only interest in his activities was in ensuring myself a steady supply of brandy. He assured me we can expect no more trouble."

Florrie smiled with relief. At least she could feel safe in her bed once more.

Alford prowled the room nervously, hesitating before the brandy decanter, then continuing his circuit. He had to leave, he knew that. But he would like to leave knowing Florrie thought more highly of him than she had when this all started. How, precisely, could he convince her that he now wanted to make something of his life? He finally sank down in one of the chairs flanking the fireplace and stared glumly into the flames.

"How does your head feel?" Florrie asked. An inane question, but one could not exactly ask what he had meant by that kiss this morning. Even though it was the thing she most wished to know.

"It feels fine," Alford replied.

"Did you—?"

"Are you—?"

Alford laughed. "Ladies first."

Florrie took a deep breath. "I was curious about the book you are reading. The one about agriculture."

"Oh." Alford smiled sheepishly. "Agriculture is one thing my father is not interested in. I thought I might convince him to allow me to make a few changes at Swinton."

"Is Swinton the only property with a farm?" Florrie asked.

Alford nodded. "There are a few other houses, here and there, but none have enough land to make a farm worth bothering with."

Despite her literary proclivities, Florrie had difficulty conjuring up the picture of Alford as a contented country landowner. "You would prefer the country to London?"

Alford paused. "They both have their attractions," he said evasively.

He had talked about his interest in politics, but Florrie was now uncertain how serious he was. Would he rather grow corn or formulate policy? "I imagine it is easier to keep track of politics in the city," Florrie said, hoping to draw him out.

"That's true," Alford agreed. "But what of you? I imagine this sojourn in Devon has given you your fill of country life."

"I would hardly call this isolated outpost an example of country life," she said with an ironic smile. "One usually is not beset with ghosts and smugglers in the country."

"Well, take Swinton then. Would a fortnight there bore you to tears?"

"I always enjoyed my visits there," she said carefully. Did he intend to tender her an invitation? The prospect of visiting Swinton in Alford's company was appealing. Particularly if they could be alone again.

"I don't think I have spent a full month at Swinton since I was fifteen," he said, half to himself.

"You will probably need to if you plan to make improvements," she pointed out.

"I know," he said, flashing her a rueful smile. He abruptly changed topics. "How do you think your father will get along without you in Sweden?"

"Tolerably, I hope," she said. "I own I have some reservations about how well he will manage by himself."

"It must have been an interesting life for you, moving from

one capital to another," he mused. "Did you ever miss not having a permanent house?"

Florrie smiled sadly. "Swinton was probably the closest thing to a home I ever had." She glanced at him shyly. "Did you hate it there so very much when you were younger? Is that why you were always away?"

"My father and I—" Alford broke off. There was little point in going over that again. Florrie would not care about his struggles to live up to impossible expectations. "Our interests diverged."

Florrie felt an onrush of compassion. It was difficult for her to imagine anything but a close relationship with her father. She pitied Alford for not having a more understanding sire. She could only guess at the pressures Barstow had applied to his eldest son. Alford had rebelled in the only way he could.

"I know my father was disappointed not to have had a son," Florrie said quickly. "I struggled against that for the longest time. I tried to do as much for him as I could."

"I am certain he is very proud of you," Alford said softly, envying her that close relationship. If he ever had sons . . ." He smiled sadly. "Tell me, how did your parents come to name you Florence? Is it a family name?"

Florrie laughed. "I was born there—quite by accident, I understand. I was to have been named after my grandmother. But Mama insisted on a permanent reminder of the event."

"And you, of course, are thankful they were not in Rome or Naples when the happy event occurred." Alford grinned.

"Or St. Petersburg." Florrie giggled.

An awkward silence descended. Florrie struggled for a topic that would lead him to some revelation. She desperately wished to know exactly how Alford viewed her. "Do you plan to go to Swinton when you leave here?"

"Perhaps," he said, dismayed by the question, for it only reminded him of what he ought to do: leave. Immediately. Each minute he lingered only made the pain of his eventual loss worse. He smothered a bitter laugh. One could not lose what one never had. He envied Kit with all his soul.

"I always liked Swinton in the spring," Florrie said,

recalling past visits there. ''The gardens are at their best then.''

''My mother always said that,'' he blurted out, shocking himself with his candor.

''I do not remember her very well, I am afraid,'' Florrie admitted, wondering if Alford and his father would have dealt together better if Lady Barstow had lived longer. Perhaps she could have softened her husband's criticisms, or stiffened her son's resolve.

''Neither do I,'' he said softly.

Florrie glanced at him, surprised by the mingled sadness and regret in his eyes. A tremor ran down her spine and she hastily looked away.

Alford stared at the floor. He did not wish to dwell on those who were dead—his mother and hers. Yet the future looked equally bleak, knowing he could not have Florrie. He lapsed into silence.

''The Derby and the Oaks will take place soon,'' Florrie observed. Would the lure of the gambling draw Alford away? ''I imagine you will not wish to miss them.''

Her remark startled him. Lord, he had not even thought about either race since his arrival at Hartland. And he usually had considerable sums of money riding on both. All his thoughts had been concentrated on ridding himself of her presence—or contriving a way to keep her at his side forever.

''Have you ever attended?'' he asked.

Florrie shook her head. ''Would I enjoy it?''

''Very much so, I think,'' he said, with a smile. ''It is a quite suitable race meeting for ladies.''

''Perhaps I shall go, one day.''

Alford had an overwhelming urge to catch her up in his arms, shower her face with kisses, and blurt out his declaration of love and desire until she agreed to remain with him forever. ''Shall we try a hand or two of piquet before dinner?'' he asked instead. ''Perhaps you can win back some of your money.''

Raw panic attacked Alford following dinner. What were

they to do in the hours until bed? Another halting conversation like the one earlier would be too much for him. He racked his brain for some reason to keep her contentedly in the library. After last night's ordeal she would desire to retire early. He must contrive a plan.

He sat in his chair, nursing the glass of brandy in his hand, watching her while she repaired the rents in her night robe with neat, even stitches. It was a surprise to see her occupied with something other than her Spanish grammar.

"No stomach for verbs tonight?" he asked lightly.

Florrie glanced up in surprise. Somehow, in light of her changing attitude toward Kit, learning Spanish no longer seemed important. "I am not certain it is such a useful task," she said.

"Would you like me to read?" he asked.

Florrie looked at him with an amused smile. "More of *Otranto*?"

He laughed. "I would have thought you have had your fill of mysterious happenings."

"I have no objections to them, as long as they are happening to someone else," she replied. "I would very much like to have you read, Alford."

"You only wish to see me wearing my spectacles," he retorted, pleased he had found some way of keeping her attention.

"Quite right," she replied. "I am certain you will look like a university don with them."

Alford guffawed. "Watch your tongue, young lady, or I will enthrall you with the latest crop rotation techniques instead."

"A fascinating subject," Florrie murmured, delighted that they had been able to recapture their light-hearted teasing. "I am breathless with anticipation."

Alford wished she was breathless with some other emotion, but quickly retrieved his spectacles and the book, and launched into the further travails of the inhabitants of Otranto.

Florrie relaxed against the back of the chair, closing her eyes, listening with real pleasure to Alford's voice. He read well. She would like to spend many more such evenings in front of the fire, listening to him read. But she found it increasingly difficult to concentrate on his words.

What a topsy-turvy day! She had gone from the terror of the tunnel into Alford's arms, from vague misgivings about her future to a growing conviction that the orderly life she had planned with Kit was no longer meant for her. But how could she know if her future lay with Alford?

She examined him carefully from beneath lowered lids. He looked so very different in his spectacles. More mature. Responsible. He *had* undergone a masterful turnaround in these last days—from indolence to commanding authority. He had led their foolish first expedition into the tunnel with aristocratic aplomb, soothing her fears and finding an escape. That valiant second foray into the smuggler's den demonstrated his bravery and determination. But would the Alford who had emerged in a crisis remain when life returned to normal, or would he settle back into his old patterns?

She wished she were a gypsy fortune-teller, so that she could predict the future. Would she be happy with Alford? Kit would be the safer choice, the logical choice. And Florrie had always prided herself on her logic. She had carefully planned the course her life would take, and now one perplexing, infuriating man was turning all her plans upside down.

With a sudden pang, Florrie realized that whatever happened, she could not go through with the marriage to Kit. It would be too much a matter of second best. She had not wanted this to happen, but it had. For now that she knew Alford—yes, loved him—she would always measure Kit against him. And Kit would always suffer in comparison. It would be grossly unfair. Better he found a lady who thought the world of him than one who longed for another.

She knew Alford would never be as manageable as Kit. He would always do precisely as he pleased. It would be her task to channel his inclinations into productive paths, but she knew she could never push him into something he did not wish to do. And if he reverted to his old ways . . . there was little need for her. It might be better if she walked away now, while it was still possible.

But the very thought of walking away from Hartland, and Alford, tore at her heart. She feared it was already far too late for that. She loved him. Best to remain, and wait, and hope that her confidence in Alford was not misplaced. And pray that she could somehow capture his interest.

She had felt so secure in Alford's arms. In that nasty, dark tunnel, he had held her, comforted her, taken care of her. And she realized with a sudden shock that she *wanted* a man who made her feel that way, wanted a man she could turn to for solace and strength. A man she *needed*. She had never considered such a thing before, but now she knew how important it was. Her father, and their travels, had taught her to be self-reliant, but there were times when it was a joy to lay the burdens on the shoulders of another. Especially when they were such broad, attractive shoulders.

Florrie's cheeks flamed, and she ducked her head, praying Alford would not notice. She could not deny that physical attraction played a large part in her longings for Alford. When he had kissed her, she wished he would never stop. Tonight, sitting across from him in the library, was an exquisite torture. Every glance at his lips brought memories of their touch flooding back, along with the feel of his body pressed against hers as they clung together on the grass. She wanted him, ached for him. . . .

Perhaps it was her innocence that caused her feelings to rage in such an out of control manner. Alford had ample dealings with lust and desire—his reputation did not derive from his monkish habits. When he thought of her, was it different from the way he thought of any woman? He had accosted her that day so long ago in London without any knowledge of her identity; was one woman as good as another for him? She had seen much in her travels, but her experience with men, and the passions they engendered, was highly limited. Was she confusing love with desire?

She suddenly wished her father was here now, instead of on his way to Sweden. She could talk with him with a frankness few daughters could; he would help her make sense of all this. But he was not here, and she would have to make some sense of this on her own.

Florrie's thoughts tumbled through her brain. Alford and love. Alford and marriage. Alford and . . . Her body gradually slumped against the side of the chair as sleep overcame her.

Alford smiled fondly at the picture of her asleep in the chair. He welcomed the opportunity to study her without the need to disguise his longing. Those oh-so-kissable lips were turning upward in a faint smile. How he wished it was with thoughts of him. Poor Florrie. It had been an exhausting day. For both of them.

With a yawn, he closed the book, stretching out his booted feet toward the fire. He sat for a long time watching Florrie, noting the slow rise and fall of her chest beneath the soft fabric of her gown. It was a bittersweet moment, duty and honor warring with his personal desires. If only he could talk to Kit. Perhaps his brother was not so firmly committed to Florrie. But Alford knew that was only wishful thinking on his part.

With a sad smile, Alford rose unsteadily to his feet. Florrie would be far more comfortable in her bed. Sighing, he knelt beside her, gently shaking her shoulder. Like the gentleman he was, he would escort her to her room, bid her a fond goodnight, and retire reluctantly to his lonely chamber.

Hours later, a sudden noise intruded into Florrie's subconscious. She blinked sleepily into her pillow. It had been such a marvelous dream; what had awakened her? The darkness told her it was still night. She lay quietly, trying to recapture the threads of her dream that lay tantalizingly out of reach. Only a few more moments . . .

An icy chill swept the room and Florrie pulled the blankets closer. The fire must be out. She smelled the unmistakable odor of sea air. Odd—she thought she had closed the window. Florrie groggily rolled over, peering into the darkness.

And froze. There, silhouetted against the open window, was a Lady. Her white garments billowed about her, blown by the chill breeze flooding the room, her face obscured by the long, flowing shawl wrapped about her head. Florrie stared in wide-eyed horror as the Lady took a step toward the bed and stretched out her hand toward her.

"Alford!" Florrie screamed. "Alllllllfoooord!"

Chapter 23

Startled from his sleep by Florrie's cries, Alford burst through the door, prepared to do battle with whatever demon threatened her. He barely had time to scan the room for an intruder before Florrie hurtled herself at him, clinging to his neck as if she would never let go. He rather liked the feeling of it.

"She was here," Florrie wailed in a terror-stricken voice. "I saw her clearly. Oh, Alford, I was so frightened."

"There, there," he said soothingly, patting her back and trying to ignore the feel of her thinly-clad body pressed tightly against his. "Who was here? What did you see?"

Florrie took a deep breath to quell her quaking. "The window was open," she began haltingly. "And standing in front of it was . . . was the Lady. She was all dressed in white—just as when I saw her on the lawn. Then she began walking toward the bed." Florrie buried her face in Alford's shoulder again.

A bad dream, no doubt. Alford felt a twinge of guilt. He should not have been reading *Otranto* after all else that had happened. It was enough to give anyone nightmares. And it was all his fault, for having scared her so in the preceding days. Once again, guilt assailed him.

"Florrie, Florrie," he whispered, holding her trembling body close. "It is all right, I promise you. Whatever was here is gone now."

Alford held her tightly, gently stroking along the length of her back. Gradually, he felt her trembling ease, and the tension fled her body. She was soon still, and soft, and warm. He looked down and pressed a gentle kiss atop her head.

Florrie lifted her head from his chest and looked at him. "Thomas, I—"

"Hush," he whispered, placing a finger to her lips.

She looked at him with such trust and confidence that he nearly flinched from her gaze. *Don't look at me like that*, he pleaded silently, but by the time he thought, it was already too late. He took his finger from her lips and cupped her cheek in his hand. He gently tilted her face, and lowered his, until their lips met.

It started slowly, that kiss, building from a soft brushing of skin on skin to something more powerful, more painful in its pleasure. His lips grew demanding, hungry, as the passion he had held in check for so long bubbled to the top, seeking an outlet. Slowly, carefully, he eased both of them down onto the bed.

Florrie felt wrapped in some strange otherworld, her senses honed to a super-sensitivity that had every nerve in her body screaming with tension. Dimly, she sensed Thomas pushing her gown from her shoulders, felt his lips trail along her neck and shoulder.

"Thomas," she breathed, wrapping her hands in his thick hair, reeling with shock and excitement at the sensations he aroused in her. She wanted him, yearned for him, ached for—

A chill blast of air swept over her as he abruptly pulled away.

"Thomas?"

Alford took a deep, shuddering breath. "Florrie, I am so sorry," he said, averting his eyes from the tempting sight of her. "I swear, not a word of this will ever pass my lips. He will never know."

"Who will never know?" Florrie sat up and looked at him in puzzlement.

"Kit."

"Oh." Kit. Of course the thought of him would give Alford pause. Honor demanded it. Damn honor! Florrie took a deep breath. "I think that . . . that Kit and I will not suit after all." The dawning hope she saw rising in Alford's face caused her own hopes to soar. Was it possible that he did care for her?

Alford could hardly draw breath, so stunned was he by

her words. If Florrie was no longer tied to Kit, there was nothing to bar his pursuit of her.

Except his own failings. His lamentable past hovered over his head like a dark, threatening cloud. He had so little to offer her, compared to Kit. He was a fool to think otherwise.

"What do you mean, you won't suit?" he asked, a rough edge to his voice. "Kit is everything you want. Talented, ambitious. He'll probably end up as Foreign Minister one day."

"I do not think that is as important to me as it once was," she said quietly.

"Oh? And what is?"

Florrie looked down at her hands, although she knew Alford could not see her eyes clearly in the shadowed room. "I do want a man with talent, and ambition, who has a sense of purpose. But I also want someone who wants to protect me, care for me."

"Kit would do that," he said.

She shook her head. "No, he wouldn't. Not in the way I would wish. Kit and I . . . well, he looks upon me in far too brotherly a fashion."

"And how would you like a man to look upon you?"

Florrie lifted her head and dared a glance at him. "Like a lover would."

"Oh, Florrie," he whispered, his hand reaching out to stroke her cheek.

Florrie watched the swift play of emotions that crossed his face. Did that darkening expression mean he was not pleased, realizing the implications of their very compromising position? She pulled her gown closer, desperately needing some reassurance from him. Was she merely a convenient female?

Alford was beset with impatience. He knew it would take weeks, if not months, to win her approval, her admiration. Yet she sat there in such an enticing display, her eyes beseeching him for he knew not what. And he could not wait another minute. He had to know. Now.

He shifted to draw his face closer to hers, so he could see

clearly the look in her eyes, know her first reaction to what he asked.

"Florrie, I . . . I do not wish our marriage to be annulled," he said hoarsely. "I want you to remain . . . my wife."

"Your wife?"

"I love you, Florrie," he said simply. There, it was out. He could only wait, and hope.

"You do?" she squeaked.

He nodded, searching her eyes for some indication of what she felt. "I promise I shall do my best to earn your admiration, to be a man you can be proud of," he said hastily. "I will defy my father and take up politics, or run the farm at Swinton; whatever you wish me to do. Anything. Everything."

Florrie continued to stare at him in bemusement. What had he said? He loved her? A slow smile of realization spread over her face. She reached out and drew him to her again. "I would be honored to be your wife, Thomas," she said with a wide smile.

"You would?" he asked, delight dawning on his face. He did not even allow her a reply but took her up in his arms again, kissing her in such a way as to make certain she was firmly convinced of his intent.

"I shall take you back to London," he promised, when he could speak again. "We shall have a proper wedding this time." And time to change her mind, if she so wished.

"We are already married," she whispered, running a finger along his jaw line, stopping at the faint cleft in his chin.

He wanted her so badly his body ached from the effort to control his desire. But what had begun quite by accident must be finished with cold deliberation.

"Are you certain?" he asked, searching her face. "You can think on it, Florrie. If we . . . if I . . . we will not be able to go back. You must be certain."

"Make me your wife, Thomas," she pleaded as she pulled his head to hers for a kiss. "Tonight. Now."

"Oh, God," he groaned. He captured her lips again in a searing kiss, while his hands sought to free her from the confinement of her gown. He trailed kisses across her face and neck, dipping his head lower until he captured the tip of one breast in his mouth, tasting her heated skin, reveling in her smooth flesh.

He felt Florrie's fingers teasing under the neck of his shirt, skimming across his shoulders, feeling soft and smooth against his skin. He groaned in need and want. Slowly his hand slipped down her side, feeling her ribs, the curve of her hip, the silky skin of her thigh.

The first rush of panic welled within him. He wanted Florrie so badly he was ready to explode, yet in the very act of making her his forever, he would cause her pain. The thought nearly unmanned him. He ran a tentative hand over the soft curve of her belly, stroking lightly while he lifted his head to capture her mouth again. While his tongue danced along her lips, he inched his hand lower and lower, toward the apex of her passions.

Florrie gasped at his shocking touch, overwhelmed by the strange and surging sensations coursing through her. She felt hot and flushed, with something building inside her.

"Thomas, Thomas," she murmured, half in wanting, half in apprehension.

"It is all right, love," he whispered, coaxing her legs apart, seeking her warmth with his fingers. He groaned at the wetness of her, knowing he must be patient, must prolong his pleasure to bring her hers. If he did not die first. His fingers stroked her in a rhythmical motion that sent his lower body into flames.

Florrie arched her body against his caressing hand, her mind devoid of any thought beyond the mad pleasure he brought her. His mouth and tongue burned a path of liquid fire over her breasts while that wicked hand teased and stroked her into ever higher spirals of pleasure. A white-hot heat flooded her body as she arched and twisted with shuddering tremors. "Thomas," she gasped.

Alford could hold back no longer. Slipping a hand under her hip, he drew her to him as he slowly eased his way into her softness.

"Ah, Florrie," he groaned as her heat enveloped him. He

kissed her nose, her cheeks, her lips as he fought against his desire. "I swear it will hurt only this one time," he whispered, as he cautiously began his gentle thrusts. He felt himself press against her barrier, then steeled himself for what he must do. With one hard jab he made her his, his lips covering Florrie's as her gasp broke out. He did not dare move for fear of hurting her more.

"Thomas," she whispered.

"I am sorry," he groaned.

"It is quite fine," she said, with a comforting smile. She tenderly kissed his cheek.

"Oh love, I do not deserve you," he whispered, then his body took over, his motions quickening while he held her to him. He could not tear his eyes away from her face, afraid to close them for fear she would somehow disappear from his vision. Then he felt that convulsive tightening in his loins, the flash of heat through his body, and his release.

Alford lay wrapped in her arms for several minutes, still stunned at the enormity of the love and protectiveness he felt for her, and the exquisite pleasure she had brought him. Florrie. His wife.

"Thomas?" His long silence disturbed her.

He reluctantly raised himself, resting on his forearms, while smiling down at her. "Yes, love?"

His words brought a smile to her lips. "I love you," she whispered.

Alford leaned down for a long, languorous kiss with his lady wife.

Mrs. Burgess gave no sign of surprise at finding Alford in Florrie's chamber when she brought the tray of tea and chocolate in the morning. Alford retrieved his robe and insisted upon serving Florrie himself. It was a difficult task, for he could barely keep his eyes off her as she sat propped against the pillows, her honey-gold hair splayed across her shoulders. She looked so deliciously wanton. And she was his.

He handed her the cup and turned back for his own, glancing at the window as he did so. "Look, Florrie, here is the cause of all the problem last night," Alford announced in a triumphant voice as he handed her a white, filmy shawl. "This was caught in the window latch; the breeze must have made it look like a figure."

Florrie ran her fingers over the soft, white folds. "It is lovely," she whispered, then looked up at Alford with widening eyes. "But it is not mine."

He stared at her in consternation. "Then who . . . ?"

A faint, musical laugh emanating from the empty air floated across the chamber.

Chapter 24

"My lord?" Burgess stood at the library door. "Visitors have arrived."

Alford looked up from his book, reaching automatically to remove his spectacles. "Visitors?"

"A Mr. Cole, and party."

"Seb!" Alford jumped to his feet. "See them in, Burgess. And bring some brandy and glasses."

He turned to Florrie. "You remember Seb Cole, don't you, love? He was at the wedding."

Florrie wrinkled her nose as she tried to put a face to the man. "Tall and blond?"

Alford shook his head. " 'Fraid not. I wonder who is with him?"

"Alford, Alford," Seb greeted heartily from the door. "Your salvation has arrived at last. And we brought you an added present in the bargain." He waved his arm with a flourish.

Lewiston Hervey walked into the room, a lady on his arm. He handed Alford a packet of papers. "The annulment papers. All they need is your signatures and—" he nodded to Florrie—"the lady and you are free." He patted the woman's hand. "And a special present to celebrate your freedom."

Alford hoped his face did not look as sick as he felt. He glanced quickly at Florrie, then looked at the lady simpering on Hervey's arm. Nanette. Oh God.

From Alford's reaction, Florrie had a very good idea just who this unknown woman was. His London trollop.

"I—uh—I," Alford babbled. "What are you doing here?"

"I was concerned about you, Thomas," Nanette said with an artful pout. "When I received that mysterious letter . . ."

"So we asked her to come with us on the trip," Hervey interjected. He smiled at the lady at his side. "Right nice traveling companion, too."

Alford thought he blanched an even paler shade, if there was such a one.

Seb laughed. "Buck up, old boy," he said, clapping Alford on the back. He turned to Florrie, bowing low. "You probably do not remember me, Miss Washburn. Sebastian Cole." He jerked a thumb at his companion. "Lewiston Hervey. And Miss Nanette La Pierre."

Every ounce of diplomatic skill that Florrie had acquired over the years came to the fore. "How do you do," she said, a false smile pasted on her face. "Would you like to sit down? I know you have had an arduous journey." She stared pointedly at Alford. "Perhaps you would care to ring for refreshments for *our* guests, my lord?"

Alford still stared dumbfounded at the new arrivals, his hands convulsively clutching the papers he held. How in the deuce was he ever going to explain this to Florrie? Someday he would kill Seb and Hervey.

"Alford," Florrie said sharply.

"Refreshments. Yes," he stammered and raced from the room.

"Rustication can do that to a man," Seb said, taking a chair near Florrie. "I trust he has not been too much of a trial, ma'am?"

"We managed to reach an accommodation of sorts," she said with a wry smile. "How is it that you have the annulment papers?"

"We ran into Barstow at the club and he told us they'd been finished. Then explained about the—uh—error in the housing arrangements."

"Could have knocked me over with a feather when he told us you and Alford ended up at the same house," Hervey said as he seated Nanette. "Figured he'd be dead by now. Seeing what you did to his nose that one time."

"Do not think I haven't been tempted," Florrie said from between gritted teeth.

Alford reappeared at the door. "Uh—Florrie, could I speak with you for a moment?"

Florrie smiled graciously. "You will excuse me?" She followed Alford into the hall, closing the door behind her.

Alford felt sheer, utter terror sweeping through him. There had been so little time—only a few days. Would Florrie believe him, would she trust him? How could he convince her that Nanette was the very last person in the world he ever wanted to see?

"Interesting friends," Florrie said, enjoying his obvious discomfort. "Miss La Pierre seems particularly . . . intriguing. I wonder I have not met her before."

"Of course you haven't, she's—"

"Your mistress?" Florrie finished.

"No! Yes! I mean, she was, in a way, but not for a long time."

Florrie stifled her urge to giggle. Alford's discomfort was amusing. But not quite amusing enough to gloss over the real worry she felt. She knew many unmarried men kept mistresses. But so did many married ones. Would Alford do the same? Old habits could be difficult to break. "Do go on," she urged.

"It was long before I—I mean—I wrote for her to come when I wanted you gone," he explained jerkily. "I thought her presence would encourage you to leave."

"Astute observation," Florrie said dryly.

"But I do not want her here now!"

"Are you certain? There are men I know who would love to have both their wife and mistress in residence. So convenient."

"She is not my mistress!" Alford reiterated. "It was never that formal an arrangement."

"She must have been somewhat convinced of your interest if she traveled all the way to Devon," Florrie said sharply.

Alford hung his head. "I may have made a few wild promises . . ." he mumbled.

Florrie took pity on him. "I know. You really should be more careful about what you put to paper, Alford."

His eyes narrowed. "How do you know?"

"I read your letter," she replied simply.

"You what?"

"And it is really very awful of you to use your father's frank for your private letters, Alford," she chastened him. "It only increases postal costs for the rest of us."

"You opened my letter and read it?" Alford stared at her, mouth agape.

"It was a trifle shocking, I will own," Florrie said with an impish smile. "That is why I thought it had best be put on the fire."

"You burnt it?"

"Only the letter. I sent the franked envelope on."

"Florrie!" Alford stared at her in amazement at her audacity, then burst out laughing. "You wretch," he cried, gathering her up in his arms. "You adorable wretch."

"Am I really?"

"What?"

"Adorable?"

He squeezed her hard. "Yes, you are," he said.

"More adorable than Nanette?"

Alford sighed. He placed his hands on Florrie's shoulders and held her away from him. "I do not wish any lady in my life but you," he said. "Forever."

"That is a mighty grand promise, Alford," she said, her expression growing serious. "I would rather you not promise anything you will be hard pressed to follow."

He grabbed her up in his arms again. "I think, Lady Alford," he said, as his head bent toward hers, "that you will be all the female I can handle."

Florrie stood on tip-toe to meet his kiss.

"What do you suppose happened to Alford?" Seb asked idly while he refilled their glasses. "And Miss Washburn?"

Hervey shrugged. "Who cares?" He cast an admiring glance at the glass in his hand. "This is damned fine brandy."

Burgess entered the library, carrying a tray, with a packet of papers under his arm.

"Lord Alford extends his apologies," Burgess said. "He is occupied with a rather pressing matter at the moment." He set the tray down and handed the papers to Seb. "He requested that you burn these for him."

Seb stared at the papers. "These are the annulment forms!" he exclaimed. "Are you sure Alford said to burn them?"

"Those were his exact words," Burgess said.

Cole and Hervey exchanged incredulous glances.

"Lord Alford also wished me to point out that there is a tolerably fine inn in Clovelly. He says you will have plenty of time to reach it before darkness." Burgess took a deep breath as he rattled off the rest of his speech. "He regrets that he and Lady Alford will not be able to see your departure."

"Lady Alford? Who's Lady Alford?" Hervey asked in confusion.

Seb tossed back his head and roared with laughter. "That rogue!"

"Departure! I am sick to death of traveling," Nanette pouted. "It is far too cold and damp in Devon."

Seb and Hervey exchanged glances.

"I think we can find a way to keep you warm, Miss La Pierre," Seb said smoothly, offering her his arm. "Perhaps we can discuss it on the way to Clovelly?"

"We were intolerably rude, not saying goodbye to your friends," Florrie whispered in Alford's ear as she snuggled closer against him.

"Ah, but think what trouble it would have been to dress again." He grinned and kissed her brow. "They will understand."

"Poor Nanette," Florrie said. "She came all this way for nothing."

"I am certain that Seb and Hervey will see that she is amply rewarded for her touble," said Alford.

"Do you suppose they will tell all London what happened?" she asked, tracing swirling designs across his bared chest with her finger.

"Undoubtedly," he replied.

"People will say shocking things," she said.

"Then we will simply avoid London until the talk dies down," he said, taking her hand and drawing it to his lips. "It should not take more than four . . . perhaps five months."

Florrie giggled, her lips hovering a scant distance from his cheek. "And shall we spend the entire time like this?"

"Most certainly," he said, turning suddenly to pin her beneath him on the bed. "In fact, four or five months may not be nearly enough time." He trailed kisses from her brow to her chin. "Oh, Florrie, how I adore you."

"Mm," she replied, her eyes fluttering shut and a contented smile upon her face. Four or five months would be perfect. Just in time for the fall opening of Parliament—and all manner of intriguing political opportunities.

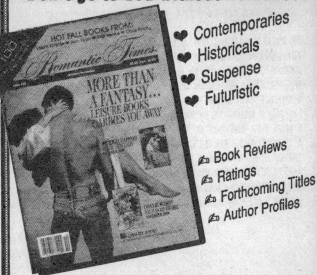